A PLACE
BETWEEN
WAKING &
FORGETTING

Also by Eugen Bacon

Fiction

Secondhand Daylight
Languages of Water (ed)—cross-lingual hybrid
Serengotti
Broken Paradise
Chasing Whispers
Mage of Fools
Danged Black Thing
The Road to Woop Woop & Other Stories
Ivory's Story
Hadithi & The State of Black Speculative Fiction (with Milton Davis)
Claiming T-Mo

Poetry

Texture of Silence (with Steve Simpson)
Saving Shadows
Speculate (with Dominique Hecq)
Black Moon: Graphic Speculative Flash Fiction

Non-Fiction

An Earnest Blackness
Writing Speculative Fiction

Published by Raw Dog Screaming Press
Bowie, MD
First Edition

Book design: Jennifer Barnes
Cover art: Bizhan Khodabandeh
mendedarrow.com

Printed in the United States of America
ISBN: 978-1-947879-78-2

Library of Congress Control Number: 2024939898

www.RawDogScreaming.com

A PLACE BETWEEN WAKING & FORGETTING

Stories by Eugen Bacon

RAW DOG
SCREAMING
PRESS

Contents

A Poetic Introduction: Forgetting, Walking Between

by Linda D. Addison

We buy books to learn something new, to be entertained, teleported somewhere else, uplifted, safely frightened; all of these things in Eugen Bacon's book.

Walking on each word, forgetting my purpose, curious to find what I will in this Place, I walked and found…

The devil, all hair and a ghost dog,
you running, then blows coming,
anger, knives, you kick, connect…
You seen death. So much, you could sail in it,
so you sold your soul to the devil & his Killer dawg
"Only the devil wanna live in a place like this,"
he were no more a devil than you.

SKY is falling…universe is split into embracing & unshackling,
everywhere is scorching. But nothing is black or white,
unwrap an embrace bracelet, being undecided was not safe
teacher divvied up seating in columns of embracers & unshackled,
safe and lost, secretly unshackled or something moderate,
fighting about collecting orgasms, embracers & unshackled
hated each other all the way to the dark web—see a world
that's a bloody beauty, and safe—this is a start.

wish life was more interesting? If life were a film, footage would be deleted, show would start with 'My Country', wrap heart around a beautiful, soulful thing that didn't exist, "always loved this show", "Fucking jungle is a hive mind", been abandoned. Now doing the abandoning, studio is walled, outside looking in. The door s-w-i-n-g-s …

Right now, tranquil. Later—worry about everything that can go wrong in space, skin is cracked in places where crawled from crevice to crevice, fleeing robopets —came unprogrammed. Robopet owners in tatters and sprawl. A woman leaking crimson, her eyeball dangling…man crawling…autopilot brought rocket capsule to a stall, hardened with time and space, survivors floating beyond distant edges of outer galaxies, insensitive to time and space...

A multiverse is an impossible world, silence, catching light and shifting, found in a natural forest, collected in pieces the mystery, a place between waking, forgetting in a forest full of stars, smelled of paradise. Tasted of heaven, seek meaning from shadows scatter alongside foliage, tanzanite eyes caught light gave nothing away, what was behind them…

Face to face like that, a prelude to a kiss in open moonlight, only stories remained. Nothing was left of the ocean. Each day began worrying itself to nothingness, standing outside warmth of a shouting wind, technology accelerated grief, propaganda for products of lunacy killed a whole ocean, blood and bones fuel a trading empire, tormenting ethics and sky, dust and dust, banging at the afflicted.

Then one broken pot prancing, chanting on dusty ground won't change a thing, sun, earth, moon imperfectly aligned, a yellow moon crossed earth's shadow, arms glimmered with cowry shell trinkets—red, green and yellow. Dancers pranced, swayed heads tight with feathers. Everything put together masterfully, firmly: 'Adaeze means princess', recovered grace, fondly known as fastest in the village, stars trapped inside, first to become a teacher, a bridge between two worlds. The sun, earth and moon imperfectly aligned…

Godé shared language with white tornado full of lightning, he crawled into tornado, next time tornado tossed him into ocean, then he was a water serpent, water velvety gray, did not resist the waves. Balance and grace are a choice…

…world needs to feed on eternal bread,

before any of that,
be a mother god,
find out what peril happened,
make conversation,
search with growing intensity,
in a flash of hope
the crushing began.

Wake up, linger a moment longer in The place where weird things happen…

I give this book back to you, what will you find in this Place?

The Devil Don't Come with Horns

IT WERE the second day of summer, a sunny day that cast its own shadow, when you seen the devil. He slipped quietly into your neighborhood. He stepped out all hair, sunnies and a bandana. A ghost dog and a moving van too.

They came in a rush.

You were running down the road, the wind giving you speed as you cut through the field towards Baridi's house at the end of the neat suburb when the boys jumped you. One minute they were sullen, smoking ciggies on the stump that was once a red oak by the footy field. Next, they were swinging fists at your ribs as you writhed on freshly mown grass in a forgetting town that the council and volunteers kept spotless.

Forgetting. Because that's where your pa fled to forget.

"What you gone hit me fer?" you cried, shielding your face.

Mad, the Cormont boy—a good looker, but all mean—spoke through his puffs. "Ain't no dawg but me," he said, and chewed on the smoking dart at the side of his lip.

Neat wore white shorts and a grubby mop on his jet-black head. No big-name heritage—he were a Clanger, and his mother part of the neighborhood watch. His brother Langdon, also in white shorts, had orange curls so tight they were a fist. The littlest Clanger, Jowls, had friendly eyes that asked fer a ciggie, offered you a puff, but he were as random as his socks, one beige, one crimson-striped, and a don't-argue vest that tradie folk somber about their business wore.

All this went through your head in slow motion as the punches fell in real time.

Soul Parchment, the compact one, had the body of an ox. He yelled *Fucketty!* as he whooped you. He were the angriest of the pack, made him the meanest.

But Mitch Lightfoot unsettled you. His folding knife had an ebony handle. He wore a rucksack and stayed away from lil' fights—just big ones where he flicked open and closed the glint of stainless steel, the blade's flicker as gray as Mitch's danger eyes.

Waterman stayed away from fights too. He were a Nielsen lad, skipping tricks on a hemp rope. Alternate foot, jump jump, cross, boxer step, jump. He kept skipping as his mates smashed you.

You tossed a kick that connected. Neat yelped.

"Got loose at the right time," hissed Mad. His fist flattened you *slam bow*. "Lie down, kid," he said, as you started to rise.

Something smashed into the pack, and Baridi was fighting your war. The boys fell away afore she spoke. "Let him go." She stood there in leggings and a tank top. Heart face. Tiny eyes. Braids.

"Or what?" Mad rubbed his lip with a thumb.

She stared him down. "Yer the courageous one?"

"Weak uns run from this." He pulled a body-builder pose, muscles ripped through a pale polo shirt. The way he said it, you knowed that he liked her.

She ignored him, gave you a hand.

The bravery in a small girl surrounded by big brutes awed you, and it stupefied the boys, except Waterman, who was still skipping, and Mitch, who dropped the rucksack from his back, pulled out *Metal Glo* and a rag, and polished his blade.

The sound of the pocketknife's flick as you walked away, then: "Wait up!" said Mad. "Ye forgot yer ball."

"Toss it," said Baridi.

'Nah. Yer come git it."

She ran back, but he dribbled, bounced away, and then sprinted. Baridi chased, chest out in her leggings and tank top. She ran hard and fast, little legs rolling. Mad gave his best to keep the ball, turned it over to Langdon.

Baridi held the heat, Mad dodging. Soul Parchment got involved, then Jowls, the boys outnumbering Baridi 4 to 1, then 5 to 1. She plowed through body traffic, dragged the ball with her foot, scooted away with it.

"Fortune changes," she called out, laughing.

"I ain't never change fer nobody," shouted back Mad.

"Is everything about yer?" She rolled the ball on the ground at speed. "Then come steal it. I'm *weak*." She hit a long one into the distance, raced after it.

Mad gave up first, then the rest.

She were full of panting when you reached her. "That's how it's done."

"Kick a ball?"

"Beat bullies." She tumbled the ball, grinned at your laughable attempt to catch it with a foot. "Want me to kick it to myself?"

"I got two lefties."

"They's *club feet*."

"Is that what yer think?" You positioned, paced to the ball and back.

"Don't reason with the ball. Just kick it."

"Sometimes, yer got to reason." You gave the ball another look, searched fer a target in the distance, and shot. The pack behind howled at your flying boot, the ball on the grass still.

Baridi took the kick. She thumped, strong shin to boot. Bent the ball across the quiet street to the cottage at the end of the world where death happened.

You seen death. You fell into it. Happened when you rushed into the kitchen in Downs where you lived, when you burst onto Maw lying on the floor. She pressed a hand to her stomach as if pushing back guts. Her hazel eyes held deep surprise, maybe at the smell of wet soil and metal.

So much blood, and it were growing. So much, you could sail a boat in it.

You dialed Emergency and they cleaned her good, put her in the hospital bed, white sheets and all, then Pa came. But there was nothing left of your maw's strawberry and freesia scent, just a dying smell of nail polish and bleach. Gray lips replaced her glitter smile that made you think of a large diamond. You held her cold hand. Her eyes were half-open, teary. There was no gentle tinkle of her laughter, just gasps, then a rattle. When her skin went porcelain, a nurse came and pulled white linen over Maw's face.

The moving van was up by the cottage's driveway. A three-seater cabin with a ramp. Somewhere near the cottage, *ting!* the peal of a bird.

"What yer bring us here fer?" you asked Baridi.

"Now yer give me stupid? I got yer out of a tangle!"

"Wouldn't call it that."

"A spectacle then?"

"Only a small one."

"That were some desperation, kid. They was killin' yer back there."

"Nothin' of the sort. And yer a kid yerself. Ye git me out of trouble, put me back in it with that ball. What we doin' here, anyways?"

"That's what I'd like to know," said the black chap with sunnies and a bandana, who'd crept out of nowhere. He stood on the stone steps that led up to

14

the derelict cottage and its stained wooden door peeling paint the color of olives or mold. Halloween windows with the eyes of a ghost looked out at a wilting dawgwood tree on the yard.

"Need help finding something?" He tawked with a whole cherry inside his underlip. That's how he sounded. He held out the ball, but neither you nor Baridi moved to take it. "You got a good look, did you?"

"Nana said—" Baridi cast you a glance. She raised a brave face and announced: "We don't tawk to strangers."

"Nana is wise. You like Skittles?"

"Why Skittles fer?" you asked.

"Settle nerves." He pulled a tin can from his pocket, clasped open the lid.

You helped yourself and popped a sour mandarin in your mouth. "If yer scared, why move here?"

"Who said I'm scared?"

"They dug up all them bodies, some whole, some hacked," you said.

"A year back," he said. "The real estate bloke told me already."

"Shrouded in them burlap sacks," you said.

He raised a brow.

"Nana said they found bones of seventeen pepo, the tiniest a bub," said Baridi.

"Tiny hole packed like a pyramid," you said. "IDs, jackets, rings, teeth, crosses, watches, a gold necklace."

"What are you talking about, nigger?" It weren't a question.

"Is it okaywise?" asked Baridi.

"Okaywise to do what?" he asked.

"Callin' folk niggers that ain't black pepo."

"Aren't you a nigger?" He looked at you.

"Oh, no, sir," you said, and shook your head firmly.

"Who is, then?"

"I don't rightly know, sir."

He stooped to eye level. "Then I say you are." He poked you on the chest with a beautiful finger, perfectly shaped. Held your gaze, then straightened up. Offered you another Skittle. "What else Nana say?"

You swallowed a pinkie—sour raspberry. "They was dining chairs, coffee table, queen bed, carpet—ain't good no more."

"I like pineapple—the yellow one." He studied as you popped the Skittle in your mouth. "What if she got it wrong?"

"Who did?" Baridi stretched a hand, and he shook a perfect rainbow—red, orange, yellow, green, blue, indigo, violet—onto her palm.

15

"What if Nana got it wrong?" he said.

"She my grammy," said Baridi.

"And that's enough?" He laughed.

Baridi folded her arms. "Yer ain't seen her."

"Place still smells rotten," you said.

He turned his beard face on you. "I bet you can conjure some magic with this ball."

"She can." You pointed at Baridi with your chin. "Give yer a good run."

"Show me," he tossed the ball and Baridi caught it.

Right foot, the ball sailed. It curled towards the footy field. The watching pack didn't stir or grab the ball. Mad smoked. Waterman skipped. Mitch flicked the knife.

Baridi ran to fetch.

"And she's a left-footer," you said. "What yer reckon she got if she put a left boot to it?"

"I won't argue with that," he said in that cherry-lip voice.

"She don't miss, Mister—"

"Baba," he said. "Just Baba."

"She don't miss, Mr Baba."

"I thought an accident brought you here."

Were he tawking about your maw's dying—how could he know—or Baridi's ball? You shrugged. "She don't kick that ball no place she don't want it to go."

The silence felt off, so you broke it. "What happen to yer dawg? I seen it in when you moved."

"She's having a dream."

"Kin we see her?"

"Come by tomorrow."

"Chill."

"Make it early."

"How early?"

"Real early."

Baridi put the ball on the boot and kicked it home. "What were yer tawkin' about?"

"Nothin'." You looked at her. "He could be yer fahver."

She laughed. It were easy to forget she were different—her mixed race weren't there 'til you looked fer it. To you, she were just Baridi. A girl with plentiful courage to take one or all them brutes out there, and they knowed it. "Pity my maw's not here to tell."

"Yer kin find her in the city."

"Maybe. But yet again…" Her eyes challenged you. "What if I ain't got no maw?"

"Like Nana make it up? About yer maw run off with some black boy and leave yer here?"

"Maybe Nana *made* me?"

Your eyes grew big. "With a spell?"

She laughed, and ran into the house. But you wondered if Nana could grow creatures. You'd seen her power, how she could heal. What if she had more power inside?

You stepped into a fresh whiff of baking. Nana's house was full of softness you never got from your pa, and it were nothing to do with the vintage velvet on her dining seats, or the turquoise plushness of a Persian rug rolling all the way from the doorway, or the perfect ribbons that held the waists of quilt curtains, handsewn. Perhaps it were more to do with the powder softness of Nana's skin, despite her smell of vegetable soap—freshly cut greens. Hers were a softness that promised home, or its memory.

"Something's off with you two," she said, but didn't press.

She had barometer eyes that told of her mood. Warm green were what you wanted. It got you square donuts, iced like heaven. Candied fruit—clementines mostly. Prune tarts with custard cream. Peaches in white wine syrup. Ice blue, not so much. When Nana's eyes got blue, you knowed to scoot.

Today her eyes was lit green. "Give me something to work with," she said, like she did when she wanted a yarn.

You thought of Baba and his dreaming dawg.

Nana shuffled on one leg around the chestnut table, served iced tea and new croissants filled with home-made chocolate and hazelnut butter. You and Baridi wolfed them down. Nana was a Shield, so you reckoned that made Baridi a Shield too. It weren't public what gave Nana the shuffle.

"What someone gone drive all the way to Alexandra fer?" you asked on the third gobble of a second croissant.

"Same thing that brought you and your pa from Downs," said Nana.

'Ain't the same. Pa were grieving when he took a turn yer don't take at the freeway."

"What's wrong with turnin' into Alexandra?" asked Baridi.

"The sign's all broke."

"It didn't stop your pa," said Nana.

"Yer know what makes a person who works fer a finance company called Coin swap the suit fer a rain cheater and a bicycle to peddle them letters?"

17

"Grief." Nana's green eyes stayed warm.

"Damn right. The kinda grief that makes yer hide from truth, even yer own self."

"Maybe fate brought you and your pa to Alexandra," said Nana. "Look at you and Baridi here. And your pa, remember when the fever took?"

Yeah, a year ago. Your pa were cooking, sweating a stew when Nana rang the doorbell, shuffled up the stairs to his bed and put a touch on him. She muttered, her eyes all bug, big toads in her throat, and a blue ocean pushed from inside wanting to come outta her skin 'til your pa went cold.

"I knowed he weren't gone," you said quietly now to Nana. "Same way I got them feels, and knowed Maw weren't gone stick long in this world."

Pa walked through the front door, no happy postman smile, nobody saying, "Darling, I'm home!" He came home like a funeral. He wore the long face of a ranger, eyes distant through invisible sights. Maw was dead and that was that, but Pa didn't get it.

"Nana say hello." You pointed at the big microwave. "She make truffle-buttered quiche fer yer."

He grunted.

You watched, hand on cheek, cross-legged on the floor in the open living room. He dropped the satchel from his shoulder, opened the fridge and popped a beer on the fridge door. Unlike the apartment in Downs, your place in Alexandra was sparsely furnished as if you'd just arrived or were leaving. No one threw a carpet over the wooden floorboard. Pa slumped into the lone two-seater, cold beer in hand. He flicked a glance at you, and then away. There was no television or dishwasher. The fridge, mostly packed with beer, was all that counted. The microwave too, a little, and maybe the toaster. The walk-in pantry was nearly always empty.

Upstairs, Pa slept in his room on a futon, and you on a stacked mattress in the attic.

They said robbery. It were theft, all right—stole your maw fer good. Your pa too. First, he were confused, slept a lot. Then he took one last heave, packed a bag fer himself, a bag fer you, hesitated, then allowed you to snatch a pillow, and drove, drove, 'til he seen a wonky sign that led off the freeway towards the lip of a town called Alexandra.

It were a town where pepo nosed into other pepo's business, and dead ones like Maw became everyone's business. What they hadn't reckoned on was that many deaths would happen right under their noses. A serial killer bested them. Chose to live in this quiet town that had neat tarmac walkways and grassy curbs, one café called Messy Chef, a newsie call Quik Ezy at the corner near the roundabout where the Cormonts sold cheap ciggies. Waterman's mother, a registered nurse, did births, needles, prescriptions, footsies and dontics, but was unable to help your pa. Nana could. It weren't a plush neighborhood with its Pattersons, Nielsens, Lightfoots, Parchments, Cormonts—Belgian or Swiss heritage, Shields…and now a Baba. It were Alexandra, the town your pa chose to go walking dead.

Up in the attic, you sunk your face on the pillow that was your maw—it felt like her, brought back her smiles, smells and glitters. You fell asleep and she visited wearing purple-gray skin inside a collapsible coffin.

You waited fer Pa to shave and chomp cereal. You heard the bang of the door, then a bicycle's bell. You brushed your teeth—Maw wouldn't like it if you didn't—threw on shorts and a t-shirt, peddled out on speedy feet and whistled.

Baridi flew from her house bouncing the ball on her boot. She flicked it, and you gave it a thumping kick that drove it closer to the wooden chalet and its weedy lawn.

"I'm better than yer think," you gloated.

"That were just a lucky break."

The ball went off her foot, bent and zipped right onto the stone steps of Baba's cottage. You stopped short. The yard looked as if an ogre had stamped it in a rage, made careless mounds in a corner over there.

Ting! The bell bird again, somewhere in hiding.

Baba was bustling to and fro with a wheelbarrow, tidying up or making a mess. A ghost-coated dawg loped about in playful leaps with a waggy tail.

Baba took off his sunnies, clear black eyes looked at you straight, and he smiled.

"Her name's Killer. A big softie."

You whistled and Killer paddled to the road, tail wag-waggy. You dropped to your knee, and her body relaxed to let you scratch her neck under the collar. The sand on her tongue found your face all licky.

"What dawg is she, Mr Baba?"

"She's a mastweiller."

Baba put a scraper to the wood on the door, and stripped down the peeling paint. You watched as he dragged the scraper top to bottom along the surface, then began sanding.

Baridi was all quiet, uneasy around Baba. Occasionally, she bounced the ball on her foot, danced with it, ball whispering along the vacant road, as Killer panted happily around your face. She were a fat-pawed 200-pounder with pale moon eyes, her mouth all droopy.

"Watch out, nigger, she's a heartbreaker," said Baba. "You like her too much, she'll say see you later!" He grinned. He looked at Baridi and stretched out the scraper. "Want to help?"

"Sure." She dropped the ball, her heart face unreadable. She tucked the hands of her unzipped jacket, exposing her wrists.

Pa grunted when he came home, and you tried to tell him about Baba and the dawg, how Killer was good-natured and keen to please. He nodded without listening as you told how she got up on two legs and hugged your face. Maw listened, head bent, silken hair over her face. When she lifted her head, black holes instead of eyes looked at you without expression.

You sold your soul to the devil and his Killer. You were smitten with the sturdy dawg and spent much of the summer helping Baba. Killer brought you twigs to throw and loped heavyset after them, her face wrinkled, white drool falling from her lip. She wore a soft sheen, velvet gray like Nana's chairs, and her coat glistened like that of a racehorse's. She put her head on your knee, nuzzled into the crook of your arm and shed a lot. You reckoned you smelled dawg—Nana said as much, but your pa didn't notice.

When Baba joined you to scratch Killer's neck, she went all floppy-eared, tail a high waggy, tongue licky and holding his gaze. You noticed his immaculate hands, long handsome fingers, and you knowed the devil don't come with claws or horns.

What you also noticed was how Killer avoided the dark patch of the yard soil near the dawgwood tree shaped in a witch's claw. The tree was all curled and gnarly right about where they'd pulled out body after body in burlap sacks falling apart. Nothing else grew there near the tree—because deadness poisoned the soil, Nana said. But, strangely, mushrooms began to sprout. They started right after Baba stood near the dawgwood, scurried bark beetles that looked at him and fled, and he finished the rest with a pesticide. He patted mulch around the patch, and what do you know?

It shook mushrooms out of dead-people ooze in the postapocalyptic house, as Baridi called it. "Zombie mushrooms," she said.

Weren't long afore Nana started shuffling by. She dropped Baba pickles and dills in jars, crumbed oven-baked tomatoes in casserole dishes, even brought trays of baked potatoes and smoky chicken, skin all crisped, lemons tucked inside.

One day she took some mushrooms and made a mean pie right there in Baba's home. You didn't want to enter the kitchen, because old sixpences stuck in your throat and a taciturn darkness overwhelmed you as soon as your feet crossed the threshold. You stood with a black circus and a clock in your head, not knowing if the shadows and their funny-voiced finger puppets were inside or outside you. All you knowed was that the three-bed with awning windows, grill-barred, was just another story with a terrible hush that a blade cut, and somebody's dream became other people's nightmares.

They started tawking mushrooms, Nana and Baba. The shrooms grew from deadness and put paradise in your stomach when Nana cooked them. Earth flavor, sea flavor, meat flavor—all of it came from demon gods. Shrooms carried all the dead people vitamins. You could eat all the carrots and spinaches, gobble salmons and livers, and not get as much nutrients as came from those shrooms, Nana said.

"This here are button mushrooms," she explained. "See how plump they get."

They were dome-shaped, pale brown, different from the cup mushrooms that were larger, partially open, and intense-flavored whether you ate them raw or cooked. The oyster mushrooms were nice to look at, flute-capped, as were the forest mushrooms with their dark, broad hats. But pine mushrooms got you and Baridi squealing—they grew wilder than the rest, saffron milk caps all bright orange, the taste rich and nutty.

"Strong bone too, less sick," Nana said. "Shrooms make your heart beat right."

Ting! The bell bird agreed.

All this while, the lads at the footy pitch gave you no mind, just looked from the distance as if plotting something. Waterman skipped: alternate foot, jump, jump, cross, boxer step, jump. Mitch: the sound of scraping as he honed his knife. Only smoke, not much words, came out of Mad's mouth. He didn't need to shout, "What yer doin' with that nigger?" cos you seen it in the contempt in his eyes. Sometimes Mad spat when you passed, but you knowed he still liked Baridi even though her pa were black.

Your pa still drunk beer and stared at the walls.

You slept in the attic, hugged your maw as she embraced you back with mottled skin. Blue-black beetles fell in and out of the holes in her stomach.

It happened at the cottage yard three days afore the end of summer break. Started with Nana's midday casserole, washed down with a cuppa and walnut-crusted cheesecake. The taste of mountain lemons and fresh earth lingered on your tongue.

Nana was inside Baba's house, washing up, and Baridi was helping to dry them. You didn't want to get inside the house that killed people. So you kicked the dawg a ball but, like always, it were a wonky kick that didn't go as planned.

The ball rolled to the cursed ground near the dawgtree that now had yellow-green leaves. This tree that never bloomed 'til Baba showed were beginning to sprout blood berries and snow-white flowers.

"They're just pretty leaves," said Baba in his cherry-lip voice. "Not real flowers."

The dawg chased the ball a bit, but was fearful, you could see. She perked up ears as she approached the darkened ground.

"Killer!" you clapped your hands. "Fetch!"

She whined, whimpered, and stopped moving. You had to fetch the ball yourself, and her by the collar. As you stepped away from the ground's pulse, a branch raked your face. You touched your cheek, and your hand came out wet.

Away from the tree, Killer was still shivering as if stained with the mark of death. Baba walked out with a first aid kit. "Here." He put a smiley band aid to stop the bleed.

"Only the devil wanna live in a place like this," you said.

He considered you fer a long time. "That what you think?"

Killer stayed all mopey. She refused a treat, her yellow moon eyes all squinty. Even the bell bird was quiet.

You whistled at dawn, and Baridi tumbled out of the house with her ball. You scattered to the day, white mist in the air. A single *ting!* of a bell bird in the distance. Rain started to form, a drizzle in the vista. You peddled on your feet, as if you were carrying demons on your backs. A torrent chased hard. The fingers of a damp demon touched you, first on the forehead, then on the neck. You raced up the stone steps, huddled by the door washed in a silence of the weather's pout. Then floodgates opened and, with it, a rush of sound. A distant buzz of racing cars. A chorus of chimes, cheeps, warbles of the rained birds. Then *gribble!* Frogs. You lived fer the summer, and this day held a curse.

You seen it first—a blob of tar hanging down the branch. The dawgtree leaned from its weight. The tar disintegrated as the rain arrived, the buzz louder as large blowflies dispersed in a cloud that changed itself and soared into the sky. You leaned closer to look at what was left behind. A worm beast. Fat writhing things, wriggled in and out of its body, skin and intestines.

Baridi threw the ball up in the air, knocked it with a boot as it fell. It whistled, *slam!* into the worm beast and some of the worms fell off in a splat. The ball lingered, stuck to the squishy insides of burst maggots. Then it bounced to the ground and you seen what the hung thing really were. Killer, dead. Hanged with a noose roped on the dawgwood, her stomach clawed open. Maggots crawled onto each other, in and out of the dead dawg. You knowed whose rope it were that noosed, whose folding knife slit her all the way down her stomach to her butthole.

You fainted, but you didn't, because you were still standing. Baridi ran, and you looked at her sprinting towards the boys starting to gather and stare in the rain as if trapped in the same summer curse. Baba fell out of the house, came running towards the tree and strong hands carried you from it.

Your lips trembled. You pressed a hand to your stomach as if pushing back guts.

Baridi lost a boot running, but she flew at the boys, uncaring of the folding knife. She barreled first into Mitch, and then Waterman.

Soul Parchment yelled *Fucketty.*

Baridi was hitting at anyone in the wet. The boys just stood as she whipped at them, and Mitch was shouting, "I didn't do nothing!" and Waterman, "It weren't us, honest to gawd."

And Mad…he just stood in the wet as it pounded.

Nana didn't lay hands on the dawg, mutter, her eyes all bug. No toads fell out of her throat in incantation, so there was no ocean pushing from inside wanting to come outta her skin to bring back Killer.

"Why can't yer?" you begged.

"Some things, boy, you don't bring back."

You watched full of empty as Baba disturbed the shrooms with a new hole in the ground.

The empty filled with something that burst when your pa got home. You gasped, "Pa."

His brown eyes fell on you. He dropped his satchel of letters, and the strides that reached you were big and long. The hands that held you were strong and tender. You choked and hiccupped as he said, over and over, in his awkwardness, "What's this, is this." His chest was out of place, his hands disconnected from his mind.

Maw was there with Killer when you slept. The dawg panted, good as new. She lay all floppy on your stomach, her black tongue licky licking your face out of a droopy mouth. Her eyes were a pale blue moon that filtered light under your door. Once or twice, you woke to Pa's footsteps climbing up the wooden steps to the attic. He stopped on the last rung, a shadow under your door. Each time he went away without coming in.

You leapt soon as morning broke and didn't whistle fer Baridi. You kept running, full of foreboding. Then you saw it: the moving van purring on the driveway, with Baba inside—clean-shaven, a bandana around his tight curls. He wore a neat jaw like you'd never seen afore on him, sat with sunnies at the wheel. You looked at his mouth, wide and honest, and you knowed you'd trust anything that came off it.

23

"Mr Baba," you said weakly, and he slid down the window.

"'Sup nigger?"

You pointed at the van. "Movin' already?"

"Yessir." There was deep sadness in his voice.

He swept a final look, reached for something in his pocket, tossed the tin of Skittles, and you caught it. He rolled the van onto the road. And you knowed that he were no more a devil than you.

Naked Earth

NAEEMA'S SKY is falling. Her universe is split into embracing and unshackling, and everywhere is scorching. Privilege is synonymous with who leads or who sponsors. And, right now, with the lefties and right wingers disconcerting the undecided with formation/misinformation, the world is more than random.

She once learnt to tell embracers from the unshackled by the bracelets they wear or don't. Embracers brandish luminescent bracelets shimmering with kilojoules from yoga, sexual intercourse or the simple act of walking home from an embrace-friendly workplace. Each bracelet transmits kilowatts to a recycling tower that helps save the planet.

The unshackled eat as they like, and wave bare arms as they jog on treadmills or in parks, dripping sweat on rubber mats, naked earth or non-embrace towels.

The undecideds wear blank amulets that sell dear and state nothing, but they incur hefty insurance premiums that are compulsory to renew.

But nothing is black or white because, in the midst of all this dichotomy, are conservatives, moderates and progressives.

The undecideds make things difficult, for instance on matters of jury selection, especially in trials where the alleged victim and perpetrator are on either side of belief. The O. Nucks case was one such conundrum—people still brawl about the not guilty verdict where guilt stood right there in the jury's faces.

Turns out it's a frequent occurrence that some undecideds firm their belief towards embracement or unshacklement mid-trial, swinging verdicts, or leading to mis-trials.

Naeema's indecision is not out of choice but from necessity.

As a child, she never questioned when Ma recycled Brian's nappies in embrace bins that a swirly ball in the sky—all clean energy—fortnightly collected. Naeema wished every birthday that she'd unwrap an embrace bracelet that put her on par with her parents, but it never happened.

"We want you to decide for yourself when you're older," Pa said the one time Naeema threw a tantrum over the matter.

Ma glowered in the way she did to say the matter was *not closed*.

Naeema learned as early as kinder that being undecided was not safe. Both embracers and the unshackled bullied the heck out of her because she was seemingly the only undecided kid in the whole class. The teacher divvied up seating in columns of embracers and unshackled, and Naeema sat alone and shunned at a corner in the back.

At primary school, still undecided, she discovered that, no matter how hard she worked, her grades got no better than a C minus. If the teacher was an embracer, students that were embracers scored distinctions. If the teacher was unshackled, students that were unshackled scored distinctions. Not a single teacher was undecided, so Naeema was pretty much fucked.

Jezza was Naeema's first kiss at high school. Jezza walked loose and relaxed, smoked ciggies and said, "Too easy," to everything. She rolled hand-made tobacco, not clean energy vapes from embrace franchises. Jezza was the kind of girl Naeema thought of as a hippie. They were washing hands in the girls' toilet at recess when Jezza locked eyes with Naeema across the mirror.

Their kiss put custard in Naeema's knees. She felt safe and lost.

The affection and euphoria she felt inside the wintergreen taste of Jezza's tobacco on her tongue was enough for Naeema to declare herself capable of decision-making.

She was thinking about the crazy tantric shit with Jezza—it was like bees making honey on her body and she buzzed and stung all over for days on end—when she firmly declared at the dinner table, "I'm unshackled."

Brian burst out into an annoying chortling laugh.

"I don't know what's the big deal," said Naeema. "I'm a free spirit."

"Tell that to your kids when you murder their world," said Brian.

Ma and Pa never stopped eating. They never looked at her once. It was as if she'd never spoken. But in the kitchen as she topped the recycler, Pa laid a hand on her shoulder, and it spoke *volumes*. For the first time in her life, Naeema wondered, truly wondered, how much of an embracer Pa was, and whether he was secretly unshackled or something moderate.

The diversity question in official forms was not about racial, sexual or religious slanting but about embracing and unshackling. She learnt the hard way that ticking unshackled cost her eligibility to government FEE-HELP for uni, because the prime minister was an embracer. Ticking embracer lost Naeema a diversity scholarship to private college because the funding body was unshackled.

Several times in her life Naeema underwent metamorphosis as she figured herself out, tried to manage, or was simply getting over Jezza and her plaited braids gone gallivanting with a backpack across the world.

The term 'better half' or 'other half' took on new significance for intermarried couples. Those who survived found synergy in their differences. Others took matters in their own hands, and divorce was not always the positive outcome, as happened in the O. Nucks case.

Introducing digital passports compelled choice. But one could stay 'undecided'—the least favorable option with the mandatory insurance premium so costly to annually renew. The undecideds also incurred a 3.25% surcharge on everything: education, recreation venues, visa applications, cafés, restaurants, pharmacies and surgery.

Naeema met Ponty who was a footy player and kicked a ripper. He knew exactly where the ball would go and was a premiership player whose team was a household name. He was totally an embracer and recycled the kinetics of his athleticism into a bracelet.

But already Naeema was fighting with him about collecting their orgasms.

"It kills the moment," she cried and refused to have sex with him. "Abstinence is better." What was the point of sustainable sex that saved the planet if a bracelet gobbled up her oxytocin, dopamine, serotonin? Rather than a floating pleasure that rushed her head—like she felt with Jezza—all she worried about now was how many kilojoules were going into the damn bracelet. She wanted to feel fullness, the kind that came with a giddy tornado that stretched and warmed, almost painful yet so sweet. She wanted to feel underwater and gasping, yet in the clouds and wallowed in sweet velvet, the way it was when her legs entwined with Jezza's.

"What does that *even mean?*" laughed Ponty when she tried to explain why they should try intercourse without him wearing his embrace bracelet.

She gave it a good go: embrace lotions, embrace-friendly eggs, nuts, seeds, cocoa, lip balm, even an embrace apartment with its recycled clean energy. She tolerated a bit more sex with Ponty though it left her feeling like someone had died.

Then came elections and embracers and the unshackled hated each other all the way to the dark web, and Naeema realized it was safer to stay undecided. She learnt to use benign phrases like, "It's a colored topic," or "It's a matter of growth curvature," when someone pointed at her bland bracelet and demanded she pick a side.

Now Naeema's sky is falling because she doesn't feel love or hate. She misses what she had with Jezza and misses Ponty's good intentions. In truth she does love them both in their own way. She adores her parents and her brother Brian—who now works as a sustainable ambassador.

Brian sells 'guaranteed embracement' in aged care homes, emergency wards and palliative care facilities, handing out embrace bracelets in hushed wards. He speaks to relatives in sterile corridors, waiting rooms or chapels as they light candles and pray for their loved ones' speedy recovery. The brochures he hands out have words like 'moral compass', 'a new era of seeing the invisible', 'having true heart to save the planet'.

He's wildly successful in convincing patients to see the better future they are creating with their sacrifice, as the bracelet glows to take their death rattle. Sometimes Naeema ponders how quickly the dying die when they wear embrace bracelets. She wonders if it's the bracelet, or the peace of wearing it, that intensifies the dying in souls that might otherwise linger.

Naeema still wears a blank amulet that states nothing. It's a gamble that leaves her vulnerable, feeling like a migrant or a refugee, never quite belonging. On the plus side, it comes with a degree of flexibility on the job market. Being undecided means she's still figuring things out, so she can trial embracer or unshackler jobs, but only as a temp or on short contracts, never as a permanent staffer.

Her life has no Jezza or Ponty, and maybe she's dead to Ma and Brian.

Pa, like Jezza, one day upped and walked out with a rucksack, all the way to humanitarian work. He writes to her sometimes from a mission church, school or hospital in a place called Kitwe somewhere in Zambia or Uganda—he's never specific, but sounds in a good place, perhaps physically.

Sometimes Naeema uses embrace lotions and aromatics, and sometimes she temps as an embrace angel or a sustainable ambassador like Brian. She even rides the swirly recycler ball across the skies on contract. She rolls a joint every now and then and it takes her to the buzz she felt wrapped around Jezza.

She doesn't like beef, and that's that, but she can't be vegan or whatever because she loves chicken. If she were mortally wounded, heck, yeah, she'd totally wear an embrace bracelet, there's no doubt about that. Because deep down she's a well-meaning person who wants to save the planet.

But she's not a leftie or a right winger, and she doesn't mind the free spirited or the climate committed. She rides hoverboards because she can't afford a car, so it's not about clean energy. She feels like she's waiting with her eyes shut for someone to destroy her fears. Or perhaps her wait is for history to pattern itself into the poetics of a last crusade. She just wants to survive now because her life is now. She can only hope that—kilojoules or not—the world might become less of a mess.

What she knows is that her body is not full of pebbles and scales. She doesn't want to become a stone like her brother Brian. Dead to what it means, really means, to be human inside, animating only for a cause. History is full of contradictions, and she might watch it with irony, unsettlement, even awe. But she doesn't want her children to grow up in the languor of pale dirt country. She wants them to see a world that's a bloody beauty, and safe—something she worries that the unshackled in their denials of entanglement and responsibility might not understand. Hers is a critical distance that carries doubt and grief for a future that is closing. It's an all-language that is no language in a world so starkly divided.

The water is changing hands—on the first sip, you know. A melon is not a lemon, even though they both have a long finish, and the same letters are shifting. She makes a choice to be less random, not undecided. To find a space of transition that is both human and saving, like Pa.

She doesn't have all the answers now.

But this is a start.

The Set

JABARI wished his life was more interesting. He wished he could have an adventure just once, but no. He worked in radio, and you know what people said about radio people. The voice of an archangel, the face even a mother cannot love. Voice of an archangel was for him a stretch. And he definitely wore a face a mother struggled with.

He thought of his chin—no—that was his nose. He tried a smile in the mirror of his mind's eye, and all he saw was a snarl, empty eyes. Didn't his mother put him in a basket, place it on a doorstep for the Brothers of St Vincent to find? Same Brothers who tried to rub onto him vocation, thinking that a motherless child was destined to heal others with the fingers of a god? Not with that smile, no. Salvation came in the choir. Jabari didn't question much, and when someone put him in the choir, he stayed in it. To his astonishment, he found that he could sing like a Tickell's blue flycatcher (without its colorful personality), and that is what earned him the Brothers' fresh butter, lemons and honey to encourage a radio voice.

Now grown, Jabari saw his life in monochrome along the borders of a photograph. And it was digital—easily blurred, brushed, filtered, soft-edged or made transparent on a resizable canvas that could rotate or flip in pixel. If his life were a film, his footage would be a deleted scene in a documentary, never certainty or a prayer—where was hope? He was unimportant, a moment cluttered on a high shelf no-one would notice. He was a line, gobbled thin and bounded by gaps in a fissure between now and then. He was a memory, shuffled and mismatched.

In this monochrome, a low-flying gull *kraa'ed* an unfamiliar ballad and dropped a piece of cellophane on Jabari's face. That was *all* the lens would remember: a seagull regurgitating cellulose that was permeable to air and water.

The photo would never remember him, Jabari; what he was on the inside, or how he felt all the time—as if there was a taxi outside that had been waiting, clocking up stories all his life from the day he passed through a birth canal.

This is what Jabari was thinking at 5.43 am precisely, lying inside a blanket on his bed—despite the alarm's wail at 5 am sharp, which was an anomaly. He always set it for 6.30 am. He swung a leg and hit his toe against a wall. It appeared that overnight his house had turned. He smiled wryly. Was his self so bad, even the house turned away from it? Because that was the only way he could explain the difference.

Who was he? Jabari asked himself today, as he did other days. *Why was he?*

He hugged his knee, caressed the throbbing big toe, and glared at the damn wall. If someone snatched his personal space and put it on daytime TV, it would only exist as a scrolling ticker low on a screen in font so tiny you squinted to see it. Or as unnoticeable remnants of a soap opera played backwards with silent ads and bloopers: *Cut! Roll back!*

If he became a fly between now and everything else, would anyone notice?

Today, the shower was not right either. Jabari squealed when a squirt of scald came out where normally it spewed tepid. And the fridge! It wouldn't budge until he opened it from the right—which was pretty startling in itself.

Despite these mishaps, he was ready for his radio show. He'd already emailed the song sequence to Lamb, the sound guy at the studio:

"My Country" by Jamilla

"You Have the Roar" by Wolfbane

"Kwacha Kwacha" by Ingoma, his favorite by far: sweet chimes of the kora, the accompaniment of the *mbira*, a thumb piano, and the *tapee-tadoo-dah* of the *djembe*—tuned skin and rope ushering gods with a drum beat…

He'd also recorded his interviews with the show's special guests:

Shallow Feels—Jabari had tried to ask the muso hard questions about his anti-vaxxer stance. He (Jabari, not Feels) came out a bit inept. But it was a slot filler.

Ingoma—talking about her inspiration behind "Kwacha Kwacha", and she was ace because a) she just was b) he liked her nose ring and shaven head and c) he was impressed by the "wise" about social justice, female empowerment—the girl from the village shaking the universe kind of thing—that came out of her mouth.

He had the show order all good in his head, and in the radio planner he'd saved into the programmer. The show would start with "My Country", then a news-in-brief segment, already summarized in cue cards. He'd then play "You Have the Roar", followed by the Shallow Feels interview. Then "Kwacha Kwacha" and, finally, the Ingoma interview and a closing news summary.

Before going to the studio, he did his normal walk in the botanical gardens. He was startled that, today, there was nothing normal about the garden. First, gates that were meant to be spear-headed wrought-iron in black were now a towering platinum monolith with auto-sensors that let him through. Second, all walking paths were in sharp angles, not their normal sweep of arcs and curves. Third, the lawns were too manicured: he could have sworn they were artificial. His mental count of anomalies went on. He met no people walking toddlers or dogs. The signpost to the Visitor Center pointed backwards. Instead of the herb garden, there was a fern gully trail.

And where a visitor's café once stood was a shallow lake. He didn't mind that the café was gone—it promised a platinum experience, but the coffee there was borderline shit. You took one sip of it and spat because it tasted like something straight off a wombat's butt. Yeah, he wouldn't miss the café, but still!

And those weren't the only anomalies he saw. There were no bins—no yellows for recycled. He neared the spot where the bins once stood, squealed and fell back as a maw opened from the ground and nearly took him. Rattled, he looked around at a treeless garden shorn of acacias, banksias and eucalypti. There were no every day sounds of honeyeaters, magpies, cockatoos or galahs, but near a brand new water fountain he'd never seen before stood a google-eyed tramp bird that studied him. It was a bulbous-headed parrot cum pig with a puffed-out breast and spindly legs. Its pink tongue dangled out of the side of its closed beak. The bird hissed, barked and cackled at him and Jabari hurried away.

On his way out of the garden he should have encountered the herbarium, but in its stead stood a high-rise blinker steepling into the heavens. Jabari's knees gave, but he was unwilling to sit on the new bouncy enviro cushies in jacaranda, framboise and tuberose colors that had replaced plain army-green park benches. He walked briskly out of the gardens through the discomfiting auto-sensor monoliths, and attempted his normal coffee stop before work.

But there was nothing normal about the coffee or the stop. Every day the sign read: *Stories So Far.* Today it read: *Stories About Us.*

He was glad to see the board was still there: *Specialty coffee, bar and bottle shop.*

What surprised him was that the café was in the exact location it should be, but it now stood next to a carpark he'd never seen. He tried not to question it. Not far was a metro hub, an industry training center he'd also never seen. Jabari figured what the hub was from the signage, and the students spilling out of it. His normal café was supposed to be ensconced in an apartment building, an arched doorway leading to it. It held a homely tightness about it, and you could get a real liquored—not flavored—affogato. You could ask for premium tea or coconut

Eugen Bacon

milk. Only yesterday morning, it wasn't *Stories About Us* selling a Kennedy Shiraz special; it was *Stories So Far*—its wall rack craftily arrayed with vintage wine. He hadn't bought the shiraz, but had taken a loaf of rye, raisin, orange and fennel sourdough bread, and a bottle of pure sparkling water from the little black fridge. Today, there was no fridge in sight. The barista used almond milk for his fresh chai latte—Jabari took one sip of it and spat. Who used fucking almond milk on a chai latte? He marched outside, chucked the lot and instead ordered (and paid again) a hot chocolate for himself and a skinny latte for his co-producer Moha.

Moha was clarified butter, and Jabari was hopelessly in love. He did this all the time: wrap his heart around a beautiful, soulful thing that didn't exist because people could never love him back. He created things that were perfect in his head, but that kind of perfection did not exist. Already he had been abandoned in childhood by his own *mother*, and all his life he carried this deep and terrible fear of abandonment to such extent that his life was vanilla. Everybody loved vanilla. Mint was a risk. Buttered pecan was a risk. Cookie dough was a risk. But who the fuck didn't like vanilla? He liked to imagine Moha as the exquisite Madagascan kind, subtly floral and indulgently creamy.

He walked out of the spacious, not homely tight, café holding Moha's coffee in a styrofoam cup. He contemplated his anomalous morning, baffled at the deforming and distorting all around him, and looked back to the night before…

Jabari had first watched the news—a shooting in a suburb and all that shit—as he ate a burger with the lot. He watched a sitcom on TV, and liked how Doreen, his fave on the cast talked:

"We here…"

"They tooks…"

Doreen looked a bit like Moha with her smooth cheekbones, sophisticated intimate eyes and blond-tinted braids. He imagined going to a *doof doof* with Doreen (or Moha) somewhere with a smooth wand DJ zinging top cunt mixers like a wizard. He saw himself sipping highball cocktails of shaken rum, sugar, lime and mint.

But the last time he'd tried a night out, it was at a club called District, patrons constantly vaping and smoking darts. A bunch of tossers acting butch, but they were all pussies, didn't like his face and were too soaked in booze to be subtle about it. He reckoned that if he got any of them solo, they'd cave. Jabari left and went to a pub where he played pool, until some drunk idiot with missing front teeth and swearing "Fahkin' hell" began causing trouble and calling Jabari a dog cunt. It wasn't just a vibe. It lost Jabari the sweet on night outs, and that was that. Still, it was the most excitement he'd ever had.

33

He switched to the sports channel, watched a bit of the Sydney to Hobart sailing race, looked at different boats and how they were named *Scallywag, Gunn Runner, Fruit Gambo, Joyride*... He wanted to give himself a joyride without having to become a skipper on a 15 m sail.

Jabari switched channels and was watching cricket—Aussies trouncing the Poms—when first the TV then the house wobbled.

Now Jabari walked towards the studio finishing his hot chocolate. The morning was white and sunny. A crisp cooling breeze touched the nape of his neck just so. Studio 59 was a ground-level building near a crossing. It was embossed with a Jupiter symbol, a hieroglyph of an eagle: a curled letter Z with a line drawn through. It stood next to a bank ATM. A black-framed glass wall allowed you to look inside—well-lit and furnished in accent chairs and charcoal pillows.

Jabari peered inside. Cellar pendant chandeliers interspersed with smoked glass chandeliers splashed their light onto a mid-century fireplace, all Romeo. He looked at his watch—8 am sharp. He swiped his staff card on the reader.

The door swung open, and he entered.

Scene 1. INT. PRODUCTION STUDIO. EARLY MORNING
No Trackie Dacks in Here

The studio interior is in classic neutral colors—modern, inviting. A lit sign says: THE WEEKLY SET. Another red flasher says: ON AIR.

There's a poster of a movie actress standing in pose against a sportscar. She is holding a cigar, a whisp of smoke wafting from her Monroe kissy-mouth in photographic freeze.

Center stage is transitional furniture—suited for a home office and includes a koala sofa set in grays and creams. It's the kind you look at its comfort and want to touch your head on it.

The cameraman BOYLE *is behind a pedestal. A flood of lights is angled towards the koala sofa facing a teleprompter. The soundman* LAMB's *headphones are dangled across his neck.*

The producer, MOHA, *is restless and holding a clipboard. She looks up as* JABARI *enters.*

JABARI: (*smiling shyly at* MOHA) I brought you a skinny latte. (*offering her the coffee*)

MOHA: (*tossing her braids, snaps the coffee from his hands*) This is going to be a ripper. (*eyeing him up and down, frowning at his tracksuit and runners*) You well know you're darn late, a fucking latte won't get me happy! And what the blitz are you wearing?

34

JABARI: (puzzled) I don't know what's all the fuss for a radi—
MOHA: (turning to the costume girl) New wardrobe. Gigi!

Heavily mascaraed GIGI is wearing her short crop dyed cyan. Wordlessly, she leads
JABARI out of the set and into a room labelled: MAKE-UP.

Scene 2. INT. PRODUCTION STUDIO
Where the Fuck Is Radio?
JABARI emerges from the make-up room dressed in a sky-colored suit, double-
breasted, and made of textured wool.
    GIGI is arranging the collar of his sleek coral button-down shirt of Egyptian
cotton, all tucked in. She straightens a lavish platinum tie in silk twill.
    He looks at his watch and is surprised that the time is still on 8 am, although the
hand is still ticking.
JABARI: (entering the studio set) The runners—
MOHA: No-one will be looking at your goddamn feet.
            JABARI sits on the high stool center stage.
            GIGI dabs more powder on his nose.
            There's a large screen on the far side of the room. JABARI sees himself on
            it, a ticker with ads running at the bottom of the screen.
JABARI: (surprised) Why, it's TV—
MOHA: (rolling her eyes) Seriously.
JABARI: (raising his palms in a sign of peace) Can I have some water?
            GIGI hands him a filled glass.
            BOYLE winks and repositions the camera.
            LAMB puts on the headphones, gives a thumbs up.
            Lights come up.
MOHA: (raising the clipboard) And action!

(Techno-music playing)

JABARI: (puzzled) That's not Jamilla's 'My Country'.
MOHA: (lowering the clipboard) And cut! (glaring at JABARI). The hell!
JABARI: I emailed the song order…
MOHA: We don't do song orders. The theme song for The Set is always 'Street Ace'.
JABARI: (frowning) I don't know about 'Street Ace'. It sounds like yowling cats and
            farting alpacas.
MOHA: Gee, thanks.

JABARI: I don't question much, but if you didn't like what I sent earlier...
MOHA: Jesus Christ!
JABARI: (shrugging) Oh, never mind. (straightens his posture and looks at the camera)
MOHA: (raising the clipboard) And action!

(Techno-music playing)

JABARI: (reading from his cue cards) Welcome to The Set. We're live from Melbourne, it's another record day...
MOHA: (lowering the clipboard) And cut! (looking angrily at JABARI). The fuck are you doing?
JABARI: The usual?
MOHA: (angrily snatching JABARI's cue cards, drops them on the floor) Look straight ahead and read the fucken teleprompter. (raising the clipboard) And action!

(Techno-music playing)

JABARI: (reading the teleprompter) The crypto bank has announced a rollout of new loans for first time homebuyers... The world is in a state, with a new strain of the mutant virus body jumping and causing premature conception in women, mostly quadruplet babies, even in sterilized people. (briefly glancing in puzzlement at MOHA, but continues to read) There is major concern that the virus is especially targeting women on contraception, triggering panic across the globe. The US is no longer accepting flights to or from South Africa where scientists first discovered the new virus strain that is contagious by human touch, skin to skin...

JABARI *scratches his head at how unreal this all sounds. He casts a beseeching look at* MOHA, *who gives him a stone face.*

JABARI: (continues reading the teleprompter) Pharmaceuticals globally are scrambling to develop a vaccine to curb the baby pandemic in an already crowded world. Airline passengers are hurting with a soaring number of cancelled flights, following an increase in positive cases among crew. Testing centers are struggling to cope with the surge as women scramble for testing. In other news, anti-vaxxers are still protesting worldwide, let's take a look...

The large monitor shows a congregation of angry people chanting and roaring "Stop the fib". They are swaying placards saying, VACCINE GUMBO, MANDEMIC PANDEMIC… The scene repeats with crowds in London, Sydney, Nairobi, Luxemburg, Dodoma, Lagos, Delhi, Paris…
MOHA: *(lowering the clipboard) And cut!*

JABARI *is relieved to leave the set and find a toilet. He frowns as he discovers the Men's is not at its usual place two doors left, but rather down the corridor where the fire exit door normally stands.*

He hurries out of the toilet and blinks in surprise that he's suddenly barefoot and wearing torn trousers and no shirt. He steps through a door and…

Scene 3. INT. PRODUCTION STUDIO
It's a Bloody Comedy
…JABARI *steps into a new stage now decorated to resemble a marooning island: fake palm trees and a beach.*
(Crow squawking)
(Monkeys jabbering in the distance)
To the side is a door that leads to the stage with a live audience.
A large clock on the wall behind the live audience says it's 8 am.
GIGI *dabs more powder on* JABARI*'s nose. She opens a make-up kit.*

JABARI: *(quickly) No mascara, thanks.*

BOYLE *winks and repositions the camera.*
LAMB *wearing the headphones, gives a thumbs up.*
JABARI *opens the side door and lights dim on.*
MOHA *approaches him, wearing a sisal skirt and stringed coconut husks covering her breasts.*

MOHA: *Thank Fonz you're here!*
JABARI: *(surprised) Wow.*

(Live audience laughing)

JABARI: *I've always loved this show. Ever wondered who the heck this Fonz is that they keep thanking? I never for a minute imagined I'd find myself in one of their skits.*

MOHA: *(fourth wall performance) Babe, we're on set. (speaking loudly, pointedly)*
        THANK FONZ YOU'RE HERE!

(Live audience laughing)

JABARI *gets into character, tilts his chin in a flirty way.*

JABARI: *I like to arrive the way cats do.*
MOHA: *(coyly) Purring, rubbing and swaying your tail?*
JABARI: *(smiling) Bet it ties your tongue, hey.*
MOHA: *It does, but don't mind me—I'm just a fragment.*
JABARI: *I don't know what the heck that means, but I likey. A lot. (winking at live*
          audience)

(Live audience laughing)

JABARI: *(sniffing in MOHA's direction) Your perfume…*
MOHA: *Wild rose—I bet it's confounding.*
JABARI: *Makes my bones ache…the inner sea…this is disaster. (grabs MOHA's*
          hand) But you, darling, make it all better when you—

(Approaching drumbeats)
(Tarzan howl that grows loud, louder)

JABARI: *Babe, what the hell is that?*
MOHA: *The musicality of fiction that will set you free. Which reminds me—come!*
          (tugging him towards the edge of the setting)
JABARI: *Oooh, but where—*
MOHA: *In your absence, as you were gallivanting to god-knows-where, leaving me*
          ALL ALONE (dramatic pause)…I discovered a circumcision tree!
JABARI: *(dragging his feet) A what?! (pulling away from her grip)*

They vanish from view, but the live audience can still hear them.

JABARI: *There's no anesthetic!*
MOHA: *(firmly) Just dip that dongle in the calming water. That's what the Bantu*
          men in East Africa do. Ice-cold water for anesthetic.
JABARI: *This here is not ice-cold—it's fucking tropical!*

MOHA: Yes, and it's salty. Now, sweetheart, drop those pants.
JABARI: (gut-wrenching man howl)

(Live audience laughing)

MOHA: Shhhh! You'll wake the big fat crocs, and with all that blood… Let's dip
         into the salty water, shall we? Healing properties, and all.

Sound of MOHA and JABARI *entering the water.*

JABARI: (gut-wrenching banshee howl).

(Live audience laughing)
(Clapping)

MOHA: (offset, to the production crew) And cut!

MOHA and JABARI *return on stage,* JABARI *hobbling with a large patch of fake
blood on his crotch. They hold hands and take their bows as the live audience claps
and whoops.*

JABARI *approaches* MOHA *outside the set.*

JABARI: (grinning wide) That was fun! I can't believe I was just on Thank Fonz
         You're Here.
MOHA: (frowning) Fuck's wrong with you? (turning away from him)

JABARI *wonders woefully what is happening, where is his normal life?*

The set is suddenly too claustrophobic, and JABARI *wants to be back in the dirt. He
walks quickly out of the studio and…*

Scene 4. EXT. EXOTIC BEACH
                    A Friggin' Love Paradise
    …(Cheery islander drumbeats)
    JABARI *steps out of a beach hut and into a private islet all tropical and near the
sea. He blinks in astonishment at the real outside world, no longer on set at the studio.
He's barefoot and wearing fire-wave swim shorts in tangerine and black.*

He looks at the golden sand and beach huts all around, lights up when he sees GIGI *and* MOHA.

Heavily mascaraed GIGI *is dipping her toes by the side of a turquoise pool in a sweeping curl around palm tree islands. She's tits out, wearing cyan-dyed hair and only a dive bikini bottom in a red and white passion blend, string ties on the side. She is holding a fizzy drink in a champagne flute garnished with a sliced berry.*

MOHA *is sprawled on a swaying hammock. She is wearing a neon bikini outside a magnificently tanned body.*
(Splashing water on a fountain near the pool)
(Cockatiel whistling, smooth and sweet.
BOYLE *winks and repositions the camera from a distance.*
LAMB *puts on the headphones, gives a thumbs up.*
JABARI *approaches the girls, wondering how he got onto a Love Island skit.*

GIGI: *(sarcastic from a distance, to MOHA)* Here comes your boyfriend. He's all yours. Sorry for dumping him on you.

MOHA: *(sarcastic laugh)* Really? Wow.

GIGI: Yeah. Give him your rose at the ceremony tonight, 'cos he's not getting mine.

MOHA: Like, why not? You worked so hard to pull that dick move last night. How do you think that made me feel?

JABARI: I don't know what you're talking about. Where are you getting this dick move shit from? *(To GIGI)* Nothing happened between us! *(To MOHA)* Honest.

MOHA: Like I care.

JABARI: *(glaring at GIGI, then softly to MOHA)* Don't listen to her, babe. She's bat-shit crazy.

GIGI: *(to MOHA)* He leaves you on red every day. I can show you the text messages he's been sending me.

MOHA: That's so fucked up.

GIGI: Him, or you? What's more fucked is if you get pregnant with a cheater. He'll do everything in his power to make sure that baby never gets born.

MOHA: *(yelling angrily)* I am not pregnant! And he loves me!

GIGI: *(eyeing JABARI in disdain)* Last night didn't seem like it. I think he's ditched you like a sack of bricks.

MOHA: *(crying)*

JABARI: *(putting his arms around MOHA)* I didn't ditch you! I love you!

MOHA *(shrugging off his touch, continues crying)*

It dawns on JABARI *that this is reality TV, not a skit, and the emotions are real. He'd craved for adventure, but this? This!*

JABARI: *(looking angrily at* GIGI*) Happy with yourself now? (down on his knees and wrapping his arms around* MOHA*) Babe—*

MOHA: *(muffled) Fuck off, yeah. Don't act so angry. You've kinda become a dick.*

GIGI: *(shouting to* JABARI*) And I meant every word! You're not getting a fucking rose from me tonight.*

JABARI *walks away glum.*

He enters his cabin, sits on the bed. He rubs his temples, lies down, and closes his eyes.

JABARI: *(uncharacteristic shouting to the ceiling) It's meant to be a fucking radio show!*

(Wobbling sound)

JABARI *sits up, startled, as the bed humps and wobbles. The cabin begins to shake violently as if a griffin is having at it. The beach hut suddenly topples.*

*(*JABARI *screeching)*

JABARI *clutches about wildly as he slides downwards and slams his head against a topsy-turvy roof or a wall. He crawls to what might be a window, bashes it open with his feet, and...*

Scene 5. EXT. TROPICAL JUNGLE—MORNING
Effin' Jungle Survivor Shit

*...*JABARI *rolls out of a tilted shipwreck and plunges headfirst into a thick jungle, eerie with wilderness.*

(Tiger growling)
(The cry of a howler monkey)

A black eagle soars overhead. JABARI *sees a tiger loping down a tree out yonder. He cries out in alarm and jumps at a rustle.*

(Deer honking in the distance)

JABARI *turns towards the rustling sound and sees to his left a python wrapping itself around a forest antelope.*

Up on hill from a distance, JABARI *makes out two shapes watching, perhaps filming.*

He sees MOHA *and* GIGI *up on a fat oak in what seems to be a treehouse. They are dressed in combat gear matching what he's wearing.*

GIGI'*s face is covered in war paint. She is sharpening a tomahawk against a stone.*

MOHA *is holding a machine gun.*

JABARI *plods across mud and shrubbery in army boots and clambers up the tree.* MOHA *offers him a helping hand. A dog-like gruff-gruff of a hornbill echoes through the jungle.*

GIGI: *(scornful) What's with the poo face?*

JABARI: *Yeah. I was born with it, like seriously.*

MOHA: *(glaring at GIGI) That's just being a dick, mate. We need to be united.*

JABARI: *The fuck is this place?*

MOHA: *(pointing at a weaponry cache spilling with machine guns, katanas, throwing axes, pistols, rifles, sabers and grenades) The right question is the fuck can you use these?*

JABARI: *The hell! I mean, adventure and all, I'd take monochrome any time. Not this! Can someone just delete this scene?*

GIGI: *Better try at least one weapon, 'cos I don't see you at any moment doing praying mantis kick-type shit if it came to hand-to-hand.*

(High-pitched cry of a tapir, like the sound of a car braking)
(Growling, close now)

The three of them look in alarm in the direction the jungle.

MOHA: *(pointing the machine gun) I guess we're all going to die, but we might as well die fighting.*

HORNBILL: *Rrro-rrho!*

GIGI: *(grinning maniacally) 'Cos, like, why not?*

42

JABARI: I'm getting outta here! War is not, is never, my thing! And not with a goddamn jungle!

GIGI: Sure thing, pussy.

JABARI *grabs the nearest pistol and leaps down into the jungle. He starts running like mad towards the capsized ship in a murky river.*

(Snake hissing)

JABARI *screams as he catches sight of an anaconda slipping into the water. He fires wildly, a nothing shot—he's not good with guns.*

HORNBILL: Rrraaa!

MOHA: (shouting to JABARI) Wait for me, I'm coming!

MOHA *leaps down from the treehouse into the jungle and starts running across the water to join* JABARI *as he tries to climb back into the shipwreck.*

GIGI: Fucking jungle is a hive mind. (warning shout to MOHA) It's comin' at ya!

(Machine gun rattling)

MOHA: (screaming) Shit! Shit! It's the fucking anaconda! (beating at the anaconda with the butt of her gun) Help!

JABARI *aims and fires another nothing shot.*

(GIGI's war cry)

GIGI *is striking air with her tomahawk, facing off with a crouching tiger up on the treehouse.*

(MOHA's ear-piercing scream)

JABARI *turns to see the anaconda wrapping itself around* MOHA.

The tiger leaps and topples GIGI *under its weight.*

(GIGI grunting)

JABARI *turns and flees. All his life he's been abandoned. Now it's him doing the abandoning. He has a choice between saving Gigi or Moha, and once upon a day he might have picked Moha. But today he's choosing himself. The last thing he sees before he falls into the shipwreck is the tiger wrapping its jaw around* GIGI's *head.*

(Crunching sound)

Scene 6. INT. INSIDE THE SHIPWRECK
A Bloody Hole
(Sound of sobbing)

JABARI *huddles inside the shipwreck, arms around himself.*

(Thump)
(Thump)
(Thump)

He cries out. Something big and keen wants to get in from the jungle and eat him alive.

(Rumbling sound)

The shipwreck wobbles. JABARI *sees a hole for him to crawl in. It's not a hole, it's a cave. He sees the mouth of the cave and crawls out…*

Scene 7. EXT. OUTSIDE THE STUDIO—EVENING
The Hell?!
…JABARI *rises to his feet and blinks at the onset of dusk outside the studio where it all began. He looks at his watch: it says 8 pm.*

With a gulp, he breaks into a run.
He doesn't know where he's running to, just away from the goddamn studio, and…

…He raced past his usual café, *Stories So Far,* with its sign that said: *Specialty coffee, bar and bottle shop*—not the fake *Stories About Us* near a metro hub. He turned into the botanical garden and was glad to see it back to normal with arcs and sweeps, nothing angled, and gates that were once again spear-head wrought-iron, no stupid platinum monoliths with auto-sensors.

44

Eugen Bacon

But he couldn't trust its grass lawns, though they were real. He laughed out loud as he raced past a woman walking a dog, a man pushing a stroller. They both turned, looked at him as if he were mad. He didn't care, and waved, laughing louder now because the sign to the Visitor Center was pointing the right way. And there, right there, was the herb garden, and the visitor's café with its wombat-butt latte. And bins! He stopped to touch a yellow one for recycling, held himself from kissing it in delirious relief. He nearly cried at the sight of the lofty banksias and fat oaks, oh, and all those eucalypti! He flopped onto an army green park bench near the herbarium and hugged its back with his elbows.

He seriously questioned this godawful day, and wondered what had happened to him. He considered if it was brain fade. He pondered if he'd gobbled some hallucinatory drugs overnight and had simply forgotten about them… Or had he stepped into a multiverse portal? He wondered if, when he got home, he'd find a copy of himself sleeping on his bed, oblivious to all that had happened, and perhaps he'd have a new friend who was his own self. But how would they coexist? The more he thought and thought, the less and less understanding came to him. So he altogether gave up trying to make sense of anything, or figuring it out.

He sat on the bench a long time, emptying his mind until he calmed.

He strolled out of the gardens…the street leading to his house was nowhere in sight. There were no streets. Just one long, empty road in the middle of nowhere.

"No, no!" he cried. If this was his life getting interesting, he didn't want it!

What he wanted was his old self that watched Doreen on sitcoms, caught up on sailing, trounced the Poms in cricket. He wanted his life back, to be the Jabari who worked in friggin' radio.

"No!" he cried one more time, and started running…

Scene 8. EXT. DESERTED TARMAC ROAD—NIGHT
The Set
…*(Staccato pounding of running feet on gravel)*

The zoom starts in his mind. First on a ticking clock in his head, and its hand is on 8 pm. Suddenly he can see as if he's the man behind the camera. He zooms in on running feet, his, pound, pound, pound on an endless tarmac road. It zooms out to reveal
ankles, knees, torso
finally, the whole
of him furiously running
pound, pound, pound.

His expression brightens as the lens zooms away from him, locks in on a building in the distance. He knows the need. He runs faster, poundpoundpound. He's hoping, seriously hoping, that he's found the norm. He's hoping that it's home. He is the usual suspect, a part of something bigger—he just doesn't know what. But all he wants is to find a bed that's decent, to sleep and forget the nonsense that's just happened. He wants to watch cricket on a green wicket that's doing something. To see batsmen punchy on game, swinging balls both ways to four runs, four runs and a boundary.

To see bowlers drawing blood.

Good hands on the field…

He needs to know.

Poundpoundpound!

He tastes labor, but his relief turns to dismay. He's circled right back to the studio, yet not. This one is a towered office complex near a bank ATM. It's embossed with a Neptune symbol, a trident of hidden depths. It stands next to an acoustic center selling guitars in classics, electrics, even preowned vintages that beckon with accessories and guides. Unlike the real studio, the one he knows, the one with a black-framed glass wall

one can peer through

this studio is walled

he can't see

a damn thing.

Despite his loss, he now thinks that he doesn't have a staff card to swipe on the reader. But the studio anticipates him. It wobbles. Suddenly he can see through its walls, fading out from brick, fading into black-framed glass. He doesn't know if this is progress or roll back, if someone might cry: Cut! There's a poster, not of a movie actress with kissy lips blowing smoke from a cigar. It's an enlarged photo labelled: In Memoriam. MOHA and GIGI, each holding a champagne flute garnished with a strawberry, smiling at someone behind a camera at some event. MOHA—braids, smooth cheekbones, sophisticated intimate eyes. GIGI—mascara-gobbled eyes, a short crop dyed cyan. JABARI is outside looking in.

Chandelier light in the studio winks.

(Creaking sound)

The door s-w-i-n-g-s

O

  P

    E

    N

Derive, Moderately

AUM...OHM...

The alien chanting in Sabibu's head has calmed to a less urgent tempo. She looks at Fudge, who has finally drifted to weightless sleep. He hates the harness, being strapped down—what toddler wouldn't? Space travel is not all aurora, or Gliese—the beautiful planet. No matter how big the spaceship, and this rocket capsule isn't by any standards big, it gets claustrophobic. She is lost in this vessel that's not hers. Mali would know how to steer a rocket capsule that is not quite a spaceship. But Mali is not here. She's back home in Anko. But is she?

Sabi is past shock and denial. She's stuck in ache and guilt, sometimes wretchedness. When fury comes, as it sometimes does, she's frightened to touch the child lest she misdirects her ire. It doesn't help that her mind is always going, going, thinking bad thoughts: everything that happened. And her core feels pulled, at stretch. Her heart is pounding, always pounding, and her stomach swirls. She rubs her taut neck. She's not eating or sleeping well. They've been moving on dual nav for what seems like eons. The manual has helped some. Now the autopilot is handling the navigation on this leg.

"Momom," Fudge whimpers in his dreaming.

Sabi studies him with a frown. She wishes Mali were here. They agreed at insemination that Sabi would be a stay-at-home mom. "Social worker, right?" Sabi had laughed. Social work or not, she's inept with toddlers, especially this one strapped in. He cried as she lay him in position inside the rocket capsule, harnessed him. He cried at the rumble of the engines as they lit, then everything jolted and lurched forward to an upward pull. He cried as they blasted into orbit, the vessel's abysmal roar, its rattle and shudder. He cried, cried until he stopped breathing. He found a new cry and was purple by the time they reached orbit and there was no more terrible noise, just terrible quiet. She took off her helmet, unstrapped herself and reached him in a float.

It feels only yesterday when Sabi's biggest worry was Fudge's delayed speech. Now she's worried about his puffy face, rounded in microgravity. She worries about his apathy in food. He's always loved fruit, just not cubes and purees that taste like nothing. At first they butted heads, as she forced his mouth open and drizzled in something packaged. He cried his rage, bawled her ears out. He spat the food and it soared around in a float, got into their eyes, their hair—which made Fudge wail even more—until she vacuumed the muck. But she quickly learnt to leave him alone because, like any bub, he asks or squeals when hunger gets a bit much.

"Pom pom," and she gives him the pumpkin pie puree. "Gogo," and she peels a mango cube from its disposable package. "Gisi," and she floats a fig into his mouth. His penchants vary. Sometimes it's 'Nana'—amen for freeze-dried bananas. She worries about him never walking, losing muscle and bone strength in space.

She misses Mali, her cleverness at everything. She misses lying naked together. Mali's swell of hips, her sandalwood taste. Fairy orgasms that wiggle all the way up Sabi's spine and light her mind. What if Mali…she cannot bring herself to name that worst horror—it slams an axe into her heart.

Mali would know how to make Fudge laugh. Mali would find hilarity in a poop bag, wearing gloves and packing down feces in a trash tray. She would laugh to tears as they conversed about spitting, sweating or peeing your own water to drink it. Thankfully the child is a boy, and Mali has toilet-trained him well. Still, at first, he fought Sabi to pee in the hose so that a suction would recycle fluid through the condensate to a water station. He still fights sometimes, and it creates a hovering pissy mess until the service module gulps its water.

She unstraps, floats from the steering system to the hygiene corner. She part-undresses, dry washes with a disinfectant wipe, and dispenses a mizzle of diluted lemongrass soap onto a disposable cloth for her face. Sabi's heart glows. She knows that Mali prefers sandalwood, but must have stocked on lemongrass for her scouting missions so she could travel into space with her own favorite scent: Sabi's.

It's taken a lesson on balance and weightlessness to stop cartwheeling in slow motion in all directions. Sabi still feels dizzy at times, ash in her joints. She'll never get used to the loss of time and space. The stomach upset is a nuisance. She considers the upright sleeper, strapping in for a quick snooze. Sleep when the baby sleeps—that's what Mali always said. But Sabi wants to busy herself with vacuuming and oxygen filter checks. Anything to forget. She still isn't sleeping well, but it's better than before.

She still cries her fear when Fudge sleeps. A tear prickles her eye now. That part is not improved much. *Ohm nama…ohm nama.* The rogue chant between her ears varies in volume and tempo. It came with the pelican man, and she has learnt not to ignore its signal of danger. She looks in panic at the service module. The engine is on green. So is the power system.

The comms system is not on, as Mali advised.

"Stay offline until you reach the mushroom planet for passage to Niva," Mali yelled between her blaster going *boom, boom, boom,* as they fled a riot.

"I don't see why I should stay off grid in practically nowhere!" Sabi protested. "What if there are space pirates. Marauders? Unfriendly contact?"

Mali brushed her off with half a laugh, half a sound of exasperation. "Look at the rage happening now!" *Boom!* She fired at a new mob of robopets racing toward the launch pad. "Right now, space is the safest place to be!"

"What if there's turbulence or the service module malfunctions?" cried Sabi, Fudge in her arms. "Think of all that distance. What if we run out of oxygen? I don't know what to do!"

"You'll be fine! There's enough oxygen to get you to the mushroom planet."

"Come with us, we can outrun them!"

"*I will* find you. Go!" in a bellow. *Boom!*

"But—"

"I need you to believe in yourself," said Mali. *Boom!* "Just let me distract these fuckers!" And then she ran blasting toward the robopets.

Belief or not, the oxygen filter reading at 47% now is not reassuring.

"Momom," cries Fudge, awake now in the rocket capsule. His reaches out his arms for a cuddle.

"My sleepy sugarness." Sabi floats to him, embraces him in the harness but his crying is louder now. He wants out. "Wipe wipe first, nana, and then cuddles," she says, although Mali said it was best to speak to little ones in proper language. "They learn faster," she said.

"Let's wipe you first, then a banana, then cuddles, eh?"

"Naw!" he bawls his stubbornness. "Cuddo! Now!"

"I'll wipe you first," she says firmly. "Then a banana and then cuddles."

"Cuddo now!" he wails, loud, louder, his legs kicking in slow motion. "Now!"

She gives in to the little shit.

Fudge is calmer now. "Seek seek." He wants to play.

Hide and seek is a limited game inside a rocket capsule. Sabi closes her eyes,

Fudge in her arms still. "One…two…Are you hiding?"

"Ya," he chuckles.

"Three…four… I'm going to get you!"

Fudge titters, then stills himself.

"Nine…ten! Where are you?" Sabi pretends she can't see him. "You are so good at hiding. But I'm going to find you!"

"Naw," chuckles Fudge, wriggling to escape from her arms.

She allows her gaze to reach his face. "Gotcha!"

He squeals his glee.

"Now it's your turn," she says. "*I* am going to hide, and *you* have to find me. I'll count for you. One to ten. Come on, close 'em, cheeky one." He giggles, closes his eyes. "One…"

He opens his eyes before she gets to two. "Momom!" He grabs at her face.

She uses the pretext of a hokey pokey game to harness him into a seat. He doesn't have the balance to do it on his own on free float.

"You put your left foot in…" she hums. "No, your other left." She taps at it. "You put your left foot in, you put your left foot out…" He moves his legs every which way, banging and kicking his thrill in slow motion.

He doesn't complain when she pulls the swing out table, and they pretend to eat imaginary food with an imaginary knife and fork.

"Pom pom?" he suggests, and she gives him a slit sachet of pumpkin puree.

Right now, she's tranquil. Later when he's asleep she'll worry about space debris, solar flares, micrometeorites, propulsion system locks, running out of air, human error.

She'll worry about everything that can go wrong in space.

Her skin is cracked in places, her calves mostly, where she crawled from crevice to crevice, fleeing the robopets before Mali came to the rescue. Her face is piled with burns.

Today she's a ghost on the pilot seat, seeing monuments of a lost life in wisp with every breath. What she wants is Mali. This rocket capsule was Mali's ticket. She was going on a scouting mission to the Niva settlement, and she'd been ardently training for it. The drills, the diet regimen. Mali knows everything about the service module. Mali, not Sabi, is intimate with how the engine works, with the power system, the steering system, the comms system that Sabi must not touch until she reaches the mushroom planet.

Sabi looks at their son, secured in a harness. He's sleeping upright. In space, anywhere is up, anywhere is down. His cheeks are smudged with tears from

50

fighting sleep. She let him wail it out until he was too exhausted, too miserable to do anything but succumb. Mali would have been less anxious, more tolerant of Fudge. Mali would have focused better on the goal to get to Niva—all Sabi does is vacillate along grief, terror, panic, dullness, worry. Repeat.

She is cold, fretting that they will run out of radioactive material that heats the rocket capsule. What does Sabi know about radioisotope thermoelectric generators or heat from radioactive decay?

Mali tried to explain, but all Sabi asked was, "Why can't they just use solar?"

"Solar needs large panels that are impractical for a tiny rocket capsule," Mali patiently explained.

None of all that matters if it doesn't bring oxygen, thinks Sabi now. She looks at the oxygen filter reading: 23%.

Remembrance comes to her in slow motion, as if in microgravity. She gets memories in a float. Weightless running. Weightless screaming. Naked flashes. *Boom! Boom!* Catalogues of memory flit behind her eyes in colors that never catch light but drift in darkness.

It happened the day before Mali's mission to Niva. Mali, who was first a scientist, second a lover, third a diplomat. No, second a mother—where did Sabi fit in? Sabi, who was too tired to feel, to resist, when satellite confirmed the new settlement planet was inhabited, as was the mushroom planet in-between. The final mission would take Mali right into the mushroom planet to replenish supplies, and then on to Niva.

Preparing for it was her life's work.

But someone knocked on the door that Saturday morning, and asked questions about the robopet. He was a little man with a folder, showed a badge. Sabi told him they were just pets, many people had them—didn't he know? He wore glasses, peered at her above the rims. His look yanked from her answers to questions he hadn't asked. The pet rescue in Bruegel, she said. You can get anything you want: climbers, crawlers, flyers, gnawers. You enter specs: eye color, pre-programmed/unprogrammed, caged/uncaged, level of interaction, purpose: guide, play, help, companion, transport…

The robopet B blinked and whirred on her shoulder. She absently patted his crown. He's a flyer, she said. B—he smells of cassava and roasted maize. He came unprogrammed. House help: he vacuums, launders, errands, bakes. Self-sufficient, easy care. Uncaged as you can see, she said. Minimal maintenance. The man raised his brow. Just software, firmware updates. Antivirus, VPN. Performance checks, backup, memory. Her wife Mali, who was prepping for a mission to Niva, could answer how she did all that, but she wasn't here right now, said Sabi. Mali recharged B's batteries, taught him new apps.

The little man scribbled into his notes.

Sabi invited him in and saw his folded wings. It occurred to her that he was off. Really. Something was off about him. He resembled a pelican. He said he liked ice-cream and hum. *Do you have a hum?* he asked. She shook her head. The chanting between her ears started then. Gently, at first. *Aum... Ohm... Aum... Ohm...* The hum got louder. *Ohm nama... Ohm nama...* Louder still. *Ohm nama shi... Ohm nama shi...* B flapped his wings, screeched at her. *Ohm nama shi va...* Sabi crouched, then crawled from the robopet's beak, claws as the hum in her head grew loudest: *Ohm nama shi va ya!*

The pelican man blinked, whirred, his arms and legs spinning until she lost sight of his face. B went nuts. So the robopet strike was on the little pelican man who knocked on her door that Saturday. It was all his fault.

On fleeing she rang Mali who screamed something about Fudge and the safe room now! Mali who blasted herself into the rescue, *boom, boom*, and them out to the streets awash with blinking and whirring pelican men accompanying the robopet rampage. Robopet owners in tatters and sprawl. A woman leaking crimson, her eyeball dangling to her nose. A man crawling on his torso, arms and legs dragging in a smear. A lone head, lolling by itself on the tarmac. All the while Fudge howling, howling, and a mob of robopets targeted the tray-truck. Little pelican men blinked and whirred toward it, fast, faster. Mali put her foot on the gas and the truck soared.

At the launch pad, robopets came from every which way, pelican men with them blinking and whirring at speed. Mali's deadpan face. Her blaster: *Boom. Boom.* One by one she felled rogue robopets and pelican men with deadly accuracy. "Come on! Get here, you little shits!" *Boom. Boom.* But there were too many of them.

"Go!" she shouted to Sabi, pushing her toward the blast zone. "Get into the rocket capsule and seal the doors!" *Boom. Boom.*

"I'm not leaving you!"

"Think of Fudge. I'll be fine!" Mali ran toward the mob. *Boom! Boom!* Her last words: "It's set to autopilot. There's a manual. Press the blue and green button, go!" *Boom!*

Sabi's head was its own carnage as she shot to the skies. *Aum... Ohm... Aum... Ohm... Ohm nama... Ohm nama... Ohm nama shi... Ohm nama shi... OHM NAMA SHI VA... OHM NAMA SHI VA YA!*

The robopet strike—that was not the little pelican men, she's thinking now in self-pity. It was all on her. Yet she knows it's just victim blaming. Survivor guilt—how is she to blame for all what happened? Still, so much time on her hands…It's inevitable that some of it would make its way finding her to blame.

Sabi screams angrily, and it wakes Fudge. "Cuddo! Cuddo! Momom!"

She rescues him from the harness. Floats with him in her arms to the hygiene station. They do the wee pump, the pooper. She dry washes him with disinfectant wipes. He sucks on a puree of honey yam, opens his mouth to catch a floating chocolate—misses and cries. There's only so many times you can entertain a toddler with floating chocolate. She looks at the sachets of liquid seasoning: all spice, cinnamon, cloves, cumin, tamarind. Wonders if they might work as paint. She looks at Fudge. He's small and messy, a late developer still working on his motor skills. Pepper in the eyes—a godawful din.

She breaks a vacuum-sealed pouch and eats a cube of goat steam-dried with paprika. She does the treadmill on harness, Fudge strapped to her back. She rides the bike, her feet clipped to the pedals. Fudge is pressed close and asleep against her.

After exercise, she wants to get into bustle, but holds herself back. She tries not to worry about radar, range, propellor, heating… She shakes off the dread tucked in her belly, her fear about Mali. It doesn't take away the axe through her heart. But she's working through it, reconstructing. Today her head is silent, no hum.

They sleep together, Sabi and Fudge strapped upright. She does not cry her fear.

She wakes up rejuvenated, even though the oxygen filter reading is at 17%.

Will it hold until the mushroom planet? And if it does, what then? But she's less anxious, more connected with her plight as a refugee.

Oxygen filter reading: 9%.

Fudge's motor skills are improving. He feeds on his own with a real knife and fork, and a plate taped to his swing-out chair. They play hide and seek, Fudge bobbing and floating by himself under the cockpit, in the hygiene corner, flat against the wall alongside Sabi's upright sleeper. Sometimes he swims on air around her in silence until he can't help giggling, as she pretends to look for him. They cuddle, and she smells the lemongrass in his unkempt curls. She presses against the softness of his velvet skin.

She looks about the rocket capsule. Nothing is broken. She should have trusted Mali. She didn't need to worry about the engine, the power, the propulsion or steering systems. She praises whichever gods for not having encountered space debris, solar flares or micrometeorites. As for human error, she has survived herself. She looks at Fudge. He has survived her too.

Time and space are teaching her to be a slightly better mom with him. Calmer, sometimes euphoric especially when she and Fudge press their faces against the triple-paned windows, looking out at nothingness.

She doesn't question that they haven't seen the dwarf host stars that Mali talked about from her previous travels. No mudflats, raining diamonds or anything like that.

She smiles. At times like now she feels as if she's breathing laughing gas.

Oxygen filter reading: 3%. The autopilot has brought the rocket capsule to a stall. Sabi and Fudge press their faces to look out through the windows.

"Momom." He points. "Look."

The rocket capsule is angled toward the pored mushroom-like structures—gold, tinted with pale blue and white. He's pointing at the welcome colors after all that blackness.

"Looks like we've arrived at the mushroom planet, my cuddle sugarness. Comms time!" She says it singsong. Still, she hesitates. Looks at Fudge, engrossed with the pretty planet outside. She wonders if the inhabitants are hostile. What if they refuse to let them in?

"Momom!" cries Fudge. "Boom!"

Sabi's heart catapults. She hops in a float to the windowpane in time to see the last of the mushroom heads opening and now three fierce blasters are pointing in their direction.

It's unreal. She clutches Fudge to her bosom, closes her eyes. She expects the firing to start at any moment. Who fires at a wanderer who's lost everything? she thinks in confusion. Who attacks one whose belief may already be broken? She can't cope with more little pelican men—who knows where they came from? She resists an instinct to turn and run. How? To where? And the oxygen...

The comm system crackles.

She floats to it, dread in her mouth, as the ominous chant grows in her head. *Aum... Ohm... Ohm nama... Ohm nama shi... OHM NAMA SHI VA... OHM NAMA SHI VA YA!*

"I come from Anko. We're refugees," she cries at the system. "We're not unfriendly contact! Please..."

More silence. Just the chanting. *Aum... Ohm... Ohm nama... Ohm nama shi...*

"Please!" *OHM NAMA SHI VA... OHM NAMA SHI VA YA!* She's leaning in desperation into the console, begging for her life, her son's life. "We're refugees. Not unfriendly contact!"

Fudge floats to her, his big brown eyes set on the lit comms system. His longer, leaner body is trapped between that of a baby's and a boy's. "Gee gee," he babbles. He thinks it's a game. "Gee gee no ta."

His ease calms her fear. Slowly, the chant ebbs to a gentle *Aum... Ohm...*

"Refugees," she speaks to the comms system. "Not unfriendly."

"Gee gee no di."

"Niva. No oxygen."

"Zizi."

She holds Fudge so they are together, whatever happens. Perhaps they are hardened with time and space, survivors floating in the sweeping silence beyond the distant edges of outer galaxies. She knows there are eyes watching them, even though she can't see them.

Silence. Then the comms crackles. *Originate. Insignificantly.*

She blinks at the console.

Derive. Moderately.

What?

Occur. Mildly.

Suddenly, as the command morphs its incoherence, she begins to chuckle uncontrollably. Perhaps it's the release, the knowing that the alien voice coming and going, estranging yet familiar in her language, is trying, really trying. Perhaps it's the oxygen now finished, and they are dying at the doorstep of help. She hiccups in helpless mirth that rises and ebbs, insensitive to time and space.

Develop. Slightly.

Fudge gurgles along with her, bouncing his glee in slow motion.

Arise. Tender.

The voice in the mushroom planet tries, and tries, to learn the right words. *Emerge. Benevolent.*

Finally: *Approach. Gently.*

She doesn't know how, but she knows they'll be fine. If they die now, they'll die happy.

Human Beans

WEMA feels like this. Her life is a gust of wind, she's felt like this a long time. Displaced. Inside a great gale that swirls with longing for a dimension of something perfect. Never straight lines or corners…angles or tips. Sometimes she imagines waters—not rivers or lakes. In her dreams she sees a place full of oceans where people float, where space and time don't matter.

It's not a gray place. It's a sun-yellow, neutron-star-white multiverse that hosts no mundane. No hearts of stone. No half-lives, inert-lives. Never particles that don't fit or don't begin to matter. Nothing that shrinks to cancellation. It's a place Thanatos desires.

What she needs is a new existence, a world that's bell-shaped and full of spring. Bell-shaped because she's thinking of the sweet scent of lilies of the valley. What she wants is a realm that's the color of quetzal birds—iridescent green and red-bellied with a golden crest. Because right now her heart is a jungle full of fog. Blackbirds *squee* in rising shrills, then *conk-la-ree* in unmusical gurgles.

Her mind is an old library. It's pregnant with photographs, shadows and floorboards of blackwood. She stoops to pick her soul, but it slips through her fingers and says, I'm here, I'm there. She closes her eyes and all she hears are strangers whistling her name. And when she answers, it's in a voice that's not hers. What comes from her throat is a leafy pond full of toads.

She tries again: My name is Wema!

A cosmos echoes her name in falling pebbles: *Wey. Wey. Ma. Ma.* Lights flicker across the edges of heaven that may be ash or the Milky Way. *Squee! Squee! Conk-la-ree.*

Wema is the kind of girl who's a natural magnet. Like she's anyone's 'type'. Easy going. To fight for. Modern. Antique. Gal next door. Exotic. A grandma-will-say-yes type of girl. Prepubescent kids in high school will high-five you for her. She's the perfect date. For Idris Elba, Kate Beckinsale, Phylicia Rashad, Angelina Jolie, Barack Obama—you get the gist. She's anyone's type. You look at her and see what you want. She sits next to a couple at a chocolate and wine masterclass, and they fight. It happens all the time. In restaurants, on trains, out jogging.

People's heads get messed up. For what? She's got strong legs, set shoulders, fine teeth, a good core. What's beauty? With her golden skin and supple tone, some might say she's athletic. Others cut it down to one word—you met it a paragraph up: exotic.

Most people just want to ruffle her hair, but the afro simply springs back— the curls so tight.

Wema felt a deep and terrible sadness. People didn't get her. Sure, they *wanted* her. Doesn't mean they *got* her. It sent her searching overseas, away from family, away from the village she once called home. A scholarship helped—wasn't hard to get. The priest looked at her like she was a seraph from heaven. She thought that she was safer with a partner. That maybe people wouldn't leer as much if she dangled off someone's arm.

Wrong.

Sally lasted a mere five weeks. She sapped Wema's life, so needy that babe. What Sally needed was ten shrinks, not an exclusive relationship.

Jools might have been the one. Because he was obsessed with himself. Jools was the Barbie-Ken type, in love with his dazzle: the dangle of his fringe, the slant of his smile. He hogged mirrors. He coveted himself in the bathroom, in the lift, on his phone screen…always adjusting himself for the world.

But he and Wema fought all the time, and it wasn't about beauty. They fought about everything stupid. Like the chocolate and wine masterclass.

"I really want to do it," said Wema. "Did you know chocolate goes well with red meat?"

"Only a fool would put chocolate with beef."

"Lamb. Try it with dark, dark chocolate."

"Lamb sucks."

Wema'd grown with the texture of yams, mangoes, coconuts on her tongue. The smell of durian fruit growing wild in backyards. Jools hated textures. Couldn't stand cucumbers or mushrooms. Purpled over the cream green of avocadoes. He refused to try anything different. Bit into the orange flesh of a pawpaw, spat it out.

"Smell food first," coaxed Wema. "The nose gets you right for your tongue. You know to anticipate a nibble."

"Baaaa!" bleated Jools—the spoiled child he was.

The snatchings started the same week Wema broke up with Jools.

The events brought back childhood stories of *Jengu*, the water spirit that vanished people. *Bichwa*, the three-headed ogre that pinched naughty children in their beds—sometimes it took them. Crocodile whisperers you knew to stay away from because, if you looked at them wrong, you might get swallowed by a croc next time you swam in the river. *Nightrunners*, who galloped naked around huts as the village slept—they summoned omens and babies cried, goats got sick, people died. Like Old Ma Fayola who keeled into a grave at a neighbor's funeral. They had to send for Ma Fayola's son in the city to inherit the cows. But what did a city man need cows for? He sold them for a pittance, didn't give a cent to his sisters back in the village. At least he left the hut.

When Jools spoke his truth, how deep his pretty head had sunk into the dark web, it was their last evening together, dining out and fancy. Wema looked at him astonished.

"Seriously," she said. "You believe aliens from a galactic federation have visited Earth, and put our Prime Minister in charge?"

"He's the second coming. See how the virus doesn't affect him?"

"I'd question it. Are you planning to take the flu shot?"

"Microchips, dude. Why would I do that to myself?" He arranged his chin for a selfie.

Wema tried to remember, and couldn't, what it was she saw in him. He didn't like sex because it was 'sticky'. Being with him was worse than copulating with a mannequin that didn't want its wig ruined.

"You're an idiot, that's what," she said. "I'll be getting my booster shot."

"Everything's messed up. Cannibal pedophiles. Big Brother watching."

"You're a fockwit. There's much going on in the world already—why do you want to screw it more?"

Flash, his camera—another selfie. He checked his teeth on the shiny screen. "The reckoning is coming. Be on the good side."

She slapped her napkin on the table, pushed back her chair. "I wouldn't have touched you with an oak if I'd known your head was full of oats."

"What are you doing?"

"Leaving you. We have zero in common."

"And you know this now?"

"Until you came out of the woodwork and burbled your outlandish theories, how was I to guess you're a whacko?"

She grabbed her clutch purse, paid the bill. The meal cost a few legs. This was a place you paid the price of limbs, and then some, because it promised to 'serve

African'—but mostly what you got was a half-baked measure of Ethiopian. Today—stewed goat, spicy lentils, eggplant and dips—was the most African it got. Half her fortnightly wages had just gone down the gutter for a brain-dead pretty face who picked at lentils before asking for a bowl of thick-cut chips, no aioli.

She stamped out of the skyline restaurant, committed to being single for the rest of her life. She pressed for the lift, and the door opened. All the buttons were lit. It wasn't going anywhere. The darn thing was broken. She took the fire exit and ran down all those stairs.

But Jools had got into her head.

She did go to the chocolate and wine masterclass, only because she'd already paid for it. She smiled at the couple sitting at the front—a short-cropped brunette and a big guy with a checked shirt. Wasn't long before they quarreled.

The venue had dangler lights that looked like sun-filled balloons with silver ribbons, but the building was rather old, peeling paint on the walls. She nibbled at a platter of almonds, walnuts, strawberries and grapes before the main event—the host, right in front, and his wife, who sat next to Wema.

"Cocoa is a very versatile product," the man said. "You get sugar from the fruit and dogs eat the husk. Guess why supermarket chocolate is black?" He looked around. "Because it's burnt cocoa beans. Cheap. Burn and sugar wholesales it."

Wema studied the room and noticed the big guy with the checked shirt was gone.

"Chocolate is like tiramisu—when you make chocolate, it's better the next day. The sheen tells you of its quality."

The wife smiled at Wema, as if agreeing about quality, but it was more about the chocolate skin kind, and less about her husband's truffles.

"This one here is a grand cru. It has 75% dark chocolate and is full of cherry and red plum, a slight bitterness."

He looked at them.

"Shine means it's well-tempered. I want you to break the first piece in front of you now. A good snap tells you it's fine chocolate. Don't just chomp it, linger the piece on your tongue. Today's tasting is about contrast pairing. Our taste buds are all different."

Wema was glad Jools wasn't here.

Sun rays shone through the glass roof of the swimming pool that morning and danced jewels in the water, as Wema swam before work. The sky was teal, pillowed with soft clouds. There was an elderly person in the water, and Wema gave them a name: Basket. Because they survival swam in a back float, dead weight. It would have been okay if they'd kept to their lane, but they meandered. Their hands scooped, scooped, causing waves. It made Wema's laps difficult. Water ran up her nose as she freestyled in the next lane, causing her to splutter. When Wema did a tumble turn, Basket was gone.

She drove to the office at the fringe of the central business district. She parked and smiled at toddlers rushing and squealing into a nearby fountain's spray, as their parents watched. She swiped her secure card, and was pleased to see Axe across the partition splitting their desks. She smiled at sie.

"How's it?" said Axe.

"Groan."

Wema tried talking to Axe about Jools and Basket. Axe was solid, reliable. Wema felt safe with sie. Normally sie listened, but today Axe was focused on Wema's bland outfit. Sie looked at the soft hues—the cream of Wema's blouse, the cyan of her skirt—and said in hir barrel voice, "This. Is. Sacrilege."

Sie pulled a drawer on hir desk and whipped out a candy scarf and came round the partition.

"No," said Wema.

"Yes. You're feeling flat because you need more rainbow." Sie arranged the hand-knitted scarf around Wema's shoulders. "Now you look dope."

If Axe were chocolate or wine, sie'd be the party flavor. What Wema most liked about Axe was sie didn't talk with an agenda. Sie didn't sexualize Wema like other people did. Sie talked to her, *her*. Not to her tits. Sie saw Wema, truly. But there was an air of sadness about Axe when sie didn't know Wema was watching. Now sie took Wema's hand. "Come with me, you need coffee. We've got ten minutes before the divisional meeting."

Outside the world looked normal. Folk walking dogs, kids in strollers, cabs picking up people. A parking inspector was writing up a car. Wema's own sedan was safe in an open car park on an 'Early Bird' special. Up ahead, a P-Plater was reverse-parking badly into a single car spot. They entered Axe's favorite joint: a specialty coffee, bar and bottle shop—no smoking. It was a café with a coffee brand named Ex-Wife.

Axe was saying, "Do you know how many Earth-like planets are in the galaxy?"

"How many." Wema said.

"Six."

"That right?"

"As in some *six billion* Earth-sized planets orbiting sun-like stars."

"*What?*"

"And—wild guess this—twenty-four superhabitable worlds, yeah, some warmer, wetter, better conditioned than Earth. The Drake equation's super dope. Tells you ace info about active civilizations in the Milky Way."

"I can't even—"

"Titan's the most habitable extra-terrestrial world within our solar system. It has nitrogen and methane. It's forty percent the size of Earth."

The barista was flustered about Wema, and was apologizing for spilt coffee. A dog-haired teen studied with hungry eyes a platter of salmon cheese cream sandwiches behind the glass-topped counter.

"The haloumi avocado looks wicked," said Axe, moments before the teenager disappeared. Nobody seemed to notice.

Wema looked at Axe. "Did you see that?"

Sie blinked. "See what?"

Wema didn't know what to say.

Coffee on hand on the way back, they passed a jaywalker talking into a smart phone. An emergency vehicle striped yellow, red and blue raced past full throttle. Her mind still troubled, Wema noticed an unmarked cop car on patrol, all black. Funny—well, not funny, just a statement—cops never stopped looking like cops, even on decoy. Clipped hair, razored jaw, falcon eyes.

Back at the office, there was only a handful of staff—most people were working from home. The divisional meeting was a conference call. Simon's video was off—he was a solicitor at the firm. Pearl—a barrister and solicitor—had a fluffy rabbit icon on her profile. Only the boss, Punt—the director—zoomed up close on screen, thick brows, a chin mole, and $$ sign eyes. It was a running joke in the team that Punt could sniff a dollar up a whippet's butt, and retrieve it himself with an enema, no gloves, if a laxative didn't work. That's how much he loved money.

"Hey kid," the boss said to Wema. Nodded at Axe: "Axel." He waited a few minutes, then: "Good. Let's show and tell." Although the law firm ripped clients by thousands, it was one of those feel-good, well-being workplaces that asked you to share something fun at a team meeting.

"I did this chocolate and wine masterclass," said Wema. "The building was so old, I imagined flakes of it raining on my head." The team laughed.

"People leave you alone?" piped Simon.

"It was a husband-and-wife duo. He's a former marine biologist. A pasty little fellow, a bit shy until you got some wine into him." More laughter. "His wife had smoky gray eyes and spoke personal, like she knew you." She grew silent, suddenly remembering the guy with the checked shirt. How he was there, then he wasn't.

"I like Peruvian beans. African cocoa too," said Pearl.

Something about the way she said it made Wema uncomfortable.

"Wema broke up with her boyfriend," said Axe, trying to help.

There was an awkward pause, then Simon whooped. Pearl said, "Yes!"

"Good on ya! To move on—" said Punt quickly, as he'd already had enough trouble with his husband over Wema.

Simon shared he'd bought new noise-cancelling headsets. "Guess I look sexy, huh?"

"Your video's not even on," said Pearl. "I've got this indoor smart garden— maybe Wema you'd like to check it out? With me, solo."

Axe and hir trivia steered the show-and-tell to a meaningful conversation about taking climate change seriously. "Temperature extremes—who wants more bushfires, another Black Saturday?" Sie reminded the team about shrinking glaciers in Europe and Canada, warming seas that harmed natural ecosystems and marine species. "Coral reefs are dying. And all that flooding, yeah, Typhoon Nina, Hurricane Katrina…"

Nothing about work, really, family law and the like. The divisional meetings seemed to be mostly a general check-in.

"You guys notice anything—different?" Wema changed the subject to what was top of mind.

"Done somethin' to your hair?" quipped Simon. "Oh, your scarf, isn't it neat."

"It's dope," said Axe.

"I meant have you noticed anything *strange* happening?"

Nope. Nope. Nope. They all said. Axe looked at her with eyes that said leave it alone. Sie knew Wema was thinking about Jools and Basket.

Punt logged off as usual with a cheerie, "Pull your weight, peeps. No bludgers."

Wema felt displaced again. Melancholy. Wretched. People didn't take her seriously. But she wasn't exactly sure what she'd expected from her team. That people would start talking about vanishings?

Her smart phone pinged. It was Jools. "You got my spare keys, babe."

You're at the Post Office, reading a sign about zero tolerance on abusive behavior. You move with the line, behind a woman in blue jeans, daggy shoes and a cloth purse. There's a notice about price changes. You look from a distance at the price tags on disposable face masks, satchel liners, digital air fryers, HD LED smart TVs. There's Daniel, the all-smiley one at the counter. You know he's Daniel because his badge says so. He's chatting chatting to every customer. He's to blame for lag service. You look up. The woman in blue is gone.

You're at the supermarket. One minute the girl at the checkout is beeping a liter of milk, a slab of cheese, bread rolls on special, kitchen towels. Next minute she's gone. You have to throw a hundred dollars' worth of shopping back into the trolley and join a new queue where you're fifth behind trolley-loads. Nobody notices.

Wema listened as Axe tittered the day away with hir trivia. "A multiverse is an impossible world. It can never exist as an everything existence. Think! If a multiverse were real, this here, Earth, this now, would be a fraction of infinity."

Wema frowned at the white noise—Axe like this was unstoppable. Didn't take sie long to go on a new tangent: "Tuna is overfished along the coasts of East Africa. It affects the world. Europe, Asia and the Americas have to make informed sourcing decisions. The world needs the right research and data that informs us about how to treat human capital as an existential threat. Thousands of jobs on the line—where's sustainability now?"

Wema looked at the time. Finally!

Richmond's streets bustled with traffic at rush hour just before Wema got onto the state route. At the lights before the petrol station, a whole car vanished. It was a silver 4WD spilling with two kids and a toffee-colored Labrador Retriever—tongue out and panting at the window. The silver car was blinking to turn right, there in front of her, when suddenly Wema's sedan was ahead in the queue. She could have sworn she imagined it, but the incident was real. The 4WD was an XC60—back windshield wipers with an antenna. Number plate starting with IJW. It had a sticker that said: *Five Mart.*

Now she wasn't sure anymore. Further out she gave way to a white van at the roundabout and it evaporated before it went past. She watched in misery and trepidation at the next set of lights, at a jogger in a black t-shirt and shorts. She waited for him to be snatched before he reached the other side of the road. He wasn't. Nor was the Deliveroo boy on a yellow scooter and matching helmet with a kitty face.

Her head hurt. The office, despite Axe, wasn't an easy week.

"What makes rye bread dark?"

"I don't know, Axe."

"Cocoa."

She deleted Jools' texts without reading them. She stood and spoke to Axe across the partition. "Are we alone?"

"Everyone's WFH—"

"No. Really. *Are we alone?* In the universe?"

"NASA's taking big looks at life beyond Earth, given that other planets orbit stars. It would be selfish, even reckless, to think our solar system is the only one capable of hosting life."

You're at the bank. The woman in front is the kind you notice. Not in a sexy way. It's the beauty of her hair. Ginger, all fuzz, curls to her waist. You blink and you're number one in the queue.

At the Botanical Gardens across the woody bridge and its sign that says, 'Slippery When Wet', you notice the tourists. You know them from their hats, maps, cameras. Behind them is a toddler riding a tricycle. His parents—wearing the absentmindedness of young parenthood—are yapping at each other. The tot is a big-eyed one with soft wavy hair. Fat legs pump tiny pedals towards a curvy nature trail. He never comes out. The parents keep walking, talking to each other as though they were always alone. You sprint after them, pull the woman. But, but…your son! She shrugs off your clutch. The hell? A burly security guard pats your shoulder. Don't disturb the peace. Please go away. Now. He says it like he means it.

You're watching footy on TV, cross-legged on your sofa. There's Big Charlie, No. 49. He's a forward, best there is. Dances around the other team, open bounce, uses his body well. He lunges at the ball, knocks off opposition. He works the space well, three quick goals. One of them a bender from an impossible angle. The third is a bizarre heel goal, so good. The other player tackles him to the ground, then stands alone. Big Charlie is gone. It's as if the ground's eaten him. The other player blinks, plays on. A sub runs in from the bench as if it's a natural occurrence to replace gobbled people. You look online at the player-team chart and Big Charlie's gone. Wiped from history. You can't believe the audacity, how brazen.

She started counting people, as if they were beans. She'd enter a café, a bank, a pharmacy…look around to see how many were there and wonder how many would be taken by the time she left.

She was startled by the count.

One day she came into the office and Axe wasn't there. Axe was always in early. Wema ran to hir favorite joint, the 'no smoking' café with its coffee brand named Ex-Wife. The flustered barista shook his head. Hadn't seen Axe.

Wema dialed Punt. His face zoomed large on the screen. "Hey kid. What's going on?"

"Is Axe on leave?"

"Axe. Is that even a name?"

"Axel!"

"Sounds like you got yourself a new bloke. You move quick, kiddo."

"Punt! Please stop this. It's not remotely funny!"

"Whatever it is, it's no biggie—this Axel of yours. Shoved off to cool steam. Crook maybe. Pissed after a night with the lads. Don't stress."

"I'm not stressing!"

"Good on ya. Pull your weight, kid, no bludging." He hung up.

She pulled a sticky note, wrote 'Axe' on it, and put it on her screen. She typed hir name on her phone, emailed it to herself, suddenly afraid she'd forget sie.

She kept looking at the door, expecting sie to appear any moment. Suddenly she longed for a venison backstroke with a dark chocolate sauce. That's when she noticed the lights flicker, the room's new glow. And the man with the luminescence of a Greek god across the partition, seated at Axe's desk.

She didn't think he was *Bichwa, Jengu* or a *Nightrunner*. Not with that luster, no.

"Wey. Wey. Ma. Ma." He said her name and its honey rolled in her ears. The sound was clean and clear, gentle and loud. It reminded her of her mother's milk, of freshly brewed coffee, of newly baked bread. "Wema."

His eyes…

"The glow of a dog star. The star of Sirius."

She looked at him startled, for he hadn't spoken, yet she heard his words. "Our mind is one," he answered her question. "She's bright," he said. She felt his touch on her mind. "Yes. She's bright." Again, he answered her question. "Not the room. Her intelligence."

He was not Thanatos.

"Who are you?" She found her voice. "Where the fock is Axe, and why are you referring to me in the third person?"

"Our name is Mwalimu." His voice was a harmonica. His words swelled like a waterfall, wind blowing through trees, tide washing on a sandy beach. His aura filled her with goodness. The coo of a toddler, the purr of a kitten. "Axe has found hir home." He stood. "As will she."

He whipped his cloak and suddenly she was swirling, feet off the ground in furious rain. A roar nearly took her ears and she lost her shoes. She closed her eyes to a splash, or immersion, opened them to emerald waters and millions of bubbles racing towards her. She was in the middle of a sea. Bright green waters.

Celestial lights shimmered nearer—she realized they were creatures. One, a dolphin, leapt in a spray. She was surrounded by ripples and a glow of sea horses, turtles, pupfish, angel fish, mantis shrimp. Yellow, orange and pink tentacles of a flower blob bumped against her arm. She held her breath as if in a dive, and it was agony. She wondered if this was how drowning felt—torrents ballooning her lungs before she exploded. She opened her mouth to cry out and nothing happened. No water rushed down her throat. She streamlined, pitched her hands, and lunged upwards with a push of her legs. But there was surface.

"Find her weight." Gentle falling pebbles in Mwalimu's voice. "Breathe easy."

She remembered Basket's survival swim. Dead weight on her back. She allowed herself to float, buoyant inside the water.

Follow… Follow… He spoke to her mind in a sweetness of immortal carols. She couldn't help but follow him, nimble as a fish, wave-like, side to side. She was a tourist in the ocean, no maps. She waved in and out of what looked like an ancient city yet it was new. She swam over and below temples chiming with hanging stairways that led to gardens whose flamboyant reflections shimmered in the waters. Was that a sunset moth? She blinked as twinkling wings scattered mottled light her way.

She sidled alongside Mwalimu and his skin suit into a golden beach speckled with lilies of the valley. A quetzal bird of bright blue colors and a splash of white perched on her shin.

"Welcome to Super Earth," said Mwalimu.

"You nearly drowned me," she said happily, unsure why she felt so gleeful and in harmony with herself, and with the world around.

"Water is a conductor, the perfect portal for interdimensional travel."

She looked around, and cheerfully hoped Jools wasn't here. The new world reminded her of images she'd seen of a constellation of galaxies. It was a rainbow of colors resplendent in spiral symmetry.

"Is this a parallel universe?"

"It can't be parallel if she's a singularity." Wema wondered if Mwalimu meant she, the person, or was it the universe, as in personification? "Unless she's a gravitational singularity, an infinite distortion of space and time, in which she's here and there and everywhere."

"I am a singularity," said Wema in astonishment, as if understanding it yet questioning it.

"Would she know if she weren't? Come. We'll show her the new Earth. It orbits a neutron star hundreds of light years from the old Earth."

"Why me? Why do you choose to show me?"

"We understand her mind, her curiosity. Her displacement for perfection. We wanted to see how she might react if, unlike the rest, cataclysmic change was visible."

"I'm an experiment?"

"We're sorry for the discomfort. Human migration to Super Earth began at a pace we thought might work for the human mind. But—she will understand— one person at a time is laborious. We sped the process and are now trialing to go large scale."

"What you're doing—how is it ethical?"

"And will she ask where does right end, wrong begin? Who defines virtue and the social contracts of natural law?" He signaled towards a vast building nestled in a cliff that shifted colors when she gazed at it from different angles. "Exos, a royal retreat. Our priests study the evolution of human macromolecules, early life and development, to create optimal conditions for humankind to thrive. All subjects are willing participants, mostly those already with an…inconvenience."

Nah, Jools was most definitely not here. He'd never be a 'willing participant'— always difficult, unless it involved grooming.

She pointed. "I know that woman in jeans—she was at the post office."

"Millie has advanced heart disease. Our studies will make her new as a fresh born. Look." He showed her a city of ruins in a valley full of lilies. "This is the Lederberg. Here, our priests investigate the conditions that ruined Earth, and we counteract them. Super Earth will never suffer from atmosphere overloading, overpopulation, degraded soil, crop failures, famine and pandemics—all things that plague humankind."

They walked through a maze of gardens scattered with cherry blossoms, bleeding hearts, gazania and dahlia. Ancient wisteria, beeches draped with hanging moss, maple and giant oaks lined its elbows. "Is that—" She pointed.

"Yes, a thylacine and her cub. And that's a flying fox. If she looks closely, she might even see a Tasmanian wolf. Welcome to Extant—here, no species is superior in its demands on the other, so as to make it extinct."

"Heavens. That's the toddler in the tricycle—" He sat playing at the foot of an angel oak.

"The mother's fiancé was a serial killer. She agreed to come here too."

The child stroked the long neck of an island tortoise. Amber phantom butterflies perched on his soft wavy hair so it looked like a reddish-flushed transparent hat.

"There." Mwalimu pointed at the brow of a hill, his words a heart's whisper, the song of a woodchipper. "That is the Self-actualization Center."

Wema caught a scent of chocolate cosmos blended with sweet alyssum. Everything smelled delicious just looking at it. She saw silhouettes of people in the distance doing headstands and yoga poses, then hugging each other in the lush green hillside. "We inspire people to expand their potential."

Suddenly there was a whoop and a squeal. "Wema!" Then someone tackled her to the ground. "Here is a better world," gasped Axe in her ear. "It's giant and stable. Nothing is waste, everything's recycled."

"Oh, Axe. If…you just let me breathe—"

Sie eased hir hold. "There's no poverty. See that wish booth? You can't wish for harmful gain against others."

"But Axe," Wema looked at sie. "I thought, the test subjects. At first…that only people with—"

"An inconvenience found themselves here?"

"Yes…human beans that could be displaced, ones who nobody noticed. What are you doing here! Are you dying of leukemia? I don't think it's dementia. Not with that super processor in your noggin. Oh, dear, Axe. Do you have AIDS? I thought we were friends, that you'd tell—"

Axe took a breath. "My family disowned me when I came out."

Wema remembered the gravestones and abyss, the deep bleakness in Axe when sie didn't know Wema was watching.

"And you?" sie asked.

Wema recalled her fog. The blackbirds in jarring gurgles. "I guess I never belonged." She hugged Axe. "Well now. *We are* family, and I'm glad you're here where people like Mwalimu speak in ballads, heart flutters and bead shakes. The notes of a flute."

"You smell like vanilla and sandalwood."

"And you like rosemary—why aren't I famished? This place is surreal. Well, Trivia Machine, I thought neutron stars are white."

"To the naked eye. Something happened to our bodies when we entered the portal. The unlaws of physics. I've never felt ace like this."

"Me too. And I like that Super Earth has all my colors."

"Mine too."

She looked at hir garish red trousers and matching shoes.

Sie looked at her bare feet and the soft hues of her flowing gown.

They burst out laughing.

Axe spoke first. "This place is dope."

The Mystery of a Place Between
Waking and Forgetting

I DIALED a hotline and cried to a stranger named Deb.

"Let people in," she said. "And keep doing what you're doing."

"What exactly?" I hiccupped. "Scenic walking along flower gardens, writing poetry?"

"Yes, that. Do you have friends?"

"*Friends?*" The word sounded alien on my tongue.

"A good circle," kind Deb said. "People you can trust, talk to."

I blinked.

I am Shalok Homsi—I don't keep a *circle*. Just you, dear Watison.

But you saw me in my nakedness. Heard my dry cry that tumbled like China plates on granite. They crashed onto the parched floor of my mind, filled it with more rip and shard. Drums and brass too. You should have seen your face, Wati. How you forgot to be noble and looked as if you wanted the world to do what it failed to do those many years in the savanna: open wide and gnaw you alive. On a scale of 1–10, your eyes said, what you needed was an exorcism to scour you from what you witnessed when I broke.

Shalok Homsi, the greatest sleuth of the universe, cracking like a plate.

It was then that I turned and cried out what you already knew. "I am not well!"

Even the forensics psychology I'd learnt during my professional study had not prepared me for this. That's why I called the hotline. Then first flew, then put us on a double-ended ferry that sailed us all the way to Pemba Island.

Commercial airlines were out of the question. The dawn charter plane took two hours five minutes from Nairobi to Dar-es-Salaam. And the ferry was a seven-hour sail via Stone Town in Unguja. I wished we had more time to explore ancient architecture, the kind of historic aesthetics that restore minds.

This travel was a lighthouse, a beacon at a time of need. Even in a pandemic. *Because* the pandemic. The double-ender ferry loaded passengers on and off both ends of the vessel, switching bow to stern rather than turning. As we boarded, I looked at fellow passengers—blind fools stampeding in masks for souvenirs outside the bedrooms of sharks, mermaids and old friends. I don't know why I thought this, but I did.

Old friends...

The ferry was first class, no allocated seating. You, dear Watison, led us up the double-decker to where it was cooler and I less prone to sea-sickness. You understood how I fared poorly in water, even in a pristine white princess like the extravagant *Azam Aqua* we were on.

At times like these, I wished you could talk, Wati. No specialist found a medical reason to account for your inability to speak. There were times I wondered: was it inability or unwillingness? What did the savanna do to the abandoned you before I collected you in a sisal mat from the wilderness?

In your silence, your eyes catching light and shifting, I read an art journal laid out in a tiny library on the lounge. In it, I was astonished to find a fascinating column by a mind specialist. *Blues and greens*, the psychologist in the journal said:

There's aqua and a smiling mind in the low-pitched tu-a-woo of a mountain bluebird. Write outdoors from your gnarled mental state, let your pen weep with gladness at the turquoise scatter of a cloud-free sky. Lock eyes with the hyacinth macaw's cobalt blue, all pensive up, up on that tree on a palm swamp. Find the chimes of a lilting voice in the relaxation app on your smart phone. And, oh, how glorious the sapphire breast of an Indian peafowl.

And greens. Find them. Feel the resilience of each step into the manicured lawns all around botanical gardens. Locate growth in the velvet green of spring leaves in the overhanging branches across the paths. Invite yourself to the blue-green ice of a ringed Uranus on the journal's glossy cover. A pandemic and lockdowns—make blues and greens your personal whee.

Astounding. I put down the journal and met your unwavering gaze. As we sailed towards the white sun on the ferry, I thought strange things. Like an uncle's blood sacrifice for the flourish of his brand-new chain of meat factories in Muranga. That was the case of the woman's leg—the mystery whose solving took me to a forest where I found you.

The Pemba taxi had barely crawled past rows and rows of stone houses and sparse streets before we were on a beach front under baking yet moist heat. How easy and languid the locals walked, no hurry—like the taxi.

Kobe and his wife Njoki were old friends. I'd known Kobe from our college days at the university in Pemba. Chake University stood in the heart of the capital, Wete. It had the unfortunate history of the slave trade and was once a sultan's palace, then an 18th century fort with a museum. Finest university in continents! There Kobe did an MBA, and I took forensic criminology. We buddied around odd jobs for pocket money, including that stint together in a forest reserve—best years of my life, Watison.

Now Kobe owned the Ambassador Lodge in the Pemba Kaskazini region, up north. Down south was Pemba Kusini, with its capital at Mkoani. As the taxi slogged—I thought it would collapse like I had—I wondered if at some point we'd have time to visit my gallivanting of auld. I was still thinking this when I realized the car had stopped at the lodge's entrance and someone flung open the door.

"Shalok-y!" It was Kobe. He squeezed the life out of my hand. "I have the presidential suite just-y ready for you."

He wore a striped suit under the late afternoon's blistering heat and didn't break a sweat. I took in his pale blue shirt, a tie of pinks and blues, and the folded kerchief on his breast pocket.

"You're just what I want in those blues," I said. "So where are the greens?"

He blinked, then slapped me on the back, and guffawed. "Funny, you funny Shalok-y. I've never known you for humor."

He lifted you in a bear hug. "Watison-y! How you have grown! Come. Please."

His wife Njoki fell into my arms in an embrace before we reached the reception. "Sharok," she cried fondly, "you must tly our whisky sour."

"My dearest Njoki," I said. "I am not drinking now. Doctor's orders."

"Lubbish!" she said. As if on cue, a waiter with a name-tag that said "J"—a skinny chap with black-rimmed spectacles—pressed a tropical goblet into my hand.

"Prease," insisted Njoki. She turned to you. "Wati, when we rast saw you, you were so tiny," said Njoki. "Now you're glown."

I looked at the flute garnished with pineapple that J handed you, and I hoped to dear gods it was age appropriate. Someone stepped forward and offered a soft hand. She smelled of wild roses and wore a face mask—the only one who did in the lodge—but there was good symmetry about her head. Her eyes gleamed sweet gold.

"Ah, Shalok-y," my friend Kobe said. "Meet Tagin, our hotel manager. Her uncle at the coroner's is my friend. This girl, like her name that-y means destiny, is fated for something big."

Tagin led us into the lodge, now acting as a bell-woman, and trolleyed our cases to the presidential suite. You would expect it would tower up thirty-something stories, but this was Pemba, dear Watison, and we got no higher than the third floor.

"How long have you lived in Nungari?" I asked Tagin.

She fell aback. "But how—"

I picked a tiny lobed leaf caught in her plaits. "I know this herb," I said. "It falls from a tree nicknamed Black Poppy. Nungari borders the only natural reserve in Pemba with the right soil to grow the mallow tree—that's its real name—that could grow as tall as a baobab, and blooms these poppy-like leaves."

"Oh!" she said.

"They are quite distinct, see the lobing in the leaf and its fuzzy blue-green? Now, it's the two sepals that drop when six-petalled flowers unfold that you don't want to get near."

"Oh," she said again. She touched her hair as if there might be another rogue leaf. "I walk through the reserve from home to work every day."

The room was how I liked it. Sand-bleached. A picture of rain falling out of season on an arcade, children running as they faded to silhouettes. I arranged the canvas posture to how I wanted it on the wall. Even the dead in their mushrooming and decay, a circle of life across the universe and my sleuthing, never stayed the same. Yes, the room was how I liked it, filled with skeletons that always won no matter how many times the vacuum hummed and navigated carpets and marble floors to shining. I wondered what secrets it held.

I looked at you, Watison, and hoped that this for you, too, was respite from a reconnaissance with skulls and black roses fashioned from the abyss. I don't know which worlds you go, I thought, edges from which you tumbled as I talked to you about death and your eyes glowed.

Was it the cocktail or mocktail that left you glum? I knew you didn't like flights but, surely, we needed a way to get from Nairobi to Dar, and taking a bus was out of the question, as was driving. You'd seemed okay on the ferry but now there was a sternness on your face I couldn't tease you out of. And you were changing channels again.

I listened to the birdcall of a mangrove kingfisher, a metallic rattle somewhere outside our balcony. Only a precocious child plucked from the Ngong Hills ridged along the Great Rift Valley changes TV channels with his eyes. Yet you blinked, watched closely when it was market shares and the weather forecast. I wondered if the savanna rainforest and its thorn trees might have changed you, or perhaps you were already changed from birth.

I had a penchant for chemistry and botany, but I think it was zoology that drew me to you that day. I found you in a natural forest during that unfortunate case of a woman's leg, before we collected her in pieces: an ear, a finger, a neat chop of an ankle… A torso showed up too. But that's not what this memory is about. You were the mystery of a place between waking and forgetting. I wore a coat the color of a jewel—you know softness and sheen that's all dreamy, and one wonders if it's real? I walked hands in my pockets, and there you were.

I can't remember why, but I kept that coat. Not to pass it down when you were older, or to love the memory of natural forest and its bushbuck and crowned eagles. No identity band came with the sisal mat, and I wondered what to call you. Pip? Butter? None seemed right because even then, flat on your back, you were regal. You wore the air of the child of a black god that had lost you in a forest full of stars.

I heard the wisp of a cry, then silence as your fat legs kicked up the mat. It was as if you were waiting, as if you knew I would come for you. I speculated how long on your blanket you'd played with three-horned chameleons, leopard tortoises of the forest before I found you. What had you done to scatter cobras, adders, spotted hyenas?

Your eyes caught light and shifted like tanzanite. No matter what your mask under the color of sky, I saw you in my destination and clutched you.

And you coiled on my chest, smiled as you slept.

There are those who said you were a changeling. You know those nose danglers who look down on anything they don't understand? Those ones were loudest in their classifications and protestations of you. Others suggested you were a *bichwa*, an offspring of the moon beast that made night-runners of village folk, man-eaters of monster crocodiles. Those ones were too fearful to ruminate about you. Incidentally, it was the uncle whodunit—that unhappy case of a woman's leg. Not the servant boy who reported her missing.

As you slept in my arms, your pulse was a mouth hungry for song. You gobbled distant whistles tucked away in sleep. Your heartbeat was raw, torn in shadows. You never cried, but you grew. You studied but never spoke, even when I felt between your teeth, and wrote a rhythm on your tongue. I poked at your ribs, and wished a pirouette into your bones so you might dance and forget that someone had lost you. Because now you were found.

But dear Watison you never spoke or danced.

You cheered up at the low sweet coo and murmur of a blue-spotted wood dove on our balcony. And food was your happy place. Our hosts, Kobe and Njoki, insisted on dining with us at the extravagant restaurant, blues, pinks and golds, overlooking an s-curled swimming pool that was part of the lodge. The indulgence seemed a waste, seeing how the lodge was only lightly sprinkled with patrons. One, a lavishly dressed woman in batik wraps and the headgear of a sultan, smiled as we walked past to our table.

"That's Mme Zig—from the Democlatic Lepubric of Congo," said Njoki.

Outside, it rained.

"Amazing," said Kobe.

"How so?" I asked.

"Months and months," said Njoki, "not a spratter of lain. And then you come, Sharok—now this."

"Indeed, Shalok-y" agreed Kobe. "A visit to Pemba is a miracle when it ushers an out of season splatter of rain and a storm that rushes the island-y."

"Tly the fish," said Njoki.

"Yes," agreed Kobe. "Fresh and straight from unsalted rivers and lakes in the mainland."

I loved the freshwater sangara fish and its gamey taste, but today I had a penchant for something more local. I mulled over a few scrumptious options on a menu that included lentil sambusas, matoke—creamy banana mash steamed in banana leaves and served with ground nut sauce, and a spicy vegetable stew that comprised baby eggplant, tomato chops, chili, almonds, fresh coriander leaves, halved zucchini, dollop of yogurt. I settled for pepper and curry rice with bedeviled eggs, and a side of broiled baby goat in cow intestine.

Indeed, dinner was a feast and, you, Watison, lover of fowl, gobbled the potted apricot chicken bake plumped with rice.

"Shalok-y, Watison-y, eat!" urged my friend Kobe.

"I'll burst if I swallow a morsel more," I begged.

"You have our new cook-y to thank." He flicked a finger. "J, fetch-y Papaa!"

"No, please—" I tried.

"Lubbish!" Njoki brushed away my protestations against interrupting the cook.

I sat back and smiled. "I think your baby is hungry," I said.

Kobe and Njoki looked at me astonished.

"But-y, I haven't said anything, Shalok-y. We haven't had-y time to talk, to catch up on family and all that-y. Has my staff been gossipy about us?"

"Don't be startled, my friends. It doesn't take much from the wetness on Njoki's blouse to see that she's nursing, and her body says it's time to feed."

They laughed.

"You missed-y our wedding," said Kobe. "You were working on that-y whatnot case."

"Rike we said—here in Pemba you don't need an invitation. You just lock up," said Njoki.

74

"Yup, rock up!" said Kobe. "Eh, Shalok-y."

"The child's name is Homsi, I hope—after his godparent?" I hoped there was a twinkle in my eye.

"His name is Mugisa," said Njoki. "Sometimes I think he rikes the yaya who minds him more than me, his own mother."

"Shalok-y. I should not be surprised by a sleuth whose visit brings rain. Ah, here's Papaa."

A big hand gobbled mine. "It's a pleasure detective," said the cook. "Kobe and Njoki have told me all about you."

"Good things I hope."

"It's an honor. And I have made special desserts for you." He clicked his fingers, and J—who interchanged attending our table with Tagin, the manager, bell-woman now waitress—appeared with a tray. "Jelly swirl cheesecake for the boy and my special walnut brownie for you, detective."

"Go easy on the tobacco," I said to J as he lifted his hand from the table.

"But—" he looked perplexed.

"Those stained fingers from pinching raw snuff in a tin and rolling it to a ciggie—my grandfather had them," I said. "You're too young to be into that kind of smoko now—think of years ahead and how you might be then."

You, Watison, gave that shrewd smile that confirmed your own keen interest in sleuthing. After all, I home-schooled you—because you frightened teachers with your eyes more than the silence. I taught you every detail, seeing I'd studied forensics from the best in the world. Practical sessions at Chake Chake University took us to real, not simulated, crime scenes. I hopped onto the crime services van, acted like I was one of them, though the team wouldn't let me touch anything. I went to real courtrooms and travelled the world in an exchange program, which got me to the fingerprint division at Scotland Yard in London.

But there I was rambling in my head, dear Watison, as you quickly forgot about sleuthing and fell into the jelly swirl with relish. I caught Tagin's eye in the distance and thought of her smell of a fresh-petalled wild rose. She was a pale marigold. I hoped to spend one lifetime with a woman in an ecstasy of color distant to order or falling petals.

"Are you short-staffed, then?" I asked Kobe.

"You said what-y?"

"Tagin. She seems to have…many roles. Has the pandemic hit you this hard, my friend?"

Njoki laughed. "Oh, no, Sharok. Tagin is a jack of many tlades. Give her a bucket, a spanner, a spade—"

"Tagin is very good," said Kobe, finishing his wife's words. "Strong like an ox. Juju hands in the garden."

"Even Papaa rets her cook his seclet lecipes." Njoki's eyes glowed with the natural pride of an employer of priceless staff.

I forked the crackly top of the shiny mud square on my plate, and a moist, dense goo dripped from it. It smelled of paradise. Tasted of heaven.

Outside, the rain had stopped. Droplets swirled in the pale blue pool in its s-curl, tiny snakes swimming back and forth. Conversation flowed and we argued about Papaa's secret to the brownie.

"It's about the butter," I proposed.

"The eggs," said Njoki. "Flee-lange chickens."

"It's the origin-y—where the cocoa comes from," said Kobe.

Other than a hint, Papaa refused to tell us of his ingredients. "It's about the whisk," he said. "Keen but delicate as a lover's touch."

During our chatting, something in your gaze, Watison, directed me to observe my friend Kobe more keenly. It was then that I realized you had picked what a more astute me should have noticed. Something was on Kobe's mind, and he was dying to tell me.

I pushed my chair back. "Watison, it's been a long day."

"Shalok-y!" protested my host.

"Perhaps you might send someone to bring up some tea? Watison cannot sleep without Rooibos. Mango chamomile for me, please."

"Done. For you? I will bring-y it myself Shalok-y."

Tagin called up the lift. Sweet gold eyes and I felt something, almost chemistry.

I thought fondly back to my university days with Kobe, making student money as we pushed goat manure and vegetable compost in wheelbarrows. All the way from Darajani Market in Creek Road to the forest reserve. We understood the florae that in turn respected the labors of our hands, and the black poppy tree took our considerate attention, I dare say.

I think Kobe had designs on me but was taken aback at my specific interest on his sister Tumaini, and her graceful gait of an antelope. Ran as fast too—made the athletics team.

I shook myself from imagining a likeable mouth behind Tagin's face mask, and conceded that my mental malady was far worse than I thought.

A knock on the door and Kobe swept into the presidential suite with our teas.

"You're double-vaxxed Shalok-y, no?"

"Indeed, I am, my friend, as is Watison." I waited as he poured. "And we needed to each evidence a negative test within 96 hours of our departure to Pemba. Now, my friend, what is that grave face all about?"

He leaned from his settee. "I am losing money, Shalok-y... Bad things-y are happening to our guests and our customers are leaving. They say it's a bad spirit-y." Kobe looked around, as if to assure himself that we were alone. But, you, Watison, have a way of thinning, wisping out in a room as if you don't exist. I could see you but others didn't seem to notice you. Was it the thing you did with your eyes, the power you had to switch TV channels, and perhaps also adjust people's perception of you?

"Two patrons have died-y. One straight after dinner at the restaurant, Shalok-y. It was a child. He fell in convulsions and was dead."

"The coroner—?"

"Found nothing-y. Then it happened again. A grown man clutched-y his throat as if asphyxiating. Him too, nothing-y to tell us the cause of death."

"Mmhhhh," I contemplated.

"Then-y we had another one, she didn't die but fell in a coma for two days, Shalok-y."

"These guests—was there anything common, at all?"

Kobe thought for a moment, then brightened. "The Lethe Suite! Makes patrons feel-y like gods. It's second best-y to the presidential suite—"

"I see."

"Do you, Shalok-y?"

"I will inspect the room, if you like."

His face fell. "It is occupied-y." He frowned. "Oh, no! Mme Zig..."

I touched his arm. "For some reason, I doubt very much that the problem is the room."

Hoo-hoo hoooooo! came the call of a Pemba scops owl.

"Aish...!" My friend Kobe got visibly distressed at this. "But that's a bad omen, Shalok-y. Why is an owl-y *hoo-hooing* outside your balcony?"

"Kobe, I never knew you to be superstitious, until now." He didn't return my laugh. "But we'll keep a lookout for death."

After he left, you stood looking out the window, and beckoned me. We stared at the pristine white beach under the moon's glow. You pointed at two figures walking side-by-side on the beach. It was Njoki and Tagin. I thought for a moment they touched hands, but Njoki rocked baby Mugisa asleep on her back inside a snuggling *kitenge* wrap.

We woke to an orange sunrise, the suite aflame in its glow. We listened to the chirp, twitter, cheep and warble of the sunbird, topaz-winged and flame-breasted, on our balcony. A bright-yellow Pemba kingfisher, white-eyed, joined it.

After a continental breakfast I didn't much care for, but you did—licking chicken pies off your fingers, flecks of omelet on your lips—we walked out the lodge to the daladala terminal.

"Daladala means public minibus," I told you, "and locals here use them to get around."

I wanted you to experience the rush of street traffic and you studied with interest all the sign-boarded daladalas, each numbered with a location: Nungwi=116; Kiwenga=117; Jambiani=309; Makondeko=310; Nungari=407; Airport(U/Ndege)=505...

We boarded number 407 and it was empty but for us.

From Nungari, I walked you to the forest reserve with its overhanging greenery brushing down the sides of dust walkways. I showed you barkless trees, wispy trees and the fat cypress tree with leaves ground up. We walked past story maps—you didn't want to stop and read them like I did—and multi-directional signposts: this way to the eucalyptus forest, that way to the chai rooms, there way to mbinguni gardens, a touch of heaven. You pointed at a giant mushroom tree shaped like a toadstool.

The reserve was richer than I remembered, swollen with more vegetation, even florae jutting out of a man-made lake, browned—not with neglect. There were all-over fragments of rainbow, flowers that gave the reserve the sweet smell of a ripe durian fruit. There stood toilet sheds now—Kobe and I used to relieve ourselves in bushland.

I took in the grassy knolls where locals could picnic, but it was all quiet now—everyone hushed by a pandemic. I was pleased to see the black poppy tree where it stood noble as ever away from the footpath. The black poppy thrived in well-drained loam or sandy soil and the gaze of a full sun direct into its soul. It was a greedy tree that gobbled compost and manure as we nourished it those many years back. It was drought tolerant, kudu- and rabbit-resistant but the Pemba reserve was the only place it grew best.

I wanted to linger there the whole day, to get going only when the moon arrived at the owl's oboe and stalked the lawn of freshly-mown grass. I wanted to seek meaning from dusk and light, shadows and scatter alongside foliage. A swoop of hushed ghosts eavesdropped on the trauma that everyone was too distracted to notice in my footsteps. Yesterday a storm blew.

I listened for the owl's oboe, a hyena's *shekere*, a lone lioness' talking drum, but all I heard was the firefly's kora, a swarm of rain locusts' shakers and a sidewinder's rattle, and they were all in my head. In spite of the fog, they sang in tune a ballad in universal key. At first, I refused to sing because I felt sorry for myself. Then I joined the banjos, pipes and drums in croon. *Mang'oma!* You didn't laugh me off the dais.

We came back to a commotion. "It's happened-y again!" cried Kobe.

"Where?" I asked instinctively, although I understood what he meant. His eyes told me.

"We've called a doctor, but, Shalok-y—!"

We rushed to the Lethe Suite on the second floor where the guest Mme Zig from the Democratic Republic of Congo was rolling her eyes and foaming from her mouth on the floor.

You caught my eye, nodded. Then it was as if I was on bionic speed and everyone else was in slow motion. I dashed to Papaa's kitchen and he opened his mouth, words forming almost in echo. I shoved him from me so vigorously even *I* was astounded.

"Quick, quick!" I cried. "Where's the ginger? Mint? Nutmeg! Rosemary and saffron. I said quick!" He handed ingredients in slow motion. I pounded the mash in a pestle and mortar. "Give me sage and cinnamon! Where's the cumin?"

"Turmeric root?" he echoed, eyes that wide.

I blended it into a broth, then turned it to tea. I sprinted back to the Lethe Suite. There you were, Watison, and time unfroze. Mme Zig gasped and croaked as if someone was choking her.

A scatter of guests crossed themselves to ward off evil.

"Hold her," I barked at Kobe.

I pinched Mme Zig's nose and forced down the tea.

An ash-haired medic from the flying doctors arrived half an hour later to find Mme Zig seated on the floor, a little confused and disheveled but otherwise alive.

"How—" Kobe was murmuring to himself. "Shalok-y?"

"I'd like a word with Tagin, please," I said.

Njoki looked at me. "But why?"

"She might know a thing or two about this whole business."

Tagin hedged.

"The black poppy is both harmless and deadly," I said. "You can eat the leaves raw in a salad or the baby plant boiled whole as a potherb." I studied Tagin. "But you know a thing about sepals and petals, as I do about antidotes."

She shook her head.

"You didn't just accidentally walk under the black poppy tree," I snapped, "but deliberately sought it because it's nowhere near the footpath."

"But the coroner never found-y any poison in the two who died-y!" cried Kobe.

"The same coroner who is also Tagin's uncle?"

The whole room looked at Tagin.

She folded her arms, shrugged. "But Papaa does the cooking, the plating."

"And Papaa lets you in the kitchen," I said.

"Why would I jeopardize my position here, detective?" Her voice was calm.

"I think you're a very ambitious girl. I saw you and Njoki... I don't know how you meant to do it, secure the wife and the lodge, but you meant to create enough chaos for Kobe."

Kobe looked at his wife, aghast.

"I swear! Kobe—I knew nothing!" Njoki cried. "I'd never—!"

Tagin made to run, and you blinked twice, Wati. Tagin fell.

The police arrived and handcuffed the girl destined for something big and took her to a Pemba jail. I was weary when we returned to the presidential suite. I wondered in glumness if Kobe and Njoki's marriage would survive this humiliation. It was possible that Njoki simply enjoyed a flirtation and knew nothing of Tagin's lethal plans.

I felt suddenly hungry and wanted something familiar. I ordered sangara fish served with coconut rice, and chicken kebabs with a spicy yogurt dip for you. And two pots of tea. Rooibos and mango chamomile.

We listened to the mangrove kingfisher and its metal rattle out yonder, then the coo and murmur of the blue-spotted dove on our balcony. Blues and greens, I thought, and smiled.

"I know, dear Watison," I said, "don't look at me that way. Every mystery must have a name. We shall call this one *The Mystery of a Place Between Waking and Forgetting*."

Your tanzanite eyes that caught light gave nothing away, but I understood what was behind them. And it was not pride at my accomplishment in solving this case, no. I knew your thinking, and it was that my caliber of sleuthing was far greater than this. That I could have done bigger, better.

But dear Watison, you of all people should know.

I am not well!

A Fiddle of Whisper Music

Hyacinth played her fiddle in a shuffle by stroke. She stamped her feet to the up and down notes of a nightingale song, slowed the music at her father's approach.

"Come and see the nightingales," he said.

She stilled her music. "Where?'

He took her hand, led her into a wooden shed behind their one-bedroomed shack on Belladonna Street. The wooden-fenced plot housed a kitchen sink, bed and lounge in a small space, and a patch of dirt between the tiny shack where they lived and her father's work shed.

"I can't see the nightingales," she said. "Why aren't they singing?"

"Let me show you different," he said, shutting the door to lock them in. "Close your eyes."

"Why?"

"You'll feel free and hear the birdsong."

There were no nightingales.

When Hyacinth cried, her father whispered, "Shitah. Shitah." He left quietly, first placing the fiddle gently back into her hands.

She shuffled out of the shed, and sat on the ground feeling burn, shadow and stone. She tried but was unable to play any music. The wind whispered, "Shitahshshshsh," trying but failing to soothe the pain that burned green and orange, framed by sad light and the undertaker solemnity of a thousand marabou storks jabbing her core.

And then it rained. It started as a shower that swelled into sheets of rain roped in wind that flogged. The thunder spoke, and it said gah gah gah galley oo.

Hyacinth smashed her fiddle to the ground, and lay flat on the sodden soil. She stretched her hands to the deluge whose torment welcomed stigmata. It peeled her fragility away and rendered her obsolete.

Hyacinth could not say, or guess, how even her own mother—who arrived home with dried tubers from her job at the welfare office in Starnbergersee—

could not see the heap of all that was broken inside the homestead. What Mother did was talk and talk at her father for an hour before bedtime, on and on about finding the heart of light then maybe he'd find a job. He smiled and nodded, as he drank ale, more ale, fell asleep and snored in cracks and bursts.

Mother didn't seem to hear it, then startled at the sight of Hyacinth at her feet on the floor as if she was suddenly seeing her. Hyacinth tried to tell her that it was school holidays, and this April was a cruel month. But all her mother said was, "Why, off to bed you. Ta ta, goodnight."

"Goonight," said Hyacinth.

"Good mornin' sweet ladies," her father said at the creaky-legged breakfast table he was yet to fix. "Hurry up, it's time for work," he said to Hyacinth's mother, who gulped down her coffee and pulled her hair tight.

"I'll go to Unreal City on King William Street after work, buy Hyacinth a new fiddle," she said to no-one in particular.

"You're a proper fool, my darling," her father said. "Leave the child alone if she doesn't want a fiddle."

But Mother went to Unreal City and bought a fiddle.

What lilacs came from flowerless land in dead country that was inside? The new music was a whisper of fog at dawn, the last fingers of falling leaves, branches in stony rubbish, a rattle of bones.

Under the mist of an autumn noon, Hyacinth's father promised to tell her a story about forgetful snow that would surprise them all. He carried her on his back, and took her into the shed.

As her world changed, so did Hyacinth. One day she picked up the fiddle and found a hum of sea-wood and copper in its strings. She adjusted to its sound and gave her father a kill-by date.

The killing, when it started, surprised her. But it gave music swirling with white towers and a peal of bells.

Killing was an art.

First there was choice and, with it, size.

She started with insects, lizards, rats... Hyacinth chopped their heads with razor-sharp objects, then graduated to chicks fallen from their nests. Then it was mice. Cats. Dogs.

She took the toddler from Cupidon Park, distracted him from his mother who was wrapped in a profusion of satin, a glitter of jewels. The smell of his powdered skin, his smudge of lost tears, his sticky face crusted with oatmeal—he was difficult to resist. She'd watched him whoosh with glee down the yellow slide painted with green butterflies, lumber away and get lost, and she lured him into her arms with a crust of dried tuber.

She took him up the hill, where she smiled, tickled his chubby cheek and said, "I'm going to kill you."

"Naw!" he chuckled.

She put a palm on his face and was astonished at the strength in her hands.

The fiddle sang spring in its strings. A silver shower evaporated into moonlight that cartwheeled to touch her head.

The girl from school, Philomel, said, "Why are you doing this to me?"

Hyacinth didn't know how to reply.

Afterward, she scooped a handful of soaked soil and ate its taste of urine and blood.

That night she played her fiddle, and the music was filled with dancing nymphs and swimming dolphins. It lasted days and days, but the sea dried up, and the nymphs departed.

Only the music's memory stayed, searing her with its might.

Hyacinth took a boy, Carthage, from Mrs. Porter's class. They were reading T.S. Eliot. Hyacinth caught Carthage's yawn, and leaned forward with a smile.

"My father has horns and motors," she whispered, and his eyes sparkled. She led him towards a cry of magpies after the bell.

"Is your home up on the hills?" he asked.

She laughed and sang, "Weilala. Wailala!" Then she pounced.

She allowed him to revive for a moment, guiding him with her expert hand to sit up. She spoke calmly to him and the beating of his heart obeyed. She controlled her touch, whispered to him, "Shitah. Shitah."

He closed his eyes, and she throttled him.

She peeled away his clothes, tore into his skin with her nails, fishing inside for anything she could remove: heart, kidney, intestine, liver… She touched what was likely a lung, but it was messy to take out.

She sat upon the grass and studied him as time rusted his blood. By dusk the fluid he had leaked was ash on the soil. She took a moment to contemplate. What was it she resented?

The sound of a beating heart, her mind said. A person alive when she was nothing but bones. All dead inside, yet strong as Samson.

That night her fiddle murmured and whistled a whirlpool that rose and fell over endless plains in its strings.

Hyancinth tailed a woman she chose to call Welfare. She followed her home from the office in Starnbergersee, where Mother once worked—before the fire took her, the one branded with Father's kill-by date. That night he was soaked as a pudding in ale, but flew alert and squealed more than a pig when fire licked him—chained to the bed.

Mother slept unperturbed to her death, as the fiddle merrily sang: *Burning burning burning burning*. The fire did its work, and Hyacinth was grateful that she did not need to plant their corpses in the garden lest they bloomed.

Now Welfare's legs were folded, curled into something tragic. Her dead eyes glittered like diamonds, blank as an ocean. She had fought death. Fled and scaled furniture, but Hyacinth caught her. Welfare's knees jerked and her bowels loosened. Hyacinth listened with closed eyes, her face buried in the woman's hair, until the pulse in those veins weakened.

At some stage, Welfare groaned, "Water."

Hyacinth leaned into her face and murmured a soft recital of Eliot's poem.

Drippy drop drop. No water.

Face to face like that, until Welfare's heartbeat died, it was a prelude to a kiss.

That night Hyacinth stood in open moonlight. The wings of fireflies stroked her cheek. She swayed to the fiddle's music that rose and fell in a shooting star across an indigo night floating with no burial of the dead—just undressed bodies gorged with time, and bats with baby faces in the violet light.

Acknowledgement to T. S. Eliot

I am an immersive writer who writes on a trigger. T. S. Eliot offers cues in "The Waste Land." Text colors itself, muses itself into a tale. Outer wasteland and dilapidation are easy to write. Inner? Not so much, without self-embracing inner badlands and dilapidation. During the time of writing in the thrust of the inexorable covid-19 pandemic, it took perhaps daring and curiosity to wallow into the dirge of text that opens with "The Burial of the Dead."

But it can also be a game of chess. A castling to move the rook, bishop and knight across the board of a tale keen to suck the queen into a brilliancy of doom.

—Eugen Bacon

The Water Runner

THEIR SEX gave the whale-bone unit and its thatched roof of albatross wings a sweet musty odor like a ripened durian fruit. It was one of the many fossil houses of dry bones and cured scales that served generations, and still stood in clusters in Old Dodoma, a land of dryness that was once an ocean. Now there were only stories of the once pregnant ocean with greedy waves that humped and rippled all the way to the shore.

Yes, only stories remained.

Nothing was left of the ocean, because of a curse that rose from Mother Africa's lips in her bereavement for her lost sons and daughters, and the gods heard her cry. Men, women and children snatched from their huts and shipped as slaves in a flourishing economy commandeered by sultans and Arab leaders across the Indian Ocean all the way to Muscat and the Omani coast. Eighteenth century trade routes, running from the Swahili coastal regions all the way to Persia and Mesopotamia, stole what did not belong to them.

Zawadi had read about Tippu Tip, an Afro Omani ivory and slave trader from Stone Town. He was himself the grandson of a slave, yet did not blink at the cries of his own 10,000 slaves in clove plantations all over Zanzibar. But the gods heard, and punished the ocean. Shriveled up her womb, no waters left.

Zawadi pondered this as she lay with Mapesa a moment more on the thin bed in her one-roomer, separated from the other tenants in the government complex by a fish-scale curtain she'd wrangled from a *mtumba* second-hand bundle. A baby was crying—groaning, more like it—and Zawadi didn't want to, or just couldn't, take it anymore.

She swung her feet off the bed, and now stood outside in a blast of crimson desert sand, harsh on her skin way before sunrise. She felt thirsty and imagined cold, clean water washing down her throat. Sweet, sweetest water rushing, rushing to her stomach. She thought of New Dodoma, the world out yonder that promised such water. It also promised the sizzle of a shower like rain from a sleek chrome head in an en suite full of blinking marble and blond rustic wood.

She leant against the fishbone wall, tightened her dust scarf, and pictured rubbing the milk of shea butter on her elbow. It was extraordinary, beautiful that world, a place you got beer with a haircut. There, streets had names like Miriam Makeba Road, Fela Kuti Drive, Kidjo Avenue, Masekela Lane. Towers steepled to the sky, esplanades and water everywhere.

But in this beforehand, inside Old Dodoma, she had decisions to make—and the conclusions came along with judgments and mitigating circumstances that were too reckless to leave to chance. Mapesa was pushing for something she was not ready for.

Technology had improved on most things except housing, poverty, social injustice, the climate, inequality of women and scarcity of water. It did allow for crematorium distillates, units that pulled water, evaporating, condensing, in biological recycling to keep water alive from dead corpses.

She rubbed on the jasmine dry wash that came with moisturizer. She licked the powder that fumigated her mouth, eradicated from her tongue the taste of sleep and Mapesa.

She looked at the curtain—Mapesa's idea. "Tenants equal more credits," he'd said, not long after they moved in together after a crash wooing.

"Dear one," she said now, as he dressed into his cli-suit for work. "Let me know how you go."

"Easy," he said, the gold in his youthful eyes dancing. He flashed his suave smile, the one that softened her knees.

She followed the pings. Each ping came with coordinates. She bluetoothed her hoverboard—silent, solar-powered—and off she surfed.

Each day began with aplomb before worrying itself to nothingness.

By close of day her kinetic energy was in a stupor, the hoverboard her only answer as it followed homeward coordinates to Lyumbu.

Today's first caller was crouched in a hut in Malimbili, tucked north-east of Old Dodoma, where it was once an estuary. The woman was too broken to weep, but her face was already long way before grief ensconced itself like a fetus in her core. She reminded Zawadi of her own mother's lingering face in Nkulungu those many years ago. A sweet-looking face lean like that of a waterbuck. But this here bone and scale hut was nothing like the fresh-smelling one that housed pomegranates, coconuts, figs and nectarines that Zawadi's mother sold at the market. This hut in Malimbili smelled like a sewer clogged with feces.

The woman stretched out a tiny bundle. She unwrapped from it a puffed face with pupil-free eyes unshut in death. The tiny gray mouth was set in a straight line. The mother had covered the child in a temperature wrap to keep it cool, unreasoning that the corpse was beyond feeling or needing heat.

"What happened?" asked Zawadi.

"She's only a tiny one," the woman said. But even tiny ones were pulpable, filtrable.

Zawadi pulled out her device, logged the job. "Everything doesn't start with *No*."

"You'll take her?" The woman spoke in murmurs. Her *chitenge*—a flowing wrap—kept falling off her shoulder to reveal a leaking breast.

Zawadi pointed at the woman's chest. "That milk will sell. I can arrange for collection until you dry." She looked squarely at the woman. "It just means more credits for you—and that one." She nodded at the dust-covered boy peering from behind the *chitenge*. His hair was a rust color, his belly swollen. "Let him have a tug, it will help his kwashiorkor."

"The gods give. Why quarrel with them when they choose to take?" said the woman.

"You may have your own idioms, but this is not karma. If I had a word with the gods, we'd talk about why they are full of cruelty."

"Maybe it is a kindness." The woman, unschooled, signed with a finger on the pad.

"Instant credits when the shuttle comes to collect," said Zawadi.

She jumped back onto her cosmic hoverboard, its Milky Way whiteness a shimmer in her eyes. She soared under a red sky, no clouds. The day was yet another sizzler, you'd think the body would get used to it. It never did. Even with the government-issued cli-suit and its self-regulating system that adjusted to the environment, she never got cool enough. The suit's purpose was endurance, not comfort.

Stuck on a traffic island—she smiled wryly at the irony of the term 'island' in this godforsaken barrenness—she wondered how Mapesa was faring. He hadn't called as she'd asked. It didn't feel like a 50-50 relationship. Mapesa asked, and he got. Zawadi asked…who knows what she got?

Like her, Mapesa worked in government. He was a groomer. He dry-washed old people. Took orders on ping like her. Biochemicals and a hand-held hoover did the rest because water was so scarce who could afford to shower, bath or frolic in it as they said folk did in those stories of auld? And in New Dodoma.

They met three years ago at a government conference in Makulu Oysterbay—another hooter because there was nothing oyster or bay about Makulu. The event was a forum on water planning, where they served bite-size sandwiches pregnant with cream cheese, smoked salmon and hardboiled eggs. Uniformed waiters strutted with trays holding flutes of real, clean water.

When Zawadi saw Mapesa, she was drawn by the kink in his curls, then the gold in his eyes when he turned to look at her with a crooked smile from his tall frame. *Wowza!* she thought. A professional development opportunity that came along with dividends. It was a matter of minutes before the dividends reached her. She smelled the vanilla and wood aroma of him long before he brushed her arm.

She looked at him squarely and demanded, "What's your position on the Great Leader?"

He nearly failed. "I used to think he was a fockwit, but now ..."

She swirled to leave. "Clearly I was mistaken about you—"

But his palm hooked her elbow, and he cut her words with the right answer. "Only a fool tests the deepness of a river with both feet."

"Do you even know what a river looks like?"

Still, she smiled at his redemption. Indeed, the Great Leader was nothing but a nincompoop. He'd already taken a sixteen-year-old as his fifth wife.

Zawadi was not done with the examination.

She sneaked Mapesa to a side room at the end of a corridor. It turned out to be where they stored robot vacuums that twitched and blinked their beady eyes—not in puzzlement, more as if they understood conspiracy. There, inside the storeroom, Mapesa passed the chemistry test. She thought for days how mind-blowing his kiss, the intimacy of their tongue wrestle, how her lips trembled with new longing when he was gone.

After they hooked up, she liked the way he spined her, as she chose to call it—a run of lean, long fingers down her naked back. Aiyaiya, it gave her electricity. She loved how he spooned her, their bodies a glove fit. As they lay in a twine in afterglow, he told her stories of New Dodoma, the place where water-polished pebbles on a sandy beach were not a rare thing of history and fairy tales. There, folk had time and place to attend real schools with human teachers, not robots. Schools that had students who wore emblemed blazers and went to assembly, then took lessons on how to move in water like dolphins and whales that were now extinct. He told her of streets where music started on cue and led you to a salt spray from a humping ocean swollen with luminescent fish.

Their sex was *good*. He knew her sweet spot. He touched her and her buttocks went tight, heat and chill all over her body, pulsing between her legs, moments before the release that flowed everywhere.

It made up for their tensions.

When they started arguing and he acted all snobby, know-it-all, she nearly hated him. She found herself beginning to question his first words when they met, and wondered if his reference to the fool who tested the river with both feet was not to the Great Leader, but to Zawadi.

The lights turned.

The job in Area C was a suicide: what made a father of seven kill himself? Everything. In this waterless world that paid in credits that never lasted but dissolved unstretched in a grueling economy—e-v-e-r-y-t-h-i-n-g. One simply lost faith. Even though the father was outwardly perfect, rigor-mortised in a fetal curl of dying agony, she had to say no. The man had swallowed rust remover. His water was compromised.

The next job was in Ipagala where the ocean once jutted out an elbow and created a recreation space where lovers and families visited in throng to picnic and fish. This job was a hit-and-run. A collision with another hoverboard. Zawadi studied the broken body—the splatter of what was left at the site of the incident. This fresh, the cadaver wasn't yet releasing the putrescine odor of rot catalyzed by heat.

Unlike the first mother, this one with a pockmarked face was roaring her grief, tearing hair as bystanders consoled her. Zawadi logged the job, but there wasn't much liquid. Her manager Amadeus was not going to like this. "We're not Mother Teresa," she imagined his disdain as he muttered the name of the ancient saint. "You have no power to give what's not yours."

But whose was it?

She couldn't log the murder in Chang'ombe, but made the appearance of inspecting the body, the collapse in the matted head where the skull had fractured. The caved cavity released a creamy ooze onto the naked floor. The girl had whiplash and lacerations on the arms and legs. Blood still seeped from her nose.

"This is a matter for the police," Zawadi said. "Call me when the body is cleared."

She finished before lunch on a burn in Uzunguni. It was a wealthy neighborhood that was once fully vintage, a coveted islet on the ocean. Now on it stood neat rows of identical thermal-controlled bungalows inside a fenced complex. The houses were built of phase change material that absorbed latent heat and gave cooling. Housewives drew leisurely strolls with robot poodles on manicured lawns.

Zawadi stubbed her toe on an ancient shell. She picked it from the ground where it had pushed itself up, and studied its turquoise and white swirl inside which a breathing creature had once lived. She put the shell back aground, not in her pocket as she really wanted to. She walked along a garden speckled with the pink blush of peonies, the yellow stretch of leopard orchids with reddish-brown rosettes, the milky dash of impala lilies gilded in red velvet, the snowy blossom of baby's breath. But the flowers and their ultra-sheen were all fakes that would never wilt. No real flowers grew in Old Dodoma. At least here there was no lingering of nosy neighbors like you might find in the cheaper suburbs. Shades, paints and glazes—you couldn't see a thing until you stepped across the threshold.

Inside one of the bungalows, a gas burner had exploded. She looked at the cooked skin peeling off the woman's body, her chin and neck like melted plastic, clusters of charcoal on her torso. But the burn had sealed her water—Zawadi logged the job. The husband would get good credits.

She rubbed her temples. Her head hurt, so did her muscles. Day in, day out, body after body. How much longer could she do this? Did Tippu Tip's slaves ask themselves this question, over and over, as they slogged under whips? She checked herself—what she had was not good, but it was better than what those slaves had endured.

Back in the office in Chamwino, she let herself into the shoebox that housed two desks and a TV on the second floor of a warehouse that manufactured nutrition pills. It was an embedded warehouse, a concrete and timber hybrid buried in the ground like most corporate buildings in Old Dodoma—built to stay cold as a stone church.

Her boss Amadeus had gone missing. She hadn't seen him for days and wondered if he'd gone on a getaway to New Dodoma. *He* could afford such luxury, but she wasn't sure *how* on the meager income they both earned. It had to be a side hassle on the black market. The two of them ran the water business, coordinated with body collectors, factories, reservoirs and the banks.

But it was only a matter of time before robots took over. They were everywhere. Robots diagnosed patients in pop-up clinics, and printed prescriptions from their mouths. Robots tutored children who weren't home-schooled by parents, and ran online modules for those who were. Robots ran walk-in drycleaners—they swallowed dirty clothes and spewed them out ironed. They were all part of Robotix, the Great Leader's own company.

Talk of undeclared conflict of interest!

Lunch was two reds: bland pills full of protein, vitamins, minerals, water and carbs. Zawadi swallowed them whole, grateful she could afford them, but not the water she recycled from dead people. She was still thirsty despite the nutrients in the pills. The swooning in her head told her she was tired. Yet only half the day had passed. Today time was not playing kind.

On days she felt extravagant, she took purple pills that came rich with magnesium, calcium, phosphorus and potassium—this diet balanced her water, fed her skin, polished her hair and her nails, and she stayed strong on iron and selenium.

On frugal days (she and Mapesa were saving to migrate to New Dodoma), it was the grays—a carb hit that kept her brain functioning. But mostly she could stay with the blues, cheaper than the reds and just enough protein to tease the right hormones and antibodies to keep forming.

She grabbed the remote and turned on the TV to the sight of the Great Leader with his hippo head and rat brain. Nearly two decades later, he was still denying climate change. 'I don't believe it,' he was saying to a reporter.

"Don't you believe about the ocean, how it once existed?" the reporter asked.

"It's all a hoax. We all know it's rubbish that Old Dodoma was once the Indian Ocean."

"It's charted in the records of history. Are you saying our ancestors were wrong? Scientists and scholars too?"

"Prophets of doom, that's what they are. They should be lynched."

Like he'd lynched the economy. Like he'd lynched opposition and democracy. Declared himself the Great Leader, worked with some monarch in New Russia on the secret to longevity, bought meds from New China to resuscitate his idiocy daily. It was no doubt Mapesa was a fan. And he kept harping about harvesting clinics. That the government was growing babies.

"If it's true," said Zawadi, "they're propaganda farms."

"Give the Great Leader a break. What's wrong with creating children of the state?"

"For what?"

"All you have to do is register and we get rich," said Mapesa. "I'd do it tomorrow if I was a woman."

"I'm not doing the harvester."

"Know how many credits that is? Two hundred and fifty thousand. More than ample for two one-way shuttle tickets and a settlement bonus to New Dodoma. Think of rippling waves smashing on a beach."

Zawadi thought about it, but disagreed with his thinking. "Dear one," she said, "you're good in bed. But does our talking always have to end in affray?"

She couldn't shrug the desiccated human from her last job. A woman had put her husband in a grain store for a whole year, hooked him up, skinned him and covered him with salt like you cured the meat of a pig. The carcass was still pink—maybe it was pink-orange, but did it matter what color it was? All Zawadi remembered was how he was crusted in parts, tougher than bad leather. And the face, dear gods, the face.

His water was gone.

But Zawadi logged the job, slipped through some credits. She wondered about the woman, and her intent. Was it to keep him or eat him, and was it freedom or desperation that finally led to the ping? Everyone had a breaking point.

She thought of slaves laboring under a harsh white sun in clove plantations—and a wrath of the gods that took away the waters. Even the gods broke.

"Is it really true?" she asked Mapesa that night back home in Lyumbu after their reds. "The harvesting clinic?"

"Don't be stupid," he said. "Of course, it's true."

"I'd love to see some seagulls."

"Me too. But only you can do something to change our situation."

The fish-scale curtain parted. "Look who's visiting," said Zawadi.

Mapesa looked, and frowned.

It was Rafi, the tenant's toddler. She poked her head below the curtains. She had big gray kitten eyes. She was smaller than her age, that was clear, still crawling on her stomach when she should be toddling. She didn't play much, was irritable in the hours that the people of Lyumbu slept. Her cry wasn't the owh-owh of a baby, but a slow, low cry like that of a grieving old woman: 'Owwwhhhh.' It didn't take intellect to figure the child was suffering from malnutrition. Zawadi hated to imagine the teeny bub becoming another water run, feeding the mincer for condensate.

"Hello, Snotty," she said.

But the mother, whose name was Queeny or Beany, snatched in with her stink eye, taut cornrows and tattered *chitenge*. She scooped the child without a word, leaving behind her smell of the unkempt.

Zawadi couldn't put a finger to it, but the woman's husband, Jiwe, made her uneasy. There was something jiggery-pokery about him. He had the type of square face with mean eyes and a broken nose you'd pick out in a police line-up. The woman looked battered, always shouting, "Weye!" or "Acha!" to her lethargic baby who didn't need to stop doing anything.

Zawadi wondered if Jiwe was a wife-beater. She'd never heard it, but she was on the water run the whole day—who knew what the walls saw? Sometimes she called him the magician—he vanished at odd hours. He looked around with furtiveness, whispered into his handheld, put on his cli-suit and was gone until dawn.

"I can't do it, the harvesting, you know that," Mapesa was saying. "But you can."

She struggled with the thought for a long time, and finally said, "And who can we ask?"

He nodded at the curtain.

"Jiwe?" asked Zawadi.

"Haven't you wondered if he was in the black market?"

"Matter of fact, I have." She sighed. "Then *you* do it, Mapesa."

He smiled.

"Talk to him, man-to-man," Zawadi said. "Because I honestly would rather not. And I'm sick of this arguing."

"Easy," he said, and the gold danced.

She listened to their whispers—urgency in Jiwe and Mapesa's voices as they spoke. Indeed, the night had ears. Rafi was crying that old woman groan. "Owwwhhhh." Zawadi wanted to stand outside in the warmth of a shouting wind, and was about to swing her legs from the sheets when the curtain moved. Mapesa slipped back into bed.

He cuddled her in a spoon, spined her until she trembled with electricity. He was lying on his back, knees folded on the bed. She sat at his feet, her head slightly back as she faced him. She'd do anything for him, she thought. But she was hungry to forget this fact as she steadied herself against him, let him fondle the erogenous zone in her feet on his shoulders. It had taken practice to get this tantric position right, and it was perfect. His kisses and caresses on her feet felt inside her. She thought she would explode. Just when she nearly did, he pulled her to his swell, and she moaned at his thrust.

His words in afterglow breathed on her neck. They lay in a new spoon. "So, they have running water in New Dodoma—it splashes from a tap."

She turned, touched his nose. "And that is news—how?"

"They have shops where you can buy sugar, milk, bread, biscuits, even beer or soda in a can—like we read in the books, how it was long ago."

"If you say so. I said I'd do it, no need to convince me."

"I can convince you to something more," he said with husk in his voice. He knelt and sat her astride him, kissed and caressed her breasts.

She rubbed against his torso, not need much convincing on that score either.

Later, spent, his words continued to touch her in a drawl. "They have seagulls there—yellow-eyed and pink-beaked, flying low above your head and crying kraa-kroo in a happy warble."

"And Jiwe told you all this?" said Zawadi. "Has he even been there?"

"Well…er—"

"Soon you'll tell me they have shower huts in all colors of the rainbow at the beachfront. Caravan homes stacked with sun chairs by the waterfront."

"Is that too impossible to want?"

"Yes!" she snapped. "Like wanting hospitals with white sheets on a bed."

"But they do have them! And restaurants. You go in and sit and dine like a royal on a five-course menu. People wait on you every day, not just in government functions. They bring you poached chicken, boneless lamb or butternut squash balls that you chew and savor, not swallow like pills."

Zawadi had to admit she was weary of soaring over burnt soil and dry rock to collect water from dead people. She wanted to see a world with clubs and the silvery glow of streetlights. Neon signs of whatever was the rage. Back alleyways swollen with cafés on ultrawide laneways. She wanted to walk in a botanical garden with real flowers and real dogs—Rhodesian ridgebacks, big like a grown-up, sleek Azawakhs prancing like sheikhs on trimmed grass. She wanted to step out of a beachfront caravan and walk to the beach, slip her toes in wet sand and feel the water's heartbeat.

"How many credits does this Jiwe want from us?" She toyed with the tightness of Mapesa's curls, stretching, releasing. "What do we have to give for him to hook us up with the clinic?"

"I've already paid, anything for you. All you've got to do is let me take you there. Just one week is all it takes. One week, and we're frolicking in water, sipping lit cocktails on a sandy shore in New Dodoma."

"A week?"

"It's called technology. The eggs are already treated. From the moment of implanting, it's an accelerated gestation."

She thought of the dead child with a puffed face in Malimbili, the suicide in Area C, the hit-and-run in Ipagala, how the mother roared her grief.

"And who'll do the water run?"

"I can talk to Amadeus. He'll give you sick leave—hundreds of casuals are waiting in a queue."

She thought of the husband, hung up like a pig. The wife's eyes turned inward, as if searching for her soul. On the scale of things, harvesting didn't sound that bad. Not bad at all.

"Dear one," she said. "And how much credit will you give Amadeus to agree to all this?"

They soared on one hoverboard—Mapesa's. Zawadi wrapped herself around him as if she were made of tentacles. She sought an emotional connection, but she could well be clutching a plank. There was just his wood and vanilla smell from the antiperspirant, and his solid athletic frame.

The clinic stood behind steel gates, electrical fencing, double-security doors. Surprisingly, it had hospital beds with white sheets on them. She was the only patient, and there was one obstetrician in the ward. She was glad to see that he was a real doctor, not a robot. Either that or he was the perfect cyborg in a human body. A seasoned man with snow hair, a knowing jaw and eyes that told nothing.

She felt thirsty. Mapesa was hovering with a smile—not the suave one. This one was off, not reaching the gold in his eyes. It was as if he, not her, was discomfited by the whole thing. On second thought, no—the smile wasn't foolish. It was the copious one of a pauper about to get rich. At all costs. As she read and signed the paperwork, she thought of that traitor Amadeus who didn't give a hoot about Mother Teresa and would sell his employee to anybody for a few credits.

She looked up at the doctor in the room blinking with lights, and thought of a city with vibrant bustle and silver rain, water in her grasp. She understood that, much as she resented Mapesa right then, that full minute, it was her dream too. She wanted to walk into a neon-lit world whose boulevards resurrected names like Salif Keita and Yvonne Chaka Chaka.

She questioned her decision to be in the clinic, but her mind came at her with ecstatic thoughts of fun parks where she bought tickets and walked into the big mouth of a giant clown, and straight into a mirror maze or a spider ride or a supernova that churned her in the sky as she squealed her glee. She knew that she should ask about where the implanted eggs came from, who fertilized them and what happened to the babies: were they propaganda for the state, products of the Great Leader's lunacy? Suddenly it struck her, and she went cold: what if they were water harvests? Birthed, then humanely put to sleep for the crematorium distillate?

She thought of Tippu Tip and the curse he brought that killed a whole ocean. Slaves chained in planks, skin to skin on the floor like tilapia going to the market. Flesh to harvest by masters who had no claim to it. Sweat, blood and bones to fuel a trading empire on routes along the Indian Ocean from the Swahili coast to Persia, Omani and Mesopotamia…

But she closed her mind from the niggling growing into a tormenting dread that came with pondering ethics or ethos, and imagined escape from a perpetual drought that ate her inside out until it became normal, but not really. She accepted that her everyday as a water runner was too reckless to leave to chance and understood that there was nobody to save her, that she must bequeath herself with dragon wings to separate from this world with its fossil houses and ground so hard, footprints were a dream.

She thought of New Dodoma where she would never thirst again. She yearned for a cool wind that hummed year-round in a crisp breeze that summoned gulls, and they were alive not extinct. She wanted to be in a place where the ocean of pale green water unpolluted by humans and an evil trade went and went, round and round, no land in sight for miles and miles. Water so clear, so pale in its green hue, it let you see the silt and black rock on its ocean bed, as its wet tongues licked at soft, wet sand where children dug in buckets and shaped sandcastles. So instead of asking the questions she wanted, she searched the doctor's eyes, but they were black velvet. "Will it hurt?"

"Don't be stupid, you won't feel a thing," said Mapesa.

"We put you in a coma to keep your body activity minimal," said the doctor.

He hooked her onto a ventilator, and at once she felt heady. What if, from here, it was for her straight to the mincer? She saw herself as a corpse, pure, unresisting in giving water from her remnants in biological recycling. She panicked for a wild moment—already she was losing control over her own body. But before she could ask the doctor to pause or stop, the vapors took.

Sound fell.

She saw him at the edge of her vision, fading in and out. Mapesa's mouth was moving and she could make out the words "I love you," or "I have you," or "I hope you…"

Did he doubt that she'd make it? Her last thoughts as her head plummeted and a jaw of blackness devoured her.

Dimension Stone

NOW she truly understood the term "six feet under". She could feel each pull of oxygen that she drew. But she tried so very hard not to hyperventilate. She'd read somewhere that the smaller you were the longer you survived buried alive. She wasn't dead yet.

She thought of Australia. What would happen to that now?

So hungry.

She thought of the kiosk and its chicken and chips, eggs. Fresh shrimp in roasted yasa caterpillar dip. Tangawizi tea. Fanta. Safari beer. Roasted bananas. Wali nyama—rice and beef… The chimes of a lark's song against the backdrop of a finger harp, lyrics tugging her soul: "Me wanna spoil you."

"You'll not get rich by sleeping," snapped Mama from the laundry room.

"How is this sleeping?" muttered Pendo.

"What's that?" Mama's voice sharp and rising.

"I said I've finished sweeping the chicken coop."

"And the eggs?"

"All in the kitchen, Mama."

"And the goats?"

"Fully milked."

Pendo could honestly do with more hands. She threw her rucksack by the door, and gave the kitchen one last look lest some out of place pot gave Mama apoplexy.

"Acha!" Pendo bellowed at her sister Rafina to stop, sticky baby fingers already digging into the rucksack. Pendo grabbed it and peddled down the narrow lane away from the house before Mama could call her back for leaving the toddler bawling.

Out at the market just before the fruit and veggie stalls, motorbikers roared their business at her. "Bodaboda! Half-price! Free helmet. Ride anywhere!"

Indeed, bodabodas were cheaper than Ubers and shuttles, and you could ride anywhere. Each biker knew to weave the traffic and get Pendo to Shimoni Academy just before the morning assembly bell. She much preferred St Annes, where her friend Jamani went, but it cost money and Mama couldn't afford it.

She stood by the roadside and flagged down Tupo, her favorite biker. He was her stranger, non-stranger. He represented normality, certainty—someone who was not blood kin, always reliable. He was a fresh looker in that tight T-shirt she could clutch around his waist, and he didn't try to make a pass at her. He kept his lime green Kawasaki Ninja sparkling, and she wondered how he did it in all that Dar es Salaam clamminess and dust.

The motorbike bopped and thumped in a loud but not annoying roar, zipping in and out of roadways between cars and shuttles, as Pendo clung to Tupo's thin waist. She wished she wore earphones, so she could listen to the catchy beats of solo artist Smooth Lark. Chuma had introduced her to the lark's music, especially the latest hit, a sweet-tongued woo about definitions and "me wanna spoil you" against the backdrop of a finger harp.

She shut her eyes from the racing landscape and her longing for soothing music, and thought about Chuma.

They met at Africa Joy on an evening so humid, a Dar night at its worst. She wanted to throw off her blouse and walk tits out, but Jamani would, like, have a fit, if not faint. That night at Africa Joy her friend Jamani was being an outright nuisance, not fancying being out this late.

"It's not even a school night!" protested Pendo.

"Carry your water and you'll learn to love every drop," said Jamani.

"What's water got to do with dance?"

"I have to work hard to stay at St Anne's—my parents won't like it if my grades dropped."

"One night and they drop?"

"One night, two nights—with you it becomes five, ten nights, Pendo. There's no end to your lust for fun."

"And what's wrong with fun?"

"You know how it is when there are too many men around. Look at them! One minute they're laughing, next they're throwing fists, you have to duck not to get hurt."

Just then, someone behind them said, "That's fucking dope."

Pendo turned to see who it was, and there he stood with a big gap-toothed smile, moving his body to the new beat, a Smooth Lark number. He wore natural

98

sleepy eyes that put softness in her legs when their gaze met. He was bopping solo on a sparse dance floor and, mindless of Jamani, Pendo's feet took her to him. They swayed, like forever, then he took her hand and drew her to the outdoor pub linked to Africa Joy.

She looked at the menu. Fresh shrimp in roasted yasa worm dip. Pilau and beef. Tangawizi tea—but ginger reminded her of Mama and medicinal herbs.

"Whatever my mami wants," Chuma wooed her.

"I like kuku," she said. "Anything kuku."

His gap-toothed smile. "I love chicken too," he said softly, his words an endearment, each syllable brushing her skin. His sleepy eyes took her knees and, weakened, she climbed onto a barstool.

"Get you anything?" he asked. "Besides kuku?"

They laughed.

He bought her a Safari beer, and a soft drink for himself that he slurped.

"I should introduce you to my friend, Jamani—you'll get on well," said Pendo.

"Why?"

"Fanta."

He laughed. "It's because I want to behave tonight, mami."

"Why?"

His look melted her. "Because you."

"What do you do?" she asked, anything to shift attention from the intimacy her whole being was begging.

"Sokoine," he said.

She raised her brow.

"University of Agriculture, Morogoro," he said. "I study geology."

"I see," she said. "You're one of those fogwits digging tanzanite for our corrupt government and rich socialists."

"You want marriage—no?"

"Yes. No. That's the kind of ridiculous nonsense only a man would spring up in the middle of an important conversation. How does marriage have anything to do with those digging fogwits?"

"A gemstone comes with a promise, mami. I'd like to tell you how there's more to life than living in the moment. I'd like to show you how there's more to geology than cobalt, gypsum or tanzanite." Oh, those eyes. He took her hand.

"Like—" she swallowed. "Like what?"

"Like soil science, earth science, biodiversity, conservation."

"Y-yeah?"

"Yeah. Like extreme nature: earthquakes and floods. Spatial analysis and modelling too."

"So you know about volcanoes?"

"Yeah," he said. "Girls like you, mami."

Tupo's Ninja made it to Shimoni, many minutes to spare. Pendo took off the helmet, handed it back and shook her braids. She was ready for school, and yet not. Mrs Zuberi was boring as ever in the hisabati class—Pendo was not good with theorems and geometry, estimates or probabilities but was fine when it came to counting change at the kibanda called Waterbuck Café just outside the school gate, where she and Jamani sometimes met for lunch.

Waterbuck was cheaper by far than most places with its fried or roasted bananas and chips kuku—they snipped the quartered chicken for you and swapped the parts you wanted. Pendo loved a stack of roasted chicken legs, for just Tsh 100. That first night with Chuma she'd tried chicken heads at Tsh 150 each and intestines at Tsh 200, but discovered she didn't care much for those.

She was good at biologia because she needed to know how to count safe days for when she and Chuma had sex because he didn't like condoms. She loved most jiografia because it told her of places, their contours, and she wanted to get away from the sand and heat of Dar es Salaam. She wanted to climb a plane, sit on the sky and fly all the way to Nairobi, Johannesburg, Marseille or Detroit. She wanted a new life, any life away from Mama. Melbourne—she liked Australia. Mrs Zuberi said, if she studied hard, she could get a scholarship to Kenya, South Africa, Europe, USA. But Pendo wanted to go "Down Under". She read that people there spoke funny. They said "mate", "this arvo" and "bloody awesome".

Today she lunched alone, not with Jamani, who was the fierce protector, but held grudges. This week she had alienated herself over some fallout whose root cause Pendo couldn't remember. What she remembered was that it took over a month for Jamani to forgive that night of abandonment at Africa Joy with Chuma.

She remembered how the chap at the outdoor pub was adept with the fryer and the paddle. How she and Chuma watched as he tipped parboiled chips into the bottom of the fryer, added oil, and tossed. How the finger-cut chips that he served were all gold and crisp, drizzled with salt from Lake Nakuru, just as pink as its flamingos, and the potato as tender inside as yasa worms.

"Mayai?" the chap asked, and Pendo nodded. The jolly chap cracked three eggs straight into a heated skillet, tossed an omelet and threw it over the chips on her plate.

Sometimes, with Jamani, Pendo preferred her eggs separately beaten and drooled into a skillet full of chips for a stir-fried blend. But this version was ace.

100

After the meal, they walked to Serafina Beach where an old dhow was berthed along the edges of emerald water.

"The ocean is bluer at Bongo Beach," suggested Chuma.

"But we don't go there," she said.

"Why?"

"Because, clearly, you've stayed the fog away too long in Morogoro." He pretended to look hurt, then drew her to him. "So much turbulence, is why," she fell against him laughing.

Chuma took off his moccasins and convinced Pendo to toss off her sandals.

"I don't like the feel of sand," she confessed.

They dipped their toes in the greenest of waters, and she marveled at his carefree nature, his full lips, his tight curls, and that baby beard and mustache.

He *behaved*, drove her back to Mama's house in his two-seater pickup van parked at Mbezi Temboni—they walked to get there, but it was pleasant.

It was early afternoon now, school just ended.

Pendo put on her earphones and chimed to Smooth Lark. She closed her eyes to the honey *tink*! of the gourd piano and "me wanna spoil you…" She smiled, thought of Chuma, her strong-thighed gorgeous. Sure, he "behaved" that one night, the rest belonged in Mrs Zuberi's historia class. Chuma's devil took her inside a "guesthouse", where the woman at the counter frowned but took their money, asked no questions.

Pendo didn't know whether it was the natural bedroom eyes, an odd greenish-gold for a black man, or the cute gap right there where a lower canine should be. She'd at first wondered once or twice if he'd lost the tooth in a fall, or if it was a rite of passage thing, you know, like how some men circumcised, some pockmarked their faces and others pulled teeth? But he was circumcised, and she always forgot to ask the question because Chuma's voice spread butter into her knees, and his tongue and fingers occupied her eager head and body with much else.

And it was melting all the time.

Sometimes he stood and carried her against a wall. She wrapped her thighs around his waist, her arms around his shoulders and they kissed as they fucked. That position was always quick and urgent, full of thrill. Someone else would have long broken his back at their exploits, but not Chuma.

She once asked, later, much later, nestled in the crook of his arms, "How does it feel to come?"

He looked at her with amusement.

"A deep want that plateaus and my heart races twenty seconds until the muscles in my buttocks give to a forever sweetness that is a waterfall."

"Is that why you fall the fog to sleep?"

"Shit, yeah." He laughed. His look bore curiosity, and a gleam of something more. "And you?"

"It's a surge right here between my legs and it pulls from my thighs and rushes in vibrations all the way to my clit. I can't stop it," she said.

He laughed when he was happy, he laughed when she got angry. He never got angry. "Since when did a roaring lioness catch a gazelle, mami?" he would ask softly when she was feeling foul, and mostly it was about Jamani's prudishness.

Out on the horizon shone a perfect white sun. Tepid yes, but Pendo wasn't made of mud. She bopped to Smooth Lark, as she headed for the bodabodas. She smiled, Chuma sweet on her soul. That's when she felt *it*, more than saw it. A darkness overwhelmed her, and it pulsed from the ground. She opened her eyes and there, right there at her feet was the bluest eye of a god. It blinked at her. She stooped to study the ring, that's what it was, and it seemed to chameleon. At first it was a shimmering blue streamed with amber, now it gleamed amethyst. She barely touched it, but it seemed to leap on its own accord and push onto her middle finger. Her mood immediately plummeted for no apparent reason, and Pendo could only attribute the change to the ring. She could have sworn it was an opal or tanzanite, but what if it was a sacred stone?

She snatched the ring off her finger but at once craved it so badly, a deep and terrible missing, she pushed it back on and felt satiated yet fully glum. She looked around and saw a woman wrapped in batik looking intently at her from a distance, who turned and began to walk away. Pendo's mother had warned her about picking up shiny things from the road, because sometimes it was the calling of a djinn. She felt a compulsion to return the ring, because the woman might have deliberately dropped it for picking, along with whichever curse. Pendo started running after her, started calling out—what? She was startled at the growl that fell from her lips: "Acha!" The word thundered out in sync with a gruff whisper from the ring in those same words: *Stop!*

The woman turned, waited for Pendo to speak or reach her, but no words or motion came, just the ring dragging Pendo back and away against her will.

"Acha!" again, out loud in a snarl from her flouting lips.

The woman scowled and walked away.

Suddenly the ring was pulling Pendo in the opposite direction. Now she was peddling, zigging and zagging alongside traffic faster than Tupo's bodaboda. She felt herself drawn in all planes, as if she were a singularity in a multiverse where she should be many. The ring skewered her thoughts, muddied them, then crisped her mind with such clarity, it frightened. The boys out at the marketplace roared: *Bodaboda!*

Half-price, free helmet. Ride anywhere! She could hear them as if they were inside her head. Chuma saying over and over, *A deep want that plateaus and my heart races twenty seconds…* Mama, shrill inside Pendo's mind: *You will not get rich by sleeping.* Jamani speaking over them all: *Carry your water and you'll learn to love every drop, drop, drop.*

Full lips, tight curls. A baby beard and mustache.

She found to her horror that she was sprinting, unable to stop, towards Bongo Beach, the water already shouting from a distance. Much as she disliked it, she found herself pulling off her shoes and walking on the hot white sand and hurling herself into the humping waters that hungrily licked at her ankles, then her khaki skirt was all soaked. Now she was deeper and deeper into the water, beyond the waist, her head going under, the ring hauling her into a rip.

She tried swimming but she was drowning, *ghelp*, drowning. *GHELP!* This was not about connecting with nature, her last thought, as she felt terrified yet whole, as she died, yet didn't.

Pendo could only describe her state as an out-of-body experience, as they fished her body from the ocean, then she was cold and shivery, fog in her head, ice in her fingers, at the morgue. Once or twice she stopped feeling and lost consciousness, yet she always woke.

It wasn't an opal, tanzanite or a sacred stone. It was a dimension stone that pulled her along planes, put her into a singularity of many because she was here among all those dead people below her, above her, beside her at the morgue, and there, seeing the world pass by.

She saw the kibanda and its chips kuku, chips mayai where she cheaply ate with Jamani, the chap tossing an omelet in a sizzling skillet. She tried to distract herself, and thought of Chuma, how she sat on him facing outwards and touching his feet. How he leaned back on his arms, and she leaned forwards. How he put his knees below her knees, thrusting as she gently moved. How he murmured, "Love is a sin," over and over in swelling tempo until he orgasmed. She willed herself to envision Smooth Lark and his sweet zanzu, and waited for dawn to break, for anyone, anything to save her from this long and terrible nightmare.

But it was only the start.

A man cloaked in white pulled her from a cold drawer. He yanked at the ring, but it stuck. He took a knife and hacked off her finger so he could sew it back ringless, but the ring bit or scorched him and he fell back, color drained from his sallow face, and her finger with its ring was whole again.

He recovered enough to start the slicing, sawing, excruciating pain as he cut, moved things, fixed, removed. A large needle broke her skin then she watched her blood flush down a drain along the table and into the sink. Invisible tears pricked her eyes. A gurgle of the drain, then another fluid that smelled of hospitals and old people was entering her body with a burn, oh, *fuck* it burnt.

The man shoved cottonwool down her nose and throat, then sewed her mouth shut. She felt each thread of the needle as it wove in and out of her skin but could do nothing to cry out, let alone stop it. He injected something into her eyeballs, oblivious of her silent scream.

He washed her body. Brushed her hair and painted her face with dark tan angel face powder, then put her back in the refrigerator.

She was cold in the morgue—but at the same time saw folk at Mama's house. Mama, right there, her ululation of grief, Mrs Zuberi putting consoling hands around her. There were Pendo's classmates, and Jamani cooking lots of rice and pepper goat in clay pots on three-hearth stones. Men, some from Africa Joy, eating and drinking kindi—maize wine, but Pendo personally preferred chimpumu, the cassava wine, or wanzuki, the honey wine. Throngs sang and danced to a tribal ditty, not Smooth Lark, swishing sisal skirts draped over town clothes, as they moved shoulders and hips to the drumbeat.

Now she was in a coffin of striated African blackwood, handles on either side. Soft cloth inside, its lid flipped open for viewing. They had dressed her in a chitenge suit with puffed out sleeves. "It's her favorite," Mama had whispered between sobs. Only it wasn't. Pendo preferred tank tops or slim fit hoodies, lightweight—what she was wearing when she met Chuma.

It was white and lit in the sky, early afternoon—the time school ended, but here she was, instead, swathed in an open casket inside a big church. Pastor Kizito was all bouncy in sunnies, sneakers and bling—not just the gold necklace but a platinum tooth that blinked when he smiled or bellowed his hallelujahs, urging the faithful to "live like Christ", to "be Christ". Who the fog did he think Jesus was? wondered Pendo, but without rage.

She knew that she should be angry at her predicament, depressed even, but the ring had mellowed her, injected her with some form of alien tranquility. And there was whispering, always, always the whispering, and it wasn't coming from the mourners. It was from somewhere inside, outside. It came from the ring.

Pastor Kizito read from the Bible, then slammed it shut. Again, he was jumping at the pulpit, teeth all white and punctuating his hallelujahs! Runaway ripped jeans part-fell in that punk way of a street rapper down his enlightened hips, the armpits of his unholy dress shirt all sodden.

Now it was the time for viewing, Mama first, all in black.

Pendo had always thought coffins were a perfect rectangle, but she was in a hexagonal case. And there, oh, there was Rafina! Pendo wanted to reach out to her baby sister, touch her black velvet skin and big nose, stroke those neat plaits on her head. But Rafina was clasped in Mama's arms, sucking her thumb, legs astride Mama's waist.

Then there was Jamani, cowrie beads at the end of her braid tails. She was respectfully dressed—her parents wouldn't allow otherwise—in an ebony and gold batik with a matching headdress. Dear Jamani who kept grudges but was now half-crawling in grief!

And there was Chuma too, his full lips tight with a rage she'd never seen, his baby beard roughed up and fierce. His natural sleepy eyes glinted red, nothing green or gold in them. Pendo tried, so very hard tried her best to sit up in the open casket to no avail. She hoped people would see she was still alive and cancel the funeral and please, please take her home.

Six men carried her coffin by the handles. One of them was Tupo, the bodaboda guy. This was no dream, because Tupo was normality, certainty—he always reliable, this stranger, non-stranger, now here he was among kindred shouldering her casket. They paused for a herd of goats crossing the dusty path. She saw everything with such clarity, even though she was in a coffin and her eyes were sewn shut. Mourners poured into Kisutu Cemetery, nestled kilometers from the beach that took her.

In a blend of tradition and Christianity they performed rites for her safe passage into the afterworld—bloody heck, couldn't they see she was already in it? A medicine man slit a spotless rooster's throat and let its blood flow over the casket.

She listened as they said things about her that just weren't right, spoke about her kindness to her baby sister Rafina now destitute without a mentor; about her forever friendship with Jamani now desolate without a bosom buddy; about how Pendo never once answered back, her obedience to her broken-hearted mother, grief-struck by a wasteful death that had shattered the family.

Someone burst into song, the rest joined.

"You are dust, and to dust you shall return," they hummed.

Mama, then Rafina, then Jamani threw palmfuls of soil into the grave. Chuma, oh, how she loved him, kept a prudent distance from Mama, who didn't know about him, but took his turn with the rest of the men to toss a fistful of dust.

Jamani's parents, both suited, the mother veiled, offered Mama and Rafina a lift in their limousine with its tinted windows. Pendo felt a deep and terrible sadness seeing them. She longed for life, for all the traditions she had so far taken for granted: the wildness and elegance of drums and dancing, the welcoming texture on her tongue of homebrewed wine and homecooked food. She yearned for the samosas and chapatis and vitumbuas—malted rice pancakes—at her wake.

With Jamani's parents, champagne, not kindi, chimpumu or wanzuki, might flow. As the rest of the crowd departed from the cemetery, menfolk started shoveling to fill her grave. The terrible sound of the first trowel of soil hitting the coffin—only then, despite the ring, did she panic.

It was all quiet now. She felt sleepy, so tired. She tried to wriggle her toes—they'd buried her without shoes. "She loves walking barefoot," her mother said. "She wanted to study hard and get a scholarship to Canada."

No, she didn't, mused Pendo in her haze. Funny, not funny, how she wanted to go down under. Now she truly understood 'six feet under'. Each pull of oxygen... she tried not to hyperventilate. The smaller you were the longer you survived buried alive. Extreme drowsiness was claiming her despite the toe wriggles... She wished Chuma was inside her in that moment, his deep want plateauing, his heart racing as he pressed life seed into her buzz. She felt the ring's pull on her finger, the whispering, loud, louder, *loudest*.

Suddenly, as if beckoned, the ring loosened its grip on her finger.

Somewhere in her haze she faced her past and her future in a frame that morphed into a jaw. Giant lips opened and let out a broken song, the chimes of "me wanna spoil you" distorting into the drone of an unstrung harp echoing out an ominous "ooohhhhmmm". The jaws faded out, and she saw a montage of her life on a foggy canvas. There she was with Chuma—what might have been: the greenish-gold in his eyes shimmering, gazing fondly at a big-eyed toddler with full lips, tight curls hugging at Pendo's knees. The bub vanished and she saw herself alone, then with Jamani. Now they were racing up an escalator alongside other students inside a modern village with state-of-art amenities. The vertical campus soared all the way up the four-seasoned Melbournian sky.

Here, in this new montage, she wore the somber blackness of ceremonial regalia—a flowing Oxford gown with a chili red and silver trim, and a scarlet-corded trencher flat on her head. She posed with a smile and a scroll for graduation photography in the plenary of a large convention center. Flash! Flash! The photographer posed her and skillfully captured her ambition, her success along the pathway of excellence that Jamani had always steered her towards. She looked around for her studious friend, but there was just a faceless throng surging backwards to a bleak shore, seagulls lying dead on the sand.

Darkness closed in. So dark...

Pendo gave herself to a deeper, deepest calm, as something slowly but surely shuffled towards her.

106

She Loves How He Glows

IT'S A NIGHT of black flies, soft-bodied and bioluminescent, dancing their lights in a hunt or a woo. They're not the dead, no mark of a djinn branded on their foreheads. These ones walk in plain daylight. Some of them are green-leafed, pregnant with a shimmering mold. The rest are glistening with morning dew, silhouettes of bodies, holes where hearts should be.

But they all have cerulean eyes. Where they appear, birds refuse to sing and fall from the sky. Fish float belly-up in the river. The undead stagger and prowl in leaves and dew, to and from the city of lights, to, fro, as village men and women worry their naps into nightmares—until the staggerers stop prowling. Instead, they dig and step into graves scattered with fermented yams and false beer made from bush beans, not the mopane berries.

Chief Ade put the tokens inside dig-outs. Now she calls out a name,
watches as the
unbranded burst into
flames, lit by—
what was it?
cerulean eyes.

Chief Ade wonders if Weightman has anything to do with this, since she refused his hand—sure, she's widowed eons now, but *him*? If he were an animal, Weightman would be a hyena. Cunning, greedy, a pack animal. She'd never know how to navigate life with such a man. He's an excitement machine who commands adulation. Many a village woman would leap at the chance—isn't he a ruler of the city of lights? See how it glows.

But it's a city that sends out mischief, instigated by aliens who visited, splashed it with luminescence. No-one saw the visitation. The exaggeration of the intruders' luster and tallness is a myth, greater or lesser reliant on who's telling it.

…twinkled like shooting stars—

...loftier than the oldest baobabs—

It's possible that Weightman *did* cut a deal with some foreign government. His city shimmers with lights no village has seen. If a pact were struck, what Weightman got out of it Chief Ade is yet to comprehend. As far as she knows he made a deal with the devil, one she's not inclined to follow suit for her village of Kitale.

Sometimes she feels abandoned. She wishes her daughters were here in the village. Tele, the nurse, is working at a university hospital in Tongi town. Celestina, the case worker, is with the UN in a refugee camp up north in Safura for villagers fleeing the undead.

Having accomplished her magic that rids the village from unwelcome intruders, Chief Ade is not searching for truth on her way home from the river.

But the flies are restless, fast forward, slow backward, splicing the forest here, there just so. She sees in them lost children, all strays. In fact, six of them drop to the ground and claim their human form. She's at ease, they're too young to be emissaries. They are wet to their heads with the water's mud. They flee her approach, vanish behind a shrub, and then another.

Each journey begins with a step and what she feels as she treads after the children is not going or returning. It's simply enlightenment. Hers is a promise to the gods of the trees, the goddesses of the rivers, that each child will be okay at dawn, shushed from the angry buzz of glows in a hunt or a woo

that's not funny,

may be dangerous,

and never sacred.

The forest is bigger inside than it looks at the elbows where it starts. It pipes and whistles, blows its nose. It points to a space, a souvenir from the centuries, and in it is a yeti. Chief Ade blinks and the yeti is gone, just shapes and shapes of twilight that look down with scars, owl song and spent acorns.

Finally, the children step out from behind a whistling thorn tree. Quintuplets. They're spike-haired ragamuffins, nudging at each other—who'll approach first? She peers for the sixth. She can see the lovegrass on his head, the child not so well hidden. He finally peels from a bush. He's a pot-bellied toddler—well, he looks like one. She suspects he's five to ten. He has the river blindness and looks like a missing key.

He approaches as if with eyes. He gropes in the air, but knows exactly how and where to reach her. Her heart sugars with love for the cheeky imp, and the rest now taking turns to touch her hem.

She speaks softly to them, and then hums. Hers is a mother's voice reminiscing about egg yolks and chicks, nothing remaining but an omelet. She remembers

108

when she was a child how she looked everyone in the eye, so curious, like this one, the toddler, who can't look but can touch. She wants to turn away, slip away, but it's impossible in the glow of his interest that swallows her restraint. Never has longing been so bright,

> so tangible she can
> trace it with her finger
> to forever yours
> in response to
> cherry ripeness.

With her dead husband—he was a kind man she couldn't save with herbs and chants, her dear leopard, keen-minded, fearless and free—and without her daughters, free and grown to chase professions, her life has been lonely. She needs something, someone…

She looks at the boy. This child can help her make the transition. After all, he's picked her. She can unpick him any time.

The children topple in glee down the dusty road where the forest thins and gives in to a scatter of huts, some of burnt brick walls and corrugated iron roofs, others of mud and thatch. Closer to the village, the children slow and lag behind, all the way to her boma, what's left of home: an enclosure with her two cows, three goats, seven chickens, and now six children.

Already she can see hut doors opening, lanterns flickering. Curiosity lurching her way with sufficient intent. She leaves the news for the village gossips. Mish-mashed rumors, distorted, twisted inside out. They are stories about her widowhood, stories about her daughters—the first educated women to leave the village. Myths and legends on the source of her magic. They trusted her late husband because he was a man, one of them. Chief Ade? Not so much. They don't know how to contain her difference, living alone and sending girls to school. But the village welcomes her magic, is curious about it. They can't wait to get a fingernail into her life. Understandably, after all, she's their chief.

She feels waylaid, attacks on her widowhood from within, without. The morning will come with its rituals:

How are the cows? a villager will poke their head into the boma and ask.

The cows are well, she'll answer. *How are the goats?*

One is carrying a child, thank gods, the villager will say.

Tell us about your visitors, someone will finally venture.

She has no answer for them. *A gift from the forest—the goddess of the trees still giving.*

Ebo, they will accept her explanation. She's the chief.

Some visitors don't arrive for news carried in the hollow words of a greeting. They're scavengers, visiting daily, bringing along a calabash to carry leftovers home. For this very reason, Chief Ade has a potful of crushed pomegranate seeds. She sun-dries them, bakes them in hot ashes, finally pounds them. Mixed with water, they form a good paste that cooks into a meal, plenteous for leftovers. Sporadically she brings out mopane beer, but this is rare. Mostly, her special ferment might come out when a villager is bereaved or going through a difficulty—like the mother of 13 mouths whose husband was thinking to leave.

Days, then weeks pass with her new children. They chase after her to the river. She goes to find inner peace but also to inspect her borders. As the children splash about, Chief Ade harvests quiet, disquiet in forgotten speech swallowed in the halfway river that will never feel an animated stream's touch—just visits from the village gossips who talk about solitude, fear, curses and witchcraft, even though there's nothing to start a rumor about. Knowing magic is not a wrongdoing, and it protects the village from the undead ones with cerulean eyes.

At night when all lanterns are out and the hut is closed to the full moon, Chief Ade can still pick out the little one. He's lightly snoring on a kudu skin closest to the warming embers of the three hearthstones. She smiles. Wonders at how she didn't know she needed him until she saw him. Her language is now empty, no personality or experience. What's the message in its dialect, undancing in its gaps?

As with every mother, she has a favorite. He's the big-eyed toddler, not so much the quintuplets, not even Tele or Celestina. He's haired with weeping lovegrass—that's what his hair feels like. It attaches itself to everything, mostly her clothes of tempered bark. It's hair that falls, regrows. Full of fiber yet smooth. The child is the color of wet sand. His name is Gogodi, he finally says in a croak. Her heart overflows.

Today, he won't play with the rest, just clings to her skirts.

She steams yams and casavas in fresh banana leaves for her children. Stirs a pot of pigeon or groundnut sauce, serves it with pickle from the mopane berry. The gossips are still talking. She ignores them when she can. She's done this to great effect, the ignoring, but it's impossible to continue when something is picking off her brood.

It started with the quintuplets a fortnight ago. They grew pot-bellied, then seriously ill. The first one nearly died—Chief Ade had already put ash on her head—when he recovered. But the rest are vomiting and passing wet stool. She grinds ginger and cloves, mixes the concoction with honey, a crush of black baobab bark. She mutters a spell to the gods of the trees, the goddesses of the river, who bring fertility and health:

cold fog no frogs
pump and stretch
senews whole

a drop of sorghum
wine to sunned earth
ripple, ripple
perfectus agreenos

seventy heartbeats
of forgotten remembered
puff your throat

sacrifice appeasement
cold fog
no frogs
posticus tibialis.
And the children recover.

But the sickness has worsened the gossip. Villagers talk in such detail, embellished or not, and it's talk filled with fear. Some villagers boycott to sleep under their burnt brick houses, preferring mud huts under a thatched roof where 'a bad eye cannot reach'.

Complex patterns signify inarticulable longing only eyes can speak. Chief Ade never walks the past without switching off tomorrow's name. She practices speaking the nameless in front of a calabash's mirror—it's filled with magic water. But her tongue is knitted with a moment that is now. She touches Gogodi's forehead.

He's boiling. The child has refused to respond to her magic. This time she believes the ash on her head, as she did for her husband moments before he died. It's only a matter of time. She accepts the morning with its rituals, even though villagers greet from afar, mistrusting the boy she's carrying and the burnt brick.

How are the chickens? someone pokes their head through the gate.

Still laying, she answers. *How is your daughter-in-law's newborn?*

Finally suckling. But he still needs a fingertip and honey to get his mouth going.

Chief Ade has educated the women on the hazards of birthing at home, but they are still fearful of the hospital. She encourages them to go to the clinic for health advice on their toddlers. It falls on deaf ears.

Aya, what do you think our ancestors did without clinics?

Will you return the children to the forest? someone finally asks. They look fearfully at Gogodi cradled on the chief's back. *The gods are calling for that one.*

She has no answer at first, then surprises herself with an epiphany. *I'll visit my daughter, the nurse in Tongi.*

Ebo! they fall away.

The hospital will take your blood!

Even if you're not the one who is sick!

Chief Ade sends a runner to the UN camp in Safura. The young man returns as a passenger in a truck taking bags of sorghum to Tongi, to return from the city with antibiotics and bandages for Safura. The driver, an older man in a khaki suit, helps the chief into the cabin, doesn't insist on a seatbelt, but Chief Ade wears it.

In her arms Gogodi trembles in chills. First, they drop the quintuplets—boisterous in the semi-trailer—at the UN camp for Celestina to look after for a while. Celestina frowns, but accepts the children.

Now Chief Ade nods with the truck along the dusty road, until they reach tarmac when she finally sleeps.

She's a ghost, spilling from a calabash and into a cheek. She's a specter, brimming from the sun and into the wind. She's a year, lonely as a book savored by phantom eyes. She's a memory, hunting the fragrance of something lost, a pleasure forgotten. She's a seed, unimagined in a garden that whistles songs of plague.

she's a distance,

and it opens

to a wake.

I'm hungry, says Gogodi weakly from the white sheets of a hospital bed.

Chief Ade falls into Tele's arms and weeps—it's taken the boy a week to recover. It wasn't worms, or malaria, not even a virus. What they found in his stomach was a bright blob of light that irradiated the operating theater.

I am hungry too, says Chief Ade to her son when she can finally speak. *Let us get you something to eat.*

You can eat your stubbornness, Mama, Tele hisses at her when they're out of shot from the boy's ears.

112

Where is the stubbornness? asks Chief Ade.

Don't you think the boy is a spy from the city of lights?

If he were, then the sickness is a reminder that he's rejected his mission, as did the quintuplets, says Chief Ade.

Knowing this, would you have taken him in?

Yes, says Chief Ade. *Yes,* more firmly. Nurture, for Chief Ade, supersedes preservation. Always.

It's all lucid to the chief now. Weightman has been at it again. First the undead, now kiddie spies. He'll not stop any time soon, and she's not sure it's just about heart matters or something more toxic. Enchantment can mask as a tree—somewhere in the forest is an inhabited whistling thorn tree. She'll know it's inhabited because it's the only one that ants will refuse to climb. She'll destroy it, burn it with magic to its roots.

And, with the obliteration, the city of lights will lose its hold on her children. If Weightman keeps at it, she contemplates, she might consider the quiver tree. Send a message in a magicked arrow. To deter or execute? She's not sure yet.

But first she must take the truck on its return with supplies from the town, collect the others at the UN camp and take all her children home. She'll try but is not sure she'll convince the villagers to once more sleep in their burnt brick houses.

Gogodi is devouring a coconut and banana muffin, though he's never seen one in his life before. The blob of light is gone. Yet the boy shimmers. His eyes flutter, then open—awe in them at his first sight of her. He reaches for her cheek, his hand warm and sure. The river blindness was no more than the poison of a killing mission.

She hands him a vanilla milkshake whose tetra-pack carton has the face of a lost child or cat,

she looks

at her son…

from the

city of lights,

oh, she loves

how he glows.

Sleuthing for a Cause

IT'S A RED-HOT August with a slight breeze. Ja the village raven loves to watch, and today she's perched on the branch of a coconut tree overlooking the witchdoctor's boma. It comprises a burnt-brick hut, thatch-roofed, a rageful-looking billy-goat that's likely a gift, a bunch of free-range chickens pecking unperturbed on and around the bare toes of villagers, and a pile of donations by the witchdoctor's door: calabashes swollen with yams, sweet potatoes or millet brew; a spear tipped with special stone from a volcanic mountain; a fishing net that looks well-used and a little random with the rest of the pile; a sack of donkey-eared mangoes; cowrie-shell trinkets; sisal skirts resembling the one the witchdoctor is wearing, his long, hairy legs sticking out…but they're well-shaped legs, appreciates Ja.

Today, like any other day, she's more attentive to the food and drink. She likes eggshells, groundnuts, husked rice, weeping pineapples, fresh locusts, rain termites, all meats—even birdy ones—and coconut flesh. You'd think she'd have reachable coconuts easy to pluck, but (1) ravens don't pluck coconuts and (2) have you tried cracking that shell with a beak?

The villagers are lined up and waiting to see Knuckles, the witchdoctor. He's summoned his apprentice, Sita, to keep the village folk orderly in a snake queue that stretches beyond Ja's coconut tree and towards a drying-up creek.

For Ja, it's not a good fortnight. Some days are a grind, nothing pretty—this is one of those. She's been feeling especially lonely, a bit morose, sometimes with flitting memories of that Casanova Sexton, who abandoned her to fly across the oceans to a place called Wagga Wagga or Woop Woop, leaving Ja 'with egg', so to speak. As if Ja cares. Well, she does. Any raven with a mind and some compassion knows that a raven sticks around to feed his mate a whole 21 days and then some as she sits on her egg(s). So what if Ja had a clutch of one egg, not the typical five or six for a raven?

She looks with longing at the boma where she would have been a familiar had Sexton not pushed aside her tail feathers and found her cloaca. She didn't know at the time that the witchdoctor only takes virgins as familiars—ah heck, she does now. This, fumes Ja, is a bit sexist in an age of #metoo. No-one is stopping Sexton from pursuing his dreams because he's shagged! Still…Ja looks with pride at her fledgling, Chi, happily perched on the shoulder of the tight-haired orphan girl. Something good came out of the unfortunate saga with a *Sexton*, an equally unfortunate name, unlike Ja, Ze, Bo or Chi. How was one supposed to caw *Sexton*? She should have known everything about him was just wrong.

Her fledgling Chi has settled only too well into her new role as a witchdoctor's familiar. Well, a witchdoctor's apprentice's familiar, to be exact.

Kraa! Kraa! Warble! Warble. Chi is now helping the girl Sita to arrange the villagers into a perfect "s".

"No shenanigans," barks Knuckles, and glares at the queue with his good blue eye. The other eye is charcoal black and it's never clear if it can focus on a person or a raven.

The witchdoctor plucks the villager topmost of the queue. "What's wrong with you?"

"My stomach," says the boy whose name is Baridi.

Knuckles looks at the boy's protruding belly. "Did you bring a little sumthn, sumthn?" The boy's mother falls forward with a gourd. Knuckles sniffs at the neck for whatever is inside, and appears pleased—if one is to judge by the twinkle in his blue eye. He hands the gourd to Sita, who arranges it next to the piling donations.

"Now," says the witchdoctor to the boy. "Tell me what happened."

"I started feeling bloated, then constipated like a pregnant woman," says Baridi.

"Yes," volunteers the boy's mother. "His mouth moves as if he's chewing something, but there's nothing inside. And the belching! It smells like a dead impundulu—the lightning bird, gods help us." She holds her nose as if the memory of the stink brings it back. "It never stops. Even though he's not hungry."

"I see," says Knuckles. He looks carefully at the boy. "Does your family have enemies?"

Ja perks up at this.

"I don't think so," says the mother in puzzlement. Then she brightens. "Two days ago, Baridi had a fight with Kilimo over a fishing net that got lost. It's just about when the stomach started puffing up."

"Mmhh," says the witchdoctor thoughtfully. "But this Kilimo is not a witchdoctor. He couldn't have cast the spell."

115

"No," agrees the woman.

Knuckles scratches his misshapen head that must have seen too many knuckles when he was a boy. "Then this is what you must do. Take the broom with which you sweep indoors."

"Any broom?" asks the mother.

"It must be made of lovegrass—dense and tufted. Make a good beard of it and be sure it's dry."

"And then what?"

"Patience, woman!" Knuckles glares with the good eye. "Take the broom and sweep Baridi's stomach, then breathe on the broom."

"It will fix the stomach?" asks Baridi.

"How do I know unless you try it?" barks the witchdoctor and knuckles the boy away. "Next!"

Ja settles back on her branch for an entertaining display, because the witchdoctor is certainly an excitement vessel. If only she were his familiar…

"Uwiii!" cries a young woman, stepping forward. "Someone is strangling me."

"It's happening right now?" asks the witchdoctor.

"It happens at night only."

The witchdoctor knuckles her on the ear. "Get back in the queue and await your turn. Next."

An elderly man shuffles forward. "It's my wife, Mama Lawo."

"This Lawo is your first born?" asks the witchdoctor.

"He's the third one."

"What happened to the first and the second?"

"Mamba and Sengi?"

"Why is your wife Mama Lawo, and not Mama Mamba or Sengi?"

"But…but… Mamba and Sengi are girls!" cries the man in astonishment.

Ja scoffs her disdain, while the tall witchdoctor knuckles the man on his balding head. "You're the one who's making the poor woman sick with such idiocy. Is something wrong with girls?"

"No, the gods forgive me," says the man. "I had nothing to do with Mama… my wife's sickness. She shakes with chills and her legs are on fire. Her head is banging like the *ndombolo* drum at a wedding. I'll call her Mama Mamba, even Mama Imani after our youngest daughter if that will make her better! I don't want her to be sick."

"You sure about that?" the witchdoctor glares sternly. "I didn't see her queue up to get vaccinated when I was administering covid shots."

"We were right here at the boma, and you jabbed us, may the gods hear us. Don't you remember?"

116

The witchdoctor contemplates for a moment. "Ah. Yes." He looks at the man. "Tell me this."

"Anything," says the man.

"This mama of your children—girls and boys—is her stool runny?"

"How do I know? I don't follow her to the latrine."

"Is she holding down her food when she eats?"

"She's been throwing up since yesterday."

"Sit on the ground."

"*Me?*" protests the man. "But why?"

"When a witchdoctor says sit, you sit."

The man sits, knees up. Knuckles dances around him with a chant, occasionally letting out a fart and sweeping its smell with his sisal skirt towards the man's face.

"Now I want you to take the shiny seeds of a pomegranate fruit," says Knuckles when he stops prancing. "Dry them in the sun and crush them. Then make a paste with this potion—" he offers a small jar of green liquid. "Mama of your children must drink the mixture the last thing before she goes to sleep, and the first thing when she wakes. And don't forget my sumthn, sumthn—leave it with the girl." He pushes the man away. "Next!"

A woman steps forward carrying a toddler. "My child is late to walk," she says.

"How old is he?" asks the witchdoctor.

"Three, maybe four. How would I know? Take this durian wine. It's all I've got."

"It is enough—it better be good. Tonight, when you go to sleep make sure you wear old underwear. Take it off in the morning and rub the soiled part on your child's legs."

"Ebo! And it will work?"

"You're welcome to return for your durian wine if the boy doesn't walk. Next!"

A new woman steps forward. He looks at her. "You again?"

"My turn has come."

"Tell me about the night strangling," says Knuckles.

"It happens in my dreams. A man, sometimes a hyena, is strangling me, and it morphs into a black dog. When I wake up in the morning—look." She shows the witchdoctor marks around her neck. "And I have pains around my throat."

"Sita!" barks the witchdoctor. "I said no shenanigans."

"I wasn't doing anything."

"Precisely." He glares, mostly with his blue eye. "Bring the calabash from under my bed."

Sita scrambles into the hut with Chi nuzzled against her shoulder. She emerges with a calabash.

"Now sit," demands the witchdoctor.

The apprentice sits on the ground.

"Not *you*, you." He points a gnarled finger at the young woman.

She sits on the red-dust ground. There's fear in her eyes.

"I want you to be still," says the witchdoctor, and bangs her head with the calabash.

"Uwiii!" cries the young woman, and leaps to her feet. "What have I done to deserve a beating?"

"It's not a beating, you fool, just part of the cure," barks Knuckles. "Now sit, quickly, or get out of my boma."

"No. No, I'm sitting. Look."

Bang! echoes the calabash on the woman's head, as the witchdoctor dances around in a chant. Bang! As everyone falls away from the proceedings, Sita the orphan girl snatches the occasion. She's good with a coconut-beard ball, hand-made. She aims it at the coconut tree, a beautiful shape in her kick. The beard ball snares between a bunch of leaves near Ja, who garbles her disdain.

The animosity between them might have something to do with Chi. Whatever ambivalence there might have been spiraled downwards, pretty much, when the girl frogged it up the coconut tree, reached out, and the barely feathered Chi hopped out of Ja's nest and into the outstretched hand.

Finally, the witchdoctor stops prancing, both he and the poor woman spent.

"Somebody has put an evil hand on you," says Knuckles. He looks very perturbed. "There's no other witchdoctor but me in the village. Who do you think put the curse?"

The woman shakes her head miserably. Then she brightens up. "There's this man, Mfume, who wants to marry me. I said no. He might have something to do with it?"

"Mmhh…still, he'd need a witchdoctor to administer a spell. But who?"

"I don't know."

"Go home and drink virgin ash made from the branch of a mopane tree. Before you go to sleep at night, smear two-day honey around your throat and nothing will touch you."

That night, when the villagers are gone and the donations tucked away inside the hut, Ja watches the witchdoctor pace around his boma. He scratches his head.

"It can't be," he's mumbling to himself. "No. No. But how?"

Nobody answers, as Sita is doing long rangers with the coconut-beard ball, and Chi is bouncing gleefully and garbling on her shoulder.

Ja wishes she could help Knuckles right this moment. She turns over scenarios in her head but is honestly at as much of a loss as the witchdoctor.

Sita kicks a ripper that topples Ja right off the tree.

Kraa, kraa, warble, warble, rasps Chi from the girl's shoulder. Ja dusts herself, unsure if her fledgling is thrilled or dismayed at what just happened.

The next day is even more perplexing for Ja and the witchdoctor. Relatives carry a young girl into the boma. Ja is curious but watching with a cautious eye, as Sita's practice with the ball is with startling accuracy in Ja's direction.

"She has the falling sickness," the girl's aunt cries.

"Explain this sickness to me," says Knuckles.

"Out of nowhere, something on her body goes weak: her face, an arm, a leg… She wasn't born like this, gods help us. We don't know what's happening."

"Mmhh," says the witchdoctor, hand on chin. "Does she have trouble speaking?"

"But, of course. When her tongue goes weak and falls out of her mouth with drool, we don't understand what she's saying."

"And her seeing?"

"One eye sometimes goes lazy."

"Mmhh. Does she get a headache?"

"Yes! She keeps screaming about funeral drums banging in her head."

"Sita!" he glares. "I said no shenanigans."

"I was just—" Sita puts her coconut-beard ball away.

"Exactly. Bring the calabash."

The witchdoctor undertakes the exorcising calabash ritual, banging at the afflicted girl's head while chanting. Finally, he stops. "Someone has sent you a djinn."

"But why?" cries the girl's aunt.

"You tell me. Have you swindled anyone?"

"No!"

"Then think! What happened for someone to wish you harm?"

The relatives scratch their heads. Then one brightens. "She quarreled with Tabia about a broken pot at the river."

"But Tabia is not a witchdoctor."

"No."

"Mmhh. Then this is what you must do. Take her back home and slaughter a pure-black *kienyeji*—a chook that is *au naturel*."

"A naked chicken?"

"Not naked, *untainted*. Make sure it hasn't eaten anything foreign from outside the village. It must be a hen or a rooster that's spotless and has pecked only inside your boma."

"Will a pure-white do?"

"Only a black one. I can sell you that one." The witchdoctor points at one of his chooks.

"For how much?!"

"Don't question-mark, exclamation-mark me, woman," says the witchdoctor to the aunt. "It is what it is, cost me a bit. Where do you think I studied witchdoctoring?"

"I don't know!"

"Harvard!"

The next day brings along typical maladies. One woman has cut her toe with a hoe and is bleeding. She's also experiencing panic attacks.

"Pound the bark of a dark baobab tree and apply it as a paste to the toe, then wrap it with these enchanted banana leaves," says the witchdoctor.

But a couple of matters are anomalous.

"I lend people my hoe, my ox, my wife! Then I forget who borrowed them, and they don't reveal themselves. I've lost everything!" cries the young man.

"Mmhh," says Knuckles, fingers on his chin. "You have the lender's bewitchment. Your borrower is wearing a forgetting amulet. Rub stone salt on anything of value that belongs to you, and make sure you wash yourself in stone-salted water before you lend anything to anyone."

Another man, clearly distressed, is arguing with his friends. Silence as his turn arrives. "I was riding a bicycle when this woman suddenly crossed the dusty path," he tells the witchdoctor. "I swerved to avoid hitting her—she came out of nowhere and simply vanished."

"It's just bad riding," reasons a friend. "There was no-one there."

"Yes, what woman?" says another. "We saw nothing."

"Mmhh," says Knuckles. "The truth is you have been bewitched. The accident never happened. Sita! Oh, thank you," astonished, as the girl hands over the beating calabash.

Up on her tree, Ja chuckles about this bizarre incident and the witchdoctor's prancing. She's still in jollity when she witnesses one more curious case.

"I don't understand what's happening at my market stall," says a man.

"Why do you say that?" asks Knuckles.

"I have good business the whole day. People are buying the dried tilapia, sweet potatoes, donkey-ear mangoes. Truth is, I sell everything! But, at the end of the day, I look at my money tin and it's empty."

"Mmhh," says Knuckles.

Sita quietly hands over the exorcising calabash.

Finally, after the stomping and dancing, chanting and banging on the poor man's head is finished, the witchdoctor says, "Put three pinches of river reed salt on top of a piece of baby-licked charcoal inside the money tin. It will stop the witchery and you'll start seeing your money."

That night once again, Ja watches the witchdoctor's perplexment as he prowls back and forth around his boma. She'd really like to help him. He even waves at her in his state of mental disarray, doesn't mind when she dives down, cocks her head and studies him, beady eyed. He's so perturbed, he hurls a piece of cassava at Ja. She gratefully gobbles the lot and hopes he might share some of that goat stewing in a pot on a three-hearth stone fire, but he doesn't. Ja and billy-goat—a safe distance away—watch the witchdoctor chew and swallow mouthful after mouthful.

She waits him out with the patience of a raven that's sat hungry on an egg for 21 days before it hatched, and then whistles. It takes three more whistles and many garbles for the orphan girl Sita to poke her head belligerently out of the hut.

Kraa, kraa, warble, warble, gurgles Chi sleepily from the girl's shoulder.

"I have a plan," Ja tells them. "Put that coconut-beard ball away, or I won't tell you my plan."

Sita looks dubiously at Ja. "You want us to shadow Kilimo, Mfume and Tabia?"

"Why not? If they're using another witchdoctor to put spells on fellow villagers, don't you want to find out who it is?"

Kraa, kraa, warble, warble, says Chi, and looks eagerly at the orphan girl.

"Why would I care?" asks Sita.

"You don't sound very convinced but I think you like the old fart," says Ja. "Who took you in when you were orphaned?"

"The witchdoctor. But he barks at me and says no shenanigans all the time."

"Words are not stones—has he ever harmed you?"

Sita hangs her head. "I can't say that."

"And who vaccinated the entire village *for free*, without asking for sumthin sumthin?"

"Maybe you have a point. But isn't the bad witchdoctor giving the good witchdoctor good and bad business?"

"I wasn't planning on you being clever, silly girl. Do you want an adventure or not?"

"I don't know."

"Like hang out with me at a roost? I've noticed you don't have friends."

"There's Chi."

"You don't have *many* friends."

The first three nights of stalking are uneventful. The trio sits out the witchdoctor until he snores, sometimes mumbling, "No shenanigans," in his sleep.

They hide outside Mfume's hut, but not much happens other than men and women visitors coming and going. It appears that Mfume, with his handsome pockmarked face, is quite the Casanova—like one raven Ja knows. Tabia the girl who fought over a pot at the creek lives with very strict parents who will not let her set foot outside the hut at dusk. And Kilimo doesn't seem to take vengeance too deeply to heart, as he doesn't appear too keen to take further matters into his hands over the lost fishing net.

On their way back from sleuthing, Ja, Sita and Chi pass the creek that's drying up. Sita is juggling the coconut-beard ball with her foot, an excellent hopper. Ja can't help but agree how good the girl is with a ball. Things are a little awkward, because Ja and Sita don't really like each other, and neither of them knows what to answer when, out of the blue, Chi grates, rasps or croaks: *Kraa, kraa, warble, warble.*

Suddenly, Ja sees a figure by the creek wearing a shaman's cape.

"Kraa-kraa," she cries, and flies at the shaman.

She lunges with her beak, yelling and screaming and beating her wings. The shaman lunges back at her with a beak, yelling, screaming and beating his wings.

"Kraa-kraa!" he cries. "Stop it, Ja!"

She falls back in astonishment. "Sexton?"

Her rage is real as she dives at him again with her beak. "You scoundrel of a scum bug putrid piss-shit raven dickhead!"

"Kraa-kraa!" he cries, feathers askew. "Don't kill me! I know you loved me once!"

Finally, Ja and Sexton lie spent on the ground.

"I thought you vamoosed to Wagga Wagga," she admonishes him.

"I flew over the Indian Ocean, south-east and all the way to Australia, but border control insisted that I must do 14 days of hotel quarantine if I wanted to stay. I didn't trust their shuttles or hotel ventilators, so I went otherwhen to a place called Woop Woop, not quite inside Oz."

"Where did you learn to do magic?"

"I found a shaman, learnt me a few tricks."

"Sexton, I can't believe you! A witchdoctor has many roles, and it's mostly to do good things. Not...not..."

122

"I thought about being a celebrant," he explains. "But, to be honest, I'd run away with the bride—don't you think?" She slaps his face with a wing. "Stop beating me, let me explain! Performing funeral rites is out of question as I'm a bit squeamish about dead things—" she looks at him with incredulity— "if I'm not eating them. Now about interceding with the dead, do I really want to do that? Kraaa. No."

"What about mediating feuds, healing, protecting, educating, advising— that's what a village witchdoctor does."

"I'm persuasive in other ways." He gives her a knowing look.

It sets off Ja's rage, and she flaps her wings at his face. "Of all things, you chose black magic!"

"There's hurt everywhere!" he cries. "I was doing good."

"*How?*"

"In my own way!"

"Then you must undo it."

"I can't! Once it's done, it's done." He slips away and flees towards night.

Ja shouts at Sita. "Get the ball, go."

Sita leans back, steady drive in her left foot. Her hitter slams Sexton dead set, and he plummets to the ground.

"No shenanigans!" barks the witchdoctor, but his blue eye is twinkling. "Good sleuthing, you three."

"It was mostly Ja," says Sita, daring to look Knuckles in the eye.

"Was it now?"

"It was Sita who brought him down with her coconut ball," says Ja.

"Organized termites make an anthill," says the witchdoctor. "Do you know that?" *Kraa, kraa, warble, warble*, gurgles Chi.

"But we have much work to do," says Knuckles. "Look at this queue." He glances at the villagers. "Your fool ex of a raven has done enough mischief, starting with this poor woman."

The woman is jabbering and hitting out at the relatives trying to hold her down. "She stole Ndebe's rooster and ate it," pants someone as the woman flails about. "We believe she has a curse."

Knuckles looks at Sexton, bound at the feet by the hut's door.

"One of your tricks?"

Sexton nods.

"Can you undo it?"

Sexton shrugs.

Sita quietly hands over the calabash.

After the witchdoctor is done prancing and chanting around the cursed woman, whacking her now and then with the calabash, he tells her people: "Crush feverfew leaves, lemon, ginger, garlic and rooibos, goat's milk, a pinch of yellow curry and seven droplets of a newborn's urine."

"How can we remember *all that*?"

"Remember that it will fix the curse. I'm sure you won't forget. Next!"

A father carrying a boy with swollen legs shuffles forward. "Pain shoots up his leg each time he tries to walk," he explains.

"I swear I'll never steal again," cries the boy. "It was Job's farm, I stole sweet potatoes. He must have put a spell!"

Knuckles looks at Sexton, 'Your work?'

Sexton nods.

"Can you take away the spell?"

Sexton shakes his head glumly.

"The only cure for your boy is for farmer Job to decide on his punishment," says the witchdoctor. "Once the boy accepts his punishment, the swelling will go away."

It takes a while to locate farmer Job, who has been hiding for fear of the witchdoctor's reprisal. He's astonished when he hears the witchdoctor's proposition.

"You want me to decide on a punishment?"

"For the boy, yes. And then I'll figure out what to do with you for consulting black magic."

The farmer looks fearful. "Please, *you* decide the boy's punishment that will take away the curse," he begs the witchdoctor.

"The boy has suffered enough," pleads the father. "I'll take the punishment."

"Very well." Knuckles studies the boy's father. "I want you," he pokes him on the chest, "to bring the skin—"

"Of an albino?"

"What?" Slap! "No!"

"What then?" cries the man, clasping his flaming cheek.

"Bring me the freshly-shaved skin off your mother-in-law's heel after she has walked barefoot for seven days."

"She loves her sandals. The woman sleeps with them. They're from the city! Her daughter, who was married there…how will I make her walk barefoot?"

"Did your boy think of that when he went thieving?"

"But…but…how will I shave the old woman's skin?"

"Try when she's sleeping."

124

"But.. but…what will happen when she wakes?"

The witchdoctor gazes at him for a long time. "You'll find out, won't you?"

"Now what do we do with this one?" Knuckles looks at the bound Sexton on the dusty ground by the hut.

"The calabash?" suggests Sita.

"He won't survive it," says Knuckles, for once forgetting to bark about shenanigans.

"Then how do you take away his black magic?" asks Ja.

"I'm your baby daddy! How about a second chance?"

Kraa, kraa, warble, warble, screams Chi from Sita's shoulder.

"Your second chance does not come with black magic," says Knuckles. He glances at Ja. "We must cover him neck-up overnight in that billy-goat's pat. But I need one more thing for my chant to work." His blue eye twinkles. "Raven pee."

"On him?" asks Ja.

"Beak to toe."

Ja hops forward. It's the closest she'll ever get to becoming the witchdoctor's familiar. If she has to do this over again, she won't change a thing.

She moves her tail feathers. "With pleasure."

The Water's Memory

THE RED LEOPARD showed on the night of your wedding, when the sun, earth and moon were imperfectly aligned. You moved from the women's mirth, belly-deep and wholesome, undrowned by the sound of village drums. *Pom! Pom! Pom pi pom pi!*

Our son has found a maiden! began a chorus.

A nymphette from the lake.

The begetter of our offspring!

Pom! Pi! Po pom pi! Drums vibrated in a booming cantata as bare torsos gyrated, gleamed with animal fat.

Pure from the water nymph, sang the villagers.

Such wonder she shines.

A swish of skirts here, a sway of neck there. And the feet! Caked with dust, toes tapped their dance in sync to the drums. A spray of soil from the ground formed a cloud that lifted to the horizon where a yellow moon crossed the earth's shadow.

Fresh like the smell of rain!

Pure like a newborn,

Younger than morning dew.

Your arms glimmered with cowry shell trinkets—red, green and yellow. Dancers pranced to fever pitch, swayed heads hugged tight with feathers. You admired your cousin Achieng, a young, free spirit with the biggest sway, her neck of an ostrich, her eyes of a gazelle.

You sat under a stringy bark tree with the rest of the young women, all virgins gleaming with animal fat rubbed on their skins. You sat next to the children. A handful of babies first perked to *pom! pi! pom!* then surrendered to sleep. Mosquitos, mellowed with drunken blood, swooned to the ground and trembled their feet. Fireflies flickered orange wings and played with a faint-hearted wind.

You stretched your legs, away from the fire. Lowered yourself into a bush near the forest. A tiny pool formed at your feet as your droplets fell. Aroused by wetness, a green snake slithered close to your big toe.

'Spirit of my fathers, bearer of good charm,' you whispered to him.

He slithered into tussocks of grass.

The bush rustled. Crouching still, you parted the leaves and peered at the night. Amber eyes peered back at you from the shrub. A leopard hissed, snarled and leapt over you. You plunged to the ground and considered for a long time his long, athletic body marked with scarlet rosettes. And you knew at once that you would bear a firstborn daughter, who would die first, and then you.

Everything had been put together—from the payment of a dowry of two bulls, three cows, one heifer and five roosters to the day, time and locale of your marriage—way before you saw the man to whom you were betrothed.

No wedding invitations were sent—they did not need sending. Sending invitations was stupid and a waste of time. Word of mouth carried faster and steadier than today's pieces of paper slipped in envelopes and containing a person's name. In the village, you would have to write everybody's name. Anybody not lifeless or unwell came to a wedding. Or a funeral. The whole village helped. Men brought the fish and meat. Women cooked it. They sizzled enough chicken, crisped enough pigs, tenderized enough cows, and trussed up enough spiced *pilau* rice, *mumi* fish, Nile perch and tilapia to carry a feast. People came and ate and borrowed pots to take leftovers home.

That day of your wedding, Isingoma—the man to whom you were promised— stood tall and fine-looking, his smiling lips the color of rich berry fruit. A streak of something thrilling cloaked him, even as he drank *toggo*, pure banana beer, with the rest of the men. They sat with stretched out legs on hyacinth mats under a mango tree. A calabash of brew travelled from one man to another.

Something about the sweep of Isingoma's eyes, each time they took the direction of the stringy bark under which you sat, stirred your interest. You tried to keep your head lowered but felt inclined every now and then to lift it and wonder about your new husband.

You never felt that finger of doubt, that claw in the gut that gripped most fresh brides. Even when Isingoma took your fist—a fist because you were impatient but unprepared for his reach, finding no time to unfold your fingers into something yielding and clasping his—you never felt trapped.

You remember the old women's laughter, sharp as whistles, and your own mother's closed face. You remember the stray dog scrounging for scraps in the courtyard, his tail wag, wagging, wagging as Isingoma led you into a newly-built hut.

You quivered at his approach, fearful of how he might initiate you into the real world of marriage. He took you masterfully, firmly. He was skilled and clinical like the fisherman he was. You submitted, because that was how you were raised: to submit. But he was also kind and affectionate in the way he brought down your shield of innocence. His touch dismissed everything you'd heard or witnessed about the formidability of men, males like your father whose approach struck only fear. What Isingoma made you feel... was not fear.

Afterwards, in soft, smoky silence that left no words behind, soft because the moon's shine was wan, and smoky because your husband had rolled up a tobacco stick and was drawing on it, Isingoma continued to caress you with his eyes. You felt fragile and whole, and just then, only then—not sooner—did you dare touch him. You reached and lightly touched that strong jaw, those smiling lips the color of rich berries.

'Adaeze,' you said.

'It means princess,' he said.

'That's what we'll name our daughter,' you said.

Outside, the women's laughter was no longer sharp or panicked. Snug in your husband's arms, you didn't mind the mosquitoes biting the inside of your leg. You wondered if your curiosity about Isingoma would ever end, if you should tell him about the red leopard.

You were still wondering when he left just before dawn to cast his fishing net into the mist of the lake.

You stare at the lake—tame, green with pollution. She's sick like you became. She no longer boasts vast diversity of fish, not since the water hyacinth invaded. The free-floating menace brought devastation on trade by blocking ports. It harbored crocodiles, snakes, mosquitoes and bilharzia-carrying snails. Still, locals found use for the weed and harvested it for paper, rope, baskets, biogas, fodder and mulch. Finally, the weed died or was eradicated to something sustainable. But the lake never recovered her grace.

You remember the days of the water's beauty, centuries of history, as the lake wove her magic through the lands. She charted her course across colonies of disparate people, wooing the Bantu whose men (and sometimes women) were circumcised; the Nilotes whose gracile bodies carried tribal scarring; the Cushites, few in number, whose fairer skin and nylon hair set them apart. But people forgot their disparity to share in the offerings of the freshwater lake: her Nile perch, tilapia, pied kingfisher and silver cyprinid, fondly known and eaten as *omena*, *mukene* or *daggaa*. The lake batted her lashes, ran her feet across settlements, enamored local communities, heartened trade.

But now, the lake is unwell. Business languishes. The village's seasons follow the water's temperament, her castings of humidity and ominous thunderheads to signal change. You remember those days, the olden days of prosperity when the once invincible African beauty was not the sick giant she now is.

Adaeze. Princess. She was a different kind of girl. The fastest in the village, the prettiest. She had the neck of a gazelle, the lashes of a giraffe. Adaeze could run miles, balancing a pot full of water from the lake without holding it. Not only was she the prettiest girl in the village but the brightest. Brighter than her brothers. By the time she could walk, she could charm the meat of a chicken or a goat, even tongues or gizzards, from her brothers' mouths. Her brothers never caught up with Adaeze. Even Isingoma ate from her hands.

Adaeze was a pioneer. Unable to stay indifferent, she contradicted the world of riddles and the mastery of men. She was the first woman in your family to see education. You were brought up to respect everything tradition and girls didn't go to school those days. Thankfully nowadays it was different. Then, girls learnt how to make good wives.

But, like the foreignness that came to the lake, suffocating the Nile perch, tilapia, kingfisher and *daggaa*, Christianity came to native lands. It suffocated the gods of the thorn tree and the mountain. Christians at the mission house baptized your mother and the other children's mothers, before turning to the children and their would-be spouses because, like the water weed, missionaries travelled. From when Adaeze was little, you watched the German Sister from a distance, as she taught village boys to read and write under the big mango tree. But little Adaeze didn't just watch. She sat at Sister's feet. No punishing could take her away from Sister's feet, or the learning. Finally, Sister saw and understood the stars trapped inside Adaeze and talked Isingoma into sending the child to a real school in Murutunguru.

Adaeze ran miles barefoot to and from a primary school daily and later became the first woman from the village to become a teacher. But despite being a *msomi*, educated, Adaeze stayed close to culture and men fell over themselves for her hand in marriage.

But she had her eye on Aloyse, the late Atanasi's son.

Atanasi Musiba, a friend of Isingoma's, came all the way from across the lake to beg Adaeze's hand for one of his six sons. To everyone's surprise, Isingoma let Adaeze choose. Nobody let you choose; a wedding was arranged, a man was brought and you married him. But Adaeze got to see her groom. She put a finger on his face in the picture Atanasi brought along and picked him, way before her wedding.

Aloyse had an honest face and eyes that looked at you direct. A thing about him encouraged you to trust him. He was also a *msomi,* educated like Adaeze. Together, they would see many places, travel wider than the village. You understood that the school in Murutunguru had done its work. Adaeze wanted to see the world.

She was a bridge between times, the coming of two worlds. Her eyes sought bigger, better. She hunted new places, travelled further than the village, explored. You thought of the red leopard and was happy that the green snake—spirit of your forefathers—had warded off the curse in the leopard's eye.

The wedding of Adaeze and Aloyse was talk of the village for days, before and afterwards. As the ceremony drew closer, hour after hour, anticipation climbed. Suddenly, that dawn, song erupted. The moment everyone was waiting for had arrived.

Dancers swished sisal skirts here, beaded shoulders there. Their toes tapped on the earth in sync to the *Ndobolo* drum. The dancers' heels made loops in the air, spraying soil each thump of the ground.

But although Adaeze's arms shone with copper and gold trinkets, she was not coated with animal fat, or wearing a sisal skirt. Her ivory gown was a gift from the mission. She looked like a queen in it. Aloyse, he wore a black suit and a tie. No villager had ever seen anything more culturally distant than that.

Unsure how to navigate their feet inside floral dresses longer than the 'Sunday bests' they wore once a week to and from church, little girls tottered along with bracelets of purple and white Jacaranda blossoms.

Aloyse had shipped in crates and crates of a strange brew called *Safari*. It came in brown bottles, not a calabash. That beer was not made for sharing: every person drank from their own bottle. People still drank it, even though it tasted like cow urine—given as medicine in finger-tip drops to babies who had the type of belly wind that pushed out bad stool and a squeal.

Villagers cheered when it was time to cut the big white cake decorated with flowers, a thing of awe that the Sisters from Murutunguru had baked. After the feasting and dancing, people watched in amusement as Aloyse carried Adaeze over his shoulder. He put her in a car, his car. When he took Adaeze away, amusement turned to fear for the children, as Aloyse's blue car bellowed like the crocodile that nearly took a child but didn't, because villagers cornered it and beat it with sticks. The crocodile's sound saved the child because the beast opened its mouth to bellow.

Adaeze ate dinner one night, took to bed and didn't wake up.

How does a woman, strong and healthy as a cow with milk, close her eyes and die? Before it happened, there was no terrible blackness in your heart. No thunder that roared like lions. A messenger from the boat brought news at dawn.

130

Eugen Bacon

Coldness ran through you when you heard. You fell to your knees and howled. One single howl that lasted a small time. You sat on the ground, face covered in ash, mourners surrounding you. Their wails carried for miles and miles, and people kept coming. The sun rose high and heat jumped. Oblivious to it, women and children tore their clothes, pulled their hair, and collapsed to the ground shuddering and rolling in dirt. The men sat silent.

Grave like the men, you did not cry. You felt ...drained. Adaeze was gone. Loss pain is meant to be a short, stabbing thing in the chest that brings out a wail. But this pain was too big for crying. A parent shouldn't have to bury a child. Your mourning did not finish; it kept coming back, like a memory. A bottomless knowing, long and winded, telling you that something was missing.

After they buried Adaeze, there was feasting and dancing like that of a wedding. Everyone danced, every movement symbolic. Men turned as one to face the setting sun. Powerful feet descended on the ground, again and again. Women did half a turn, rolling their shoulders to a drumbeat gone wild. Together, they celebrated death as they would life.

It was close to a century since you were born when you died.

The years had not been giving. Age and disease took their toll. As did the lake, you felt tired all the time. Your life ebbing, disintegrating.

Before you died, you were helpless to see. Unable to look into people's eyes, or at their hands, to find their true intentions. You understood a person from their voice and the inflection it carried. You listened to the music of words, more than their meaning, the harmony of sound, more than its source.

But you had seen much and Isingoma was a good husband. You had lived enough years together to understand each other's silences. Towards your death, you wondered if his face was wearing a strong smile or one as limp as his tread, and just as lost. You knew he needed you and worried how he would be if, if... You wondered if there was still strength in his eyes. Same honey eyes that melted you the first time you met him.

It's dusk. The sun, earth and moon are imperfectly aligned.

You stand holding hands with Adaeze. Together, you gaze at the lake—her pulse still beating. The moon will pass through the earth's shadow again.

'It doesn't matter about the red leopard anymore,' says Adaeze softly.

'No,' you say.

Aquarii

FROM when Godé was a baby, he shared language with an orange and white tornado full of lightning. He lay in his cot tucked inside a soft body suit and a leaping-fish quilt, and stared alone—away from Mother and his stepfather—at the display happening in the room of his otherwise unremarkable short life.

As his mother said amens in liturgical hours inside her chapel—leaving him on his own in a cot—blue and white waves licked out of the cloud and reached him in a spark that beeped, then zinged with thunder in a dialect he strangely understood.

The language said, "Come out ta the bloody middle," over and over.

So he crawled into the tornado.

He found himself in a water giant humping and spitting in a belching ride. He clung to its belly, rocking and oscillating, before jaws swung open and belched him out on a white beach with no sandcastles or ice creams, just rocker waves that gobbled the shore and truncated the world he knew to this water-world he didn't.

There was a forest, and glow-eyed birds wrapped on branches inside the darkness. A woman named Aquarii combed out of the jungle, sashayed from it, wisping in fog that icicled when he stretched an arm to touch it.

He crawled to her bare feet, and she scooped him from the shores.

She looked at him and her eyes dazzled blue and white. She touched him, and his wrist burnt. She took his palm, and looked at it. "The mark of a go-away bird," she said. He wondered if she were friend or peril. "Let's walk this way," she said before he could decide.

And he feared that he'd never see his prayerful mother again.

But he did. Mother found him in his cot, as always. "My love." Her fingertips touched his crown, then his heart, and she was oblivious to the tornado that had thrown itself at him and gobbled him into another woman's water-world.

The next time a tornado tossed him from his bed and wolfed him into the ocean, Godé was a toddler. Rocker waves cast him from the world he knew and onto Aquarii's bare feet at the shore. She took his palm, and looked at its glow.

"A crowned plover," she said.

She led him to the jungle that was the elbow of a city under water. It was a real city, a sprawling metropolis full of lights and glinting structures that beeped and buzzed. She was a queen, he mused, and wondered about his role in her world.

"How am I here?" he asked, on the throne beside her.

She kicked off her shoes. "Big heels are a bitch," she said.

"What yew after?" he asked.

"The ocean chooses," she said.

He was more surprised that he spoke so clearly, than that he was a little boy, no longer a toddler in this world. What astonished him more was how folk bowed when he neared, how they muttered in awe about majestic birds.

One day a memory floated, and he remembered. He was a week old, maybe less. Tiny in a baby bath. His mother's tender touch, soap suds on his arms, his legs, his stomach. "My darling love." A rain of tepid water from the tap onto the back of his head. Gentle fingers brushing his hair, easing off coconut shampoo. He remembered the whistle of a kettle from the kitchen. His mother's startled gaze. He remembered being alone, sinking…water down his throat, a burn in his chest, a slipping away…then he was a water serpent, zigging and zagging across waves and onto a woman's sand-crusted feet.

Godé knew nothing of his father, other than that he had short curly hair and clear bright eyes, a groundnut brown inside. Big hands too—Godé saw them in a photo album—hands that had never carried him because the ocean took his father. He wondered if Aquarii was bestowing upon him kindness to make up for his lost father, the one her water took.

Next it happened, the tremor and roar, he saw white and blue light, flashes of brightness and darkness. Then his cot was gone, his bedroom too. He was on the balcony of a butterfly house up on a bitch hill overlooking the caps of houses from afar. Thin trees, fat trees hedged the house a level below his room, unimpeding the water view. A shock of leaves toddled in the wind's outline. Birds sighed, wheezed and squeaked in sundown until daylight reassembled itself into dusk. He trod-walked down the hill, a boy now, not a child. He went all the way to pounding waves and the *kraa kraa* of seagulls in a huddle at the beach.

Godé... He saw his name in the birds' eyes.

The water was a velvety gray. Out there, coned beacons in the ocean's core. He stood on a steel and tarmac pier, studied the green-gray water and its whitewash, and wondered how deep it went. He understood its lick, its drag. He stood there five or seven minutes because...he didn't know why. All he knew was that he missed his mother, and felt a terrible fear that a giant wave might topple him and gobble him into the ocean.

Then he was back in his cot, clutching its rail and looking out to the darkness that buzzed and moved on wheels. The kettle that whistled. The coughing in the distance. He didn't know what had happened, but something said, *Don't dwell on the past*, over and over, until he felt hollow and cried. The woman full of tenderness—his mother—came and wrapped him in a blanket on her chest.

Her stardust scent was exactly as he remembered.

Inside Aquarii's world, his bed was an emu's nest—soft grass, baby feathers. He met birds as his companions, the ones she'd mentioned: the gray go-away bird and its crowned head. *Kweh, kweh*, it cried out, loud and nasal. Why did he have its mark on his palm? The crowned plover—red-legged. Aquarii dressed him in brown and white plumage like the bird. Sometimes she adorned him like the masked weaver—bright in yellow and black. He liked the collared sunbird—topaz and flame, as it fed on nectar and hovered like a hummingbird half an inch from his palm. But it was not his favorite bird.

His other life, the normal one, was unremarkable. His stepfather Merak wore open-zipped jackets, baseball caps. His mouth curled downward in a permanent pout, but he was kind. Still, why did he always look so guilty? His mother Riba was Afro-haired, dimple-cheeked. She read to him but when the water took him all he remembered was her big hair.

Today the sun was out on the pier, and the water dappled blue-green. It looked peaceful, a gentle lapping of waves on a sandy hump where the ocean had been. His feet sank each stride into soft wet sand speckled with white and silver shells. He stepped into big and small footprints, some paw-toed. He skipped over brown seaweed and green-gold kelp.

He understood that, for all its calm, the water pulsed with a dragging rip, a fierce ripple lurking inside. It was lighter towards the shore—he could see sticks,

134

rocks and kelp on the sand beneath the water. But the waves danced dark and ominous further out, beacons in the water still. That hill was a beast, he thought as he climbed back home, a boy safe from gobbler waves.

Then he was back in his cot, a bub.

Sometimes it was a pram, not a cot. He was sure because of a sound of wheels, someone coughing in the distance. Things often shifted like this for him. Sometimes he remembered the smell of the bath different: not coconut, but a sweet soap with the bitter undertones of a detergent. Sometimes the kettle beeped, buzzed, rather than whistled, then a soft padding of wet feet, rather than rushing footfalls in flat heels.

Today he slipped from the dream that wasn't a dream. It was a gateway that took him from his cot to where the water bopped green, silver and gold. It lapped at the foundation of the pier, and spoke to him in a murmur, loud, louder.

"Come out ta the bloody middle," over and over.

He plunged, and did not resist as the waves grew into a beast that swallowed him in a wash.

It belched him near a great cormorant, black winged on the wetlands, strutting on rocks and branches jutting out of the water, picking at baby whiting and cod. The big bird scooped him with its great beak, not to swallow him—it flew him to the water city, the metropolis with glinting structures, and swooped him onto the throne beside Aquarii.

"You're nineteen now," she said.

"Fair dinkum."

"It's time," she said.

"Fer what?"

She took his hand, and it glowed pink with black speckles.

"The age of the flamingo," she said.

"Fahkin' what?"

"Balance and grace are a choice. But it's the heart that gives you freedom."

She blew in his direction, and foam fell from her lips. It grew into pink bubbles, big, bigger, suffocating with their rich pinkness and speckles of black. He held his breath, but had to let go. He gulped down the bubbles, felt terror as his chest shattered.

This is it, his last gasp, then a flamboyance of flamingos waded long-legged and graceful necked out of the ocean. They spread their wings and swooped him from the drowning. He was back on the orange and white tornado full of lightning, somewhere out in the chapel his mother sobbing *Amen, sweet glory,* thunder speaking directly to him inside his head as he whirled: *Balance and grace are a choice, choice. The heart, heart…gives you freedom.*

He tucked his head on his back, stood on one leg and fell asleep.

He woke to a woman's voice:

…an emu's nest—soft grass and feathers…

…masked weaver—tiny, bright plumed yellow and black…

…collared sunbird—topaz and flame, feeds on nectar, hovers like a hummingbird…

…crowned plover, red-legged, brown and white plumage…

Beep, beep, beep. Coughing in the distance. A rush of feet. Someone wheeled in a new drip on a stand—he felt the needle break his skin, opened his eyes. The hospital was all silver and bleach, a glow of blue and white lights up high on the ceiling, out of reach.

A woman leapt to his side, the book she was reading falling from her lap. She scooped him from his pillow, clutched him to stardust on her breast. Her fingers touched his crown, his heart. She was afro-haired, dimple-cheeked.

"Riba," he croaked.

She took his hand softly. "Amen."

He blinked at her. "How am I here?"

"Several times we thought we'd lost you. Praise be."

"How long?"

"Nineteen days."

Then there was Merak, who was kind, now stepping out from a blind spot. He wore an open-zipped jacket and a baseball cap. Wringing his hands, a worried look on his face.

Godé blinked. Then it all came rushing at him. He remembered.

"You're not Mother," he said.

"Sweet glory…" Her hesitation. "What…do you remember?"

He looked at her. "What wives don't do." She turned from the bed, arms wrapped about herself. Her shoulders shook, her crying silent. He turned to Merak. "And blokes," the disdain was hard to keep out, "who shaft their best mates."

He remembered the holiday house in Dromana. How he loved the water view beyond the caps of cake-shaped houses. He remembered cutting short his beach walk and study of birds, the exercise that normally took two hours, today less. He remembered climbing up the bitch hill, finding the betrayal that pushed him over the edge.

Riba and Merak leaping apart at the turn of the door, their clothes in disarray. It didn't matter that they'd kissed or shagged. What mattered was the ridiculousness of their words:

"It's not like that," said Merak.

"Just this once," said Riba.

Godé pushed Merak to the floor. "Fahkin' hell, yer me bloody mate." He'd looked at Riba. "And yew!" He spat.

He remembered their pleas:

"Don't be like that." Merak.

"Please…" Riba.

He remembered run-walking down the hill, blind with tears and rage. He went all the way beyond the crossing at Boundary Road and the road signs to Rosebud. Traffic swerved around him, drivers swore at him.

He cried as he walked-ran towards the beach and its pounding waves and the *kraa kraa* of seagulls in a huddle. The birds *kraa'd* at him, and he saw his name in their eyes before he reached the steel and tarmac pier.

He studied the green-gray water and its whitewash, wondered how deep it went, understood its lick and drag. He stood there five or seven minutes because…he didn't know why he paused under the receded sun, dark clouds in a pillowy swirl up high.

He moved to the edge, walked slowly down the rump where fisher people would stand and throw their rods, reel whiting or cod into their buckets. But that day no-one was there, only him. Waves like whales rushed at him in a pattern of hiss and sighs overlapping. Murmuring, calling, calling…to him. "Come out ta the bloody middle," over and over.

The pier started to vibrate, or perhaps it was him shuddering at a gateway of decision, indecision. A surfer monster slapped at his core, and he gave himself to it. The last thing he remembered was gasping, bopping to the surface near a beacon before another wave dragged him down. Then he was a water serpent, zigging and zagging across waves and onto a woman's sand-crusted feet.

Now, as the silver hospital beeped, he looked at Merak. "What yew after?"

"I'm so sorry…mate, you can't begin to know—"

"Git out. Now."

Then a nurse in a marine blue dress strode in flats and broke the awkwardness that stayed in the room with Riba by his bed. The nurse smiled, said, "Hello, I'm Aquarii." She took his palm, felt his pulse. "Good as gold, you've come from the dead." She looked at him. Aqua and white shimmered inside her pupils. "The ocean refused to choose you. But it takes bravery to come out of where you've been. Now you must rest."

Her soft footfalls as she left. *Big heels are a bitch, a bitch, a bitch…* He looked at the floor. Her prints were wet. Godé looked at his big hands. He knew that if he asked for a mirror he would see curly hair and clear bright eyes, a groundnut brown inside.

"Godé—" Riba's voice imploring.

"Read to me again," he said quietly.

"Amen," she said. She picked up the fallen book he intimately knew. *The Habits of Birds* by Godé Amide. She sat away from him and started reading from a bookmark, unsure of herself. "The helmeted guinea fowl…is spotted with a bright blue neck and a red hanging wattle. He runs rather than flies—" she glanced at him, and back to the text, "when he is alarmed. You will…find him south of the Sahara scratching for…seeds, blind baby snakes, insects."

"Here," he said. "Closer on the bed."

He put a hand near her lap, almost touching but not reaching. He was not ready.

"Tell me about my favorite bird," he said quietly.

She nodded, smiled through her tears. She flicked, and found a page. "The African flamingo is a wading bird. She lives in tropical and subtropical climates, and loves shallow lakes and swamps. She makes her nest in the mud and can only have one chick at a time." She looked at him. "Will we…get through this?"

He shrugged.

She continued reading, more certain. "The flamingo eats head upside down in the water, her bill pointing up at her feet. She prefers fly larvae, baby fish, snails and algae—all high in alpha and beta pigments, which give the flamingo her pink color…"

Godé glanced at the floor, the wet prints of bare feet.

He thought of Aquarii and the gateway that took him to her water-world and its forest pregnant with glow-eyed birds wrapped on branches inside darkness.

Paperweight

J'S MIND was full of the librarian he was obsessed with a long time. Her name was Rukia. She sometimes came to Laneway, the café and croissanterie where he temped after hours and on weekends. It was located near the corner of Coolangatta Terrace—between Notebook, the flower shop with velvet green décor, and Briggs, the real estate joint that announced five-bedders in ads that showed charismatic gardens and oceanic pools, resort style.

At Laneway, J stood behind a sign that said *Order Here*, and Rukia did. You'd think a girl like her would order a skinny decaf mocha, but no. It was always filtered Odyssey coffee, smashed avocado on toast, and wild organic juice that had cloves and turmeric in it.

He didn't make moves on her at the croissanterie, not with hawk-eyed Marg at his elbow, in his face, peeking up his bum. Still, he got away with things. He gave Rukia the right change and never charged an extra item for himself, as he did with other customers. How was he supposed to otherwise afford lunch?

He didn't make moves on her at the Uniting Church, either, where he sometimes tailed her from a distance. She worked at the library that folk rumored had an ancient gemstone in it, something called a Bury Paperweight—that intrigued J.

The library was not far from what J liked to call God Street—really George Street—and he liked going to prayer service. The church stood on affluent land bordering tier-cake mansions with names like 'The Grove' or 'Palace Lake', and vintage cars parked in Fort Knox garages. Mansions with sports cars number-plated with pretty names like AMELIA, and their engines purred rather than roared.

One entered the church on a side road that hushed traffic with its sign that said: *Slow Street*, well-situated with an op shop where rich people donated off-shoulder fleurette and belle evening gowns. There was a clean carpark whose tarmac you could eat off, and Pastor Methuselah's house was on a top floor above the main prayer room.

Sometimes the church announced 'community lunch and chatter' in gilded letters no-one thought to pinch, but J did—not yet pilfer, but he did think about it.

He did go to some community lunches, mostly to eye Rukia from a distance as she communed with the faithful. He liked the food—they served radiance juice, elf danishes, raspberry croissants, pizza twists, escargot and lemon custard cruffins. Sure thing, he gobbled the lunch but, of course, never stayed for chatter. He'd slip out quick and try car doors in the quiet car park.

Once, he found a wallet swollen with serious dosh. Sometimes he went to the Uniting Church during Pentecost, or for baptisms—they served lunch then too—but he never let them put hands on him for prayer, spiritual resuscitation or anything like that.

J lived with his mother near Thomas Street—that he preferred to call Dick Street, because it also hosted his secondary school. Opposite was a primary school for Years 1 to 6, where a lollipop woman guided little ones to cross the street and jump on red seesaws and whoosh down yellow slides. If Rukia was crossing, he'd become a lollipop woman for her any day!

He imagined making his moves at the library where she worked. Over and over, he fantasized how he'd approach the unsmiling Rukia, reach across her stern desk at the reception and magnetize her into a date. He didn't think much beyond the reaching and wooing, as in how that would actually work out: where'd they go, who'd pay. He was just taken by the librarian's big-eyed stare wrapped in lashes that looked lathered in mascara, but J knew it was a beauty that was natural born. The fact that Rukia was unreachable, as in totally, did not hinder his infatuation—hadn't he suffered enough humiliation at the church, with the sermons, and at the library, just to gain membership?

The library housed rare books. Unpublished manuscripts by famous dead people with names like van Levin, Kwacha and Woke. It had ancient maps, uncommon microfilm and single-copy hard prints—no paperbacks—all hidden inside a honey-combed structure. The reference database said there were booklets roped in helm or burlap, not that J ever found them, but that explained why perhaps security rather than benefactor dollars might account for top steel clad in granite walls and marble-paneled windows.

Membership needed two solid referees and a statement of intent.

J's intent was clear. He wanted to murmur an oath to the librarian whose name sounded like a rare flower. He wanted to try out a wooing language that said: *I undertake not to remove from the library or to scratch or deface in any way any item belonging to this library, and to love and worship you, pash you senseless...*

Of course, he didn't write any of that in his application form. Instead, he wrote about the overwhelming attractiveness of immortalized artifacts and text that most rightly belonged in a royal museum rather than a local library. He wrote about his life in crisis and a quest to find meaning. He wrote about vision and revolution, and his craving to be a keeper of knowledge in a marriage of ancientry and modernity by learning from the best.

He said the kind of things that might work for an exotic girl like Rukia.

For referees, he'd considered asking Marg, the manager at Laneway, who pretended at benevolence but pointed patrons to the specials board above which was a sign that said *Support Local.* The croissanterie sold at the cost of a liver what J was sure were cheaply-sourced honey walnut brownies, pear and pineapple brioches and lemon meringue pies. Not that he had any proof of the ripping off, but still.

The café was unique with its photo walls, and a giant frame holding a famous soccer player's vest: Number 8. Marg rode his ass for laughable pay. No, J didn't want to engage a loser like Marg in any of his recreational activities that involved a rare library and its even rarer librarian—notwithstanding that the engagement was simply for a reference.

So he asked his English teacher Ms Tano (she told the class her name meant *five* in Swahili), who at first frowned when he approached her in the staffroom. "I am not giving you another extension," she said.

"Why are you so suspicious?" he said. "It's not about my assignment."

"Oh." She brightened. "You students—"

"Being a migrant is not easy, is it?" She frowned at him again. "I'm not here to make things harder," he said. "I just need a favor. A reference for Beehive Library, actually."

She brightened. "It's good to see you summon interest in books. You can be like Abdulrazak Gurnah who won the Nobel Prize for Literature for his book *Paradise*."

"If I write a book, it will be set in Port Sea or Arthurs Seat," said J. "I'd write about the bluest sky and a rage of topaz waters, peaks of rocky hillocks out in the horizon." Ms Tano smiled. "There'd be sounds of the wash, crashing waves and low-flying gulls," said J. "Someone toppling off a pier and the cold hitting them first before the water swallowed them whole." The teacher frowned. "Nothing about paradise."

Still, J got his reference.

Pastor Methuselah's very size affirmed the generosity of the faithful. It was hard enough getting past him through the church office door. The pastor looked at J's mambo twist braids and the blond streaks in them, his flare-hipped jumpsuit, a road-trip T-shirt and puma-soled sneakers he'd gotten cheap online, second-hand, and welcomed him with an agenda.

"Your mother—Ms Wellness, isn't it?" the pastor said. "Doesn't sound that well."

"How do you mean?"

"Being all that single, and raising a whole boy by herself. We could give her some guidance, but she never comes to church."

"She works shifts at the emergency outpatient—very busy," said J.

"Tskkk," sighed Pastor Methuselah. "So she's an absent mother too?"

"She works double time to save lives—the pandemic, you know? Things are tough."

"What the world needs is to feed on eternal bread. Tell your mother how church is a blessing. Many a match is made in heaven. Look at the choir—happy couples in it."

"You put the hottest chicks in town in the choir," pointed out J.

"You can be in it too," the pastor said.

"That would be, like, f...chill," he lied. Nearly said *fucking chill*, and J reckoned Pastor Methuselah would probably have poured holy water at him and spoken in tongues. "But today I just want a reference," he said quickly, before any of that could happen.

"Young guns like you today get all these cravings and take whatnot for confidence."

"I know, right? Blokes want to get jacked but they don't want to eat 'roids 'cos they'll grow tits. Doesn't bother me."

"That's a lot of talk," said the pastor, "and you've come to the right place for someone to listen. I really want to help you."

"Here's the reference form—" J started unfolding it.

The pastor stayed J's hand. "Love gives generously. First, I am going to invite you to come and pray with me. Is there room in your heart for God to speak to you?"

"If that's what it takes."

"Hallelujah! Let this be holy ground. We shall exalt Him, oh powerful name." The pastor looked at J, waiting.

J looked back at him. "Oh. Halle-lujah?"

"Amen! Take a posture before the Lord, receive Him right now as I pray for you. Place His throne upon your life!" He looked at J.

"Halle-lujah?"

"Amen!" He lay hands on J. "Dear Father God, we beseech You—" Pastor Methuselah cried ardently.

"It could be a mother god—"

"We seek Your Presence and Your Power. We surrender to You, Father God, rest in Your Truth because of who You are!" He looked at J.

"Hallelujah."

142

"Amen! Yes, Lord! We're on the winning side, this is our victory. Heal this lad, this sick body!" He prayed for a forever time, interjecting it with amens, some of which J mirrored, but he was glad when the pastor took both his hands, tears running down his face. "We thank You. Amen."

"And *amen*," J said firmly, and removed his hands from the pastor's clutch, making it very clear that the praying was finished.

The pastor smiled through his tears. "Liked it?

"It was pretty chill," lied J. But his heart stuttered with an imagining that Rukia was watching him, as he pretended to love God.

"There's a festive bonanza coming up, and we have just the part for you."

"Sounds ace. Now the form—" J pushed it at the pastor's nose.

The pastor wrote the reference, and patted J's back. "Don't be a stranger."

"Sure thing. One hundred percent."

What was he thinking? J wondered, even as he held the recommendation.

Now that J had membership, he didn't really mind the library's strange rules:

Keep the door closed to fools.

Bite your nails outside.

Do not take anything out with you.

Return all books to the counter.

Chew gum at your own peril.

They were five rules—maybe there was something special about the number 5.

J wondered if someone had ever tried chewing gum to find out what peril happened. But he was despondent because—other than admission into the library—nothing with Rukia had gone to plan. When he'd leaned over the desk with that charmer look, Rukia did not give him a date. Her eyes said, "Blast right off," because her holy tongue couldn't say it.

J decided not to feel screwed, and moved to Plan B.

He'd earmarked five books from the reference database to nick: *The Aardvark Boneyard* by Idris Woke. *A Polka-dot to Uranus* by Jap Bloomberg. *The Phantom of the Nubian Desert* by Mary Mboya. *The Unfound Pyramid* by Bree Kwacha. *A Pentagram in the Rift Valley* by NHK. He'd thought *Island on a Lake of Blood* by Ripples van Levin was something special but changed his mind as he didn't really like islands or blood. What he really wanted to find was the Bury Paperweight, the ancient gemstone said to be somewhere in the library—that would earn some grave coin on the black market.

In school Ms Tano asked, "How's the library going?"

"No sweat," he said. "It's a breeze."

On Saturday, Pastor Methuselah swung by the croissanterie, and looked around expectantly. "Smells of baking bread in here."

"No shit," said J, but the pastor kept smiling hard. "You got a stroke or something?"

"You're funny. Give me a skinny decaf mocha," said the pastor.

J entered the order. "You got the dole?" The pastor blinked at him. J laughed. "What? You thought it was free or something? Because of a reference? That will be five dollars, fifty cents."

"Now this bonanza—" the pastor tried to make conversation as J made the coffee.

"Go jerk yourself, mate."

"You know what, kid? You're a hoodoo."

"Nice. I had no father to teach me."

The pastor grabbed his coffee and tossed down a ten-dollar note. "See if I'll ever haul you out of trouble. Keep change!"

After he left, it was quiet at the croissanterie, J drying dishes. Just then, Marg—sitting outside under a parasol table—called him. He walked out, towel and cup in his hands to show that he was busy, and her summon a disruption.

"Pastor Methuselah looked angry. What was that about?"

"Maybe ask him. What do you want?"

"The books look a bit off, J," she said.

"More than you?" He laughed. "Bet you're too stunned to fire me." He roped and threw the towel to the ground, placed the empty coffee cup deliberately on the table and upside-down right in front of her. "Well, I quit."

His mother once told him that was the best way to bring out another person's stutter.

It worked, the way Marg stuttered.

His search was meticulous. He X-rayed the library with the growing intensity of a rejected boy. He walked from melancholy room to melancholy room, searching with the hand of a madman, the thirst of a thief. Books thudded in a pile on the floor beside him.

Rukia approached. She looked at the books he'd yanked from the shelf. "Are you going to read all those?"

"Maybe. Maybe not."

"You know you can't take them out of the library."

"Did anything about me say that I wanted to?"

"You're reading as if the world is going to end tomorrow," she said.

"Time kills love," he snapped.

"I forgive you," she said.

"Look at yourself for forgiveness." He didn't turn as she walked away.

Finally! Right there under everyone's nose in the Gondola Room, hidden in plain sight. You wouldn't notice, until you looked closer—almost needing a magnifying glass—to distinguish the paperweight holding upright five of those single-copy hardcovers by Woke, Bloomberg, Mboya, Kwacha and NHK that J no longer cared about. It wasn't the kind of thing one immediately noticed. It was just a paperweight at first, until he touched it.

The three-dimensional pentagon against which the books on the shelf leant responded when J put hands on it as people did when the pastor lay hands on their head during prayer service. The crystalline shape glowed through his fingers, and his skin shone.

Even as he amazed at it, just then the paperweight shifted itself from perfection to five unequal sides, asymmetrical angled. He felt its rough texture like amethyst, gazed at its purplish glow through his hand. At once the marble stone hued itself into a blackish prism of granite crystals, and twinkled. J felt his feet lift off the ground and he found himself ensconced in a space between the library and the heavens, stars swirling in utmost calm in a hula hoop around his frame.

An obscene ringtone shattered the silence, a grunt and moan in climbing tempo and volume. J snapped to from spinning stars the color of Saturn in his head. Someone said *Shhhhhh!* and he muzzled and tucked the rude device that had buzzed in his pocket. He'd put on that obscene tune to shit his mother, and now she was calling him. He barely saw her, the shifts she took at odds with human hours.

He ignored calling her back to find out what she wanted. Instead, he looked at the paperweight now all calm and opalescent, a moonstone smooth and pearly in his shimmering hands. He put it in his pocket and started leaving. Rukia didn't look up—she never spoke to him since when he snapped at her—and no alarm beeped.

J walked swiftly out of the library into dusk.

Outside was not a lit night. It was dull gray, somber. The streets were deserted. Few passing cars had their lights on. *Waaa! Gaaa!* Five black ravens perched on a powerline, warbled and considered him with accusation in their pale eyes until their sound and silhouettes faded. J's attention went to the paperweight that was growing heavy and heavier in his pocket. He took it out, held it for a moment, mesmerized as its color turned a deep metamorphic blue, and then it gleamed like a tiger's eyes in a new texture and luster of quartz.

He watched, first astonished, then in panic, as the paperweight shuffled itself out of his fingers and crawled back across his arm, down his stomach and into his pocket. J took it out again, and it lumbered back into the pocket. The third time he tried to take the paperweight, it burnt his fingers. He yowled and pulled his hand out of the pocket.

He looked about him quickly. The sky dissolved as he walked, then crawled, the gemstone in his pocket now true lead and chanting. *What's mine is yours*, it whispered. *Yours, yours.* He felt himself sinking and lifted a hand, reaching, reaching… But help never arrived because each of his five fingers went opaque. *What's mine is yours…yours, yours.*

J dragged himself against the pulling weight, no-one there to notice his world slipping. There was the Uniting Church on God Street. Curtains parted in the upper room where Pastor Methuselah lived. J thought, as he agonizingly crawled, that he saw a face at the window. He tried waving, hopeful, but his fingers were still marble and it didn't matter if someone had seen him. The curtains closed.

How would he get home, wondered J glumly, and—when he did—would his mother be back from work? And how, oh how, would J explain the gemstone that was lead and burning, burning in his pocket? He pulled at his jumpsuit, tore and crawled out of its shreds.

He stood in his T-shirt and boxers, uncaring if someone might see him half-naked, when he saw the paperweight shuffling towards him from the torn clothing on the street. He turned away in panic, but could do no more than belly crawl because a deep heaviness overwhelmed him. He heard the obscene ringtone, his mother calling from somewhere in his discarded pocket.

"Mum!" he cried, and reached in a flash of hope. There was a deep rumble, then a smell of sulphur. The ground started shaking, fissures forming and making an inescapable island on which he was trapped. Rocking and teetering accompanied the rumble, then *boom*!

The roadside began to crack, a long and snailing fissure moving towards him. J gave a cry and tried to crawl away, but the paperweight had already reached him and climbed on his chest, dragging him down on the island, as the earth opened.

He squealed as he fell, fell, dead weight falling, hundreds of feet falling, deeper into the boom and rumble falling. Now J was trapped and bleeding in a gorge.

It seemed like forever, maybe it was just five minutes. He looked up and saw Pastor Methuselah peeking down. "You need help, boy?"

"Amen!" cried J. "Yes, pastor. Praise the Lord!"

146

"Amen. I ain't gone say go jerk yerself. But I call it reparation. See you later."

"No. No!" But the pastor was gone. J curled back, forlorn. He looked up. Wait—there was someone else. "Is that you, Rukia?"

"Look at yourself for forgiveness," she shouted down, and stepped away from the big hole.

"Noooo!"

He regretted his choices, wished he had lived different. Contributed more to his society rather than be a weight in it. With a sob, he wondered if it was too late to change.

A roar, and the walls started closing around him. Locked in the chasm's embrace, J shrieked at the weight of dirt on his chest, the press against his ribs, soil particles in his eyes, up his nostrils.

He screamed, no-one to hear him, louder and louder.

Then the crushing began.

The Lightning Bird

A SPRAY OF PETALS mottled her ebony hair sprawled on olive grass. Fulani allowed Sebu to entwine his fingers into hers, as she gazed at a lavender sky streaked with longitudes of cloud.

"A garland of flowers," Sebu was saying.

"Ridiculous," said Fulani, and sat up. She toyed with the stained-glass pendant in the necklet Sebu had handcrafted for her.

"And that's the truth," Sebu said. He rolled, raised himself on elbows, looked at her with eyes full of longing. Charcoal eyes enkindled as coal.

She swung her hair and the tails of her long braids brushed his face. "Rubbish," she snapped. "Liken me to…flowers?"

"Exotic ones."

"Just exotic?" She glided a fiend eye his way.

"A lilium and calliandra hybrid. A rainbow fire hibiscus with mottles of peaches and cream. You are the most radiant. Such is your beauty there's no match up, I swear."

"You only say that because—" She gazed at her hands, at the rhinestone in the promise ring Sebu had fashioned.

"Because?"

"You want to touch my petticoats." She allowed herself a giggle.

"And that's the truth," he said in solemnness. "But there is more, a hundred-and-ninety-nine percent more."

Why him? she asked herself this over and over. She was beyond him. *Way* beyond.

His countenance never met her with resistance, he said no to nothing. But he was news you shut out. The last house you parked before you reached it. He was a hut—not a castle. An inn, never home. No matter his best try, he was holiday joy. Something passing, not home.

148

Her heart said, *Listen.* Her head said, *Tick-tock.*

That was precisely it.

Fulani was acutely aware of looming spinsterhood and didn't want to wind up like Old Auntie Jiwe who muttered into a sisal mat as she braided it, gossiped about the days of her sizzle and the voluptuous exploits it conjured. *He took me like a donkey.* Barren Auntie Jiwe who drank like tilapia but never lost her fins.

It came down to compromise—how far off was Fulani willing to go?

Sebu was a sun that floated on the horizon behind a cloud, never turning on its *touch.* He had no right words, at least to her, even as a door-to-door salesman. *Tick-tock.* She knew to play dumb, never dead. So, when at midnight, he fell on his knee and shone her face with a brand new ring, she transfigured.

He clasped her hand and pushed the dazzler along her finger before she could think to resist. "Dance with me, Fulani. Will you dance with me to our graves?"

Her stomach jumped.

His proposal wasn't ready, and he wasn't going to come up with a better one. "You're the lifeblood in my soul,' he cracked clumsily, so off path she couldn't conceive the measure of his knobby words. His inadequacy fell from his tongue in monstrous detail that mutated like a virus, and it yanked out cruelty.

"All I want is to block you," she surged back with the carefree and escapade of a dirt bike rider.

He blinked, unable or unwilling to comprehend her spite.

On the eve of their wedding, Sebu's mother Dafrosa came with a gift. Fulani could have previously sworn Dafrosa detested her. Why, the woman was always pointedly aloof. And yet this…this wedding gift. It was a paragon of an impundulu, the lightning bird—the kind of artifact you might find in a museum. It was more handsome than the gifts Sebu had lavished upon Fulani.

"It's passed down generations," Dafrosa said quietly. "My mother and her mother…the sacred craft of our forebearers."

"But it's an heirloom!" said Fulani in half protest.

"Shush already." Dafrosa pressed the cold gleaming sculpture into Fulani's willing hands. "I want you to have it."

Fulani cradled the paragon, a majestic bird that resembled an eagle. It was sculpted in red and gold, bright red rubies in its eye. It was the most fine-looking object she had ever seen.

People spoke of the wedding many moons straight. Shifting accounts of the same event travelled, each description sprigging Fulani's hair with whatever blooms were in flower at the time of the telling: flamingo grevillea, purple and green lobelia, sun jeweled portulaca, satin dusk sunflowers, velvet eyed daylilies…

But all narrations held one familiar thing: how the groom sparkled with cheerfulness; how exquisite the bride.

But they were a couple spread apart, a scatter of clouds.

Nothing major: just a wrong fit. It appeared to Fulani that Sebu could do nothing right, and this manifested itself in disagreements, starting frivolous, swirling into hurricanes. These arose not because Sebu, a husband now, no longer spoke with coaxing or desire of Fulani's eye-enveloping beauty. His eye still held tenderness, but she felt it was with compromise: what he truly desired were Fulani's wifely duties. And these she struggled with. Sebu was her story's end, and its beginning. He was a bad dream, a catastrophe that threatened to last years, and she almost wished for that grave he murmured about in his wedding proposal. He was a life here, a life there, ending, ending, yet always here, something there, and she was stuck with him. Her restlessness manifested itself in a craving for daily affirmation.

Fulani noticed how more unsettled she became, and how much more Sebu floundered, especially in the presence of the impundulu. Something about the bird…perhaps it was the ruby eyes that were quiet yet questioning… She found herself putting Sebu to test after test, nudging him to enhance comparisons of her beauty and how she surpassed them all:

More regal than a white peacock's tail. And that's the truth.

More exquisite than polished Bismuth crystals. And that's the truth.

More spectacular than a Koroit opal…than a meteorite…a glowing jungle…an aurora…

She trembled when he compared her perfection to the jazz of angels. "Velvety with resonance, celestial," he sighed with husk in his voice.

Sebu was useless. He was a catastrophe slipping from room to room with his own keys in her household. He was the domestic chore of a lucid dream. She sought to see in his eyes a labyrinthine ballroom that sashayed her to a mystical place. But his adoring gaze was none of that. Just soddened music in an ancient sink. A cleft bowl she didn't recognize. A mirror draped in ash, no reflection to see. A door littered with hung pockets on its hooks, but where, where were the coats?

His wife's desire for confirmation, adulation was malady.

Sebu didn't know what to do. Nothing he whispered or boomed about her beauty was shimmering enough, noble enough, extraordinary enough to satiate Fulani's craving. It infected her happiness. Her spirit plunged into darkness and she became wretched, detached. When he compared her beauty to the spectrum of a fire rainbow, to the rarity of a black sun, to a shower of red rain... Fulani roared from the kitchen and chased him with a cleaver.

Nothing sealed the abyss that threatened to swallow Fulani. Sebu never knew which place in her mood cycle she would be when he got home—whether he might find her mad or depressed. The psychosis hurled crockery and furniture at his head. The hopelessness folded her into the fetus of herself, trembling and inconsolable in a corner of their bed. When Fulani's deep, deep eyes were not darkened with warring, they were bedimmed empty.

Sebu would gaze at her with a wide smile, his eyes pleading, as he tried to remember the exquisiteness that once was. It was as if she made herself less ugly by finding ugliness in Sebu. The timber of her voice grew spiteful, the personal nature of her attacks brutal enough to silence and distance him. His hair was too long, too short, too clumpy, too dirty, too stringy. He was home too much, too little. Pleasing her was a Herculean task.

As for the subject of beauty...now he said nothing.

What could he say without risking the cleaver?

* * *

Fulani sat brooding on the bed. Sebu was away door-to-door peddling again—not that it seemed to help much. They were living in a barn that sometimes dripped when it rained. Well, then, not actually a barn—more a cottage, but what difference did it make?

Absently, she stretched her hand and stroked the sculpted bird, the gift from Dafrosa that stared blankly from the chiffonier. Once or twice, she could have sworn the impundulu regarded her sidelong.

"Sebu doesn't love me," she said to her hands, and dismissed the impundulu's personal gaze as nothing more than the edge of lunacy.

Next day, Fulani's eye again fell upon the impundulu on her dressing table, its eye like a mirror. She gazed deep into the mirror-eye, looked to catch a reflection of her beauty, and found a glimmer of it.

That night, as Sebu chewed madly at a fowl's bone, cleaned his tooth with the tip of a nail and asked between chompfuls for more gravy, Fulani hurled the half-carved bird in his direction. He ducked and the bird smacked the wall, slid to the floor, and left a trail of oil.

Fulani snatched the carving knife, and Sebu fell back.

"What is this!" he cried. The knife clattered somewhere behind him.

"You should have married your stomach!" she cried.

"But I love you," he stammered.

She fled the room, fell to her bed and cried and cried.

Sebuleni.

He was a fragment of a name, a complication. His words painted over cracks that stayed too plain to see. She woke to his unbearable adoration, and drank coffee so it would be the last thing she remembered.

She woke from restless sleep and Sebu's snoring. She flung his arm from her waist and stood. She noticed the impundulu as it considered her from the top of her chiffonier. The light from its ruby eye was no longer stone but flaming with life and catching her fingers. It engulfed her wrist, her forearm, her elbow, all the way up the rise and fall of her chest to spotlight her angled face. Fulani stilled her breathing, stood quiet as a library in the dead of the night, so the light could feel her beauty.

She started seeing lightning birds in her dreams.

"You sleepwalk naked," Sebu said. "Glowing as you walk."

She cast him a smile full of unspecified rewards. Invisible tongues lapped her body in a burn that never scorched. The eruption of light inside radiated her beauty outside. She looked at herself in the mirror and was startled by how ravishing she looked!

Sebu was off peddling again. Fulani posed herself before the paragon and said wistfully, "Who is the most beautiful?"

The red jewel in the impundulu's eye twinkled.

"You are the most fiery," a voice said.

Startled, Fulani glanced. The lightning bird sat stock-still.

"Did you…talk?" she said.

Ruby eyes regarded her evenly.

"You are the most fiery," the lightning bird said. Its eye shifted and sparkled a little more.

And though Fulani's jaw dropped in wonderment, the paragon's words clung like a cloak. She was beautiful! The impundulu said so! And she couldn't agree more. The fieriest dame! How about that?

She felt free and whole, and could barely gird her ecstasy before it overwhelmed. She danced around the room. Thrice that day, the bird watching her, she asked, "Who is the most beautiful?" Each time, the response was the same. Her bottom lip trembled. And right there, inside the mirror gaze of the impundulu, her beauty trebled.

152

That evening when Sebu came home, Fulani was sociable to him, even a little tender maybe. She touched his arm. "It will be better now," she said. "You'll see."

She did not tell him about the bird.

Days passed without Fulani interrogating the bird. Slowly, doubt and insecurity returned. One morning she waited with impatience until Sebu was gone. She mustered her question and raced to the bedroom. She stood before the impundulu.

"Who is the most beautiful?"

Cinders danced in the sculpture's ruby eye.

"You are the most fiery," it said.

Inside its gaze, Fulani caught her reflection. Her beauty had increased a hundredfold. She touched her skin. It was soft as a baby's cheek. Her hair shimmered with brightness, ebony tresses falling in ringlets to her waist.

More days passed.

One morn, Fulani woke miserable. She had to know, but stupid Sebu was taking his time leaving the house. She pushed him out the door without goodbye, and flew to the impundulu.

"Who is the most beautiful?"

The ruby eye burnt redder, brighter.

"You are the most fiery," the bird said. Its eye gleamed like a shooting star.

Fulani laughed out loud. She listened to the sound of her glee, a beautiful river. She gazed at the mirror. Sun glided in and out of her ebony locks. Wind spread sheen on her skin.

And she started seeing her shimmer again in folks' eyes when she stepped out of the cottage. Everyone sang of her radiance. She glowed as she walked, never mind the loom of dusk—she was a lantern from the gods. She forgot her limbs, how effortless her glide. Curtains parted, doors snapped open as people gawped. She was splendor, a requiem. Divine enchantment. The song of a thousand lamps, burning burning as they sang. A child lit into a hymn. Then a man stepped from the threshold of his house, and his touch on her dazzling frock borrowed or stole a piece of her sizzle. It burst into wings on his back between shoulder blades and, with a flap, he floated off the ground. His chuffed warble blazed the world like no-one had ever seen. It rumbled and thundered, the moon shimmering at a distance for a long time.

"What a spell-binding creature," folk chanted. "She is oh-so-beautiful!"

"Your aura is stellar," crooned Sebu. "Your sparkle tinkles! And that's the truth."

That night Fulani straddled him of her own accord, rode him to a rainbow of reds and yellows and blues and greens so intense it swallowed his cry of pleasure.

Sebu was euphoric to have this new Fulani. So he was thrown aback when out of the blue she said, "Take the paragon. I want you to peddle it."

"But it's a sacred gift handed down generations. Why would you suggest selling it?"

Fulani burst into tears.

Sebu was trite but confounded. "I mean, I don't know…but if, if…you feel that strongly—" he lifted the impundulu.

With a growl Fulani snatched the paragon and cradled it.

They spoke nothing more of the incident.

Fulani kept away from the paragon and lavished new attention on Sebu. She spiced his fowl with smoked bay leaves, garnished it with pineapple broth. The chili-lime combination she put on a plate for him he polished, as did he the earth-roasted bread she served with charred tomato and broccoli salad the day after.

Inside a week, Fulani was again agitated, fidgeting before the bird.

But Sebu lingered, not in a hurry to do his peddling. Fulani tugged him by the hand and shoved him out the door. He turned, astonished. She slammed the door to his face.

"But my bag!"

"There!" she flung it out the window and latched it before Sebu could think to climb back into the house.

Breathless, she faced the lightning bird and fired her question: "Who is the most beautiful in the whole universe?"

The impundulu smiled. Its ruby eye sizzled with brilliant flames.

"You are the most fiery," it said. "And to me the most desirable."

Fulani's delight reached its zenith. Her eyes glowed so bright, a blast of flame shot from them. A volcano rumbled in her core and lit the room. The flame shooting from her eyes burst into a pyre that engulfed Fulani. She screamed out loud, yet no sound came, as scorching tongues devoured her to a mound of ash.

Fulani watched aground, helpless, as the impundulu jumped from the dresser, reborn. She was a ravishing beauty of the darkest skin and blazing hair, who took one last look at the cottage and flew out to the heavens, causing thunder as she beat her wings.

Sometimes shit happened, and bad things happened to people. Fulani detested Sebu's mother, Dafrosa, and her stupid gift that was behind all this

154

badness. But she paused and wondered for a tiny moment if she had done this to herself. She quickly discarded the silly thought—how does one do *this* to themselves? Instead, she now wondered wretchedly how her husband might respond to her ashen residue. Would he gingerly scoop her and pour her into the prettiest vase, or would he take a broom and sweep her out to nearest bin?

It was early morning, the onset of Fulani's *long, long* wait for Sebu's return.

The Fable of a Monkey's Heart

ONCE UPON a lifetime you were a clever little monkey who lived with your baba. Your house was at the top of an ancient baobab tree. The tree had the brownest trunk and the greenest leaves. The tree was
    tall, tall, tall, fat, fat, fat
       and it stood on the bank
          of the stillest blackest lake.

Inside the lake was a crocodile, always lurking near the old baobab tree because for him it promised goodness.

"Be careful of the long-toothed croc," said Baba.

And you, the cheeky little monkey that you were, didn't listen and smiled to yourself. For what did grown ones know? If it were Mama, you might have listened, but she was not as clever as you—didn't she get herself eaten by the big bad croc when her lofty branch broke? It was you who told her to test the creaky branch, stomp on it a bit. But still. You saw how she fell, as if in slow motion. You saw how the croc's jaws waited, waited wide open, snapped and clamped down on her headfirst and then swallowed one half whole. The bottom half of her torso, crimson blood squirting in arcs, legs kicking as if connected to her mind, splashed into the still, dark lake, and it stayed black.

But you had a plan for what would happen if your lofty branch broke—not that you'd die in a ditch if things didn't go your way. And that's why you waited, waited like the croc.

One day, Baba went hunting for bananas, because you loved to eat bananas. You loved the baby, golden ones that grew at the elbow of the savanna. And you also loved coconuts—your baba had those for you in plenty.

"Stay home," said Baba. "Stay away from the big, bad croc."

And off Baba left, to find some soft, sweet bananas from the great big savanna for you to eat. And you sat on the edge of the overhung branch of the old baobab tree, and peered at the lake and saw the long-toothed croc swimming and swimming around your tree.

"Oi!" you yelled. "You're full of humps and lumps, and you pong like bad fish."

But Croc just swam and swam around your tree.

You peered a little more, and bellowed, "Oi! You! Your mama was so smelly she thought the month-old carcass of a hippo, green and putrid and trapped in hyacinth, was a brand-new suitor from the gods."

But Croc just swam.

Annoyed at the croc, you peered so hard that your branch *snapped!* As you fell legs first from the tree

   the big bad croc lunged

      from the murky waters

         snatched you whole in his jaws.

And he smelled rottener up close.

He tossed you in the air, so you fell again, this time headfirst into his mouth like your poor mama did, only he didn't chomp you in half right then. He threw you back in the air, again and again, each time catching you as you fell into dead shrimp, lake-fly larvae and glowing cichlids between his yellow teeth.

Finally, he tossed you onto his back, and swam you far, further, further still from the bank, and into the middle of the silent, black lake.

You looked at your hand and it was a stump, white bone jutting where fingers once danced. Pus-colored mud came from the stump, and you looked at the croc, saw how the yukky ooze snailed from his nose. His bumpy skin was slippery with slime. You slid off it, and the croc *snapped!* bit and dragged you into the water and you tried to fight, to flee, but what good was it with one hand?

He held you under the murky surface, rolled, rolled, rolled a few times. You could hear the porridge of the lake, and it was calling for you. It blinded your eyes, enfolded your nose, tunneled down your throat, plumbed your lungs, and you couldn't breathe, breathe.

You closed your eyes to sleep or die, anything to forget, if that would take the pain. You stilled yourself one last time, but Croc stopped his death roll and snatched you back onto his bumpy, slimy skin.

You were half-dead but didn't cry because you were clever. So clever. You looked at the croc and said you didn't have your heart, and the heart was the best part of a monkey for a croc to eat.

"Say what?" roared the croc.

And though your whole body hurt when you turned, or moved your mouth, you told him again that you didn't have your heart, and, oh, how yum, yum, it was good.

"And where is your heart, little monkey?" asked the croc.

"I left it in the topmost branch of the old baobab tree, up, up there, right next to the blinky stars," you said.

"And why is your heart near the blinky stars, little monkey?"

"At the topmost branch of the old baobab tree," you said, "the blinky stars can reach the heart. And when they reach the heart, the gods can spice it up with good, good things."

You saw his hesitation, how he swam round and round contemplating your words, and you understood when he swirled and swam, tail swishing this way, that way, that the silly, silly Croc believed your tale.

So when Croc snapped his jaws, let you leap across his back, and it hurt with half a hand, the ugly stump not bleeding, just covered in slime, pus and mud, you scrambled best you could all the way up to your tree.

There, you called out loud from the top:

"Open wide, dear croc, open your great, big mouth for the god-loved heart."

The big, bad croc opened his mouth, and you hurled a large coconut that went *BOOFF!* on his head.

You saw how croc's skull cracked, and a goo of milky brain, pinky blood and a smashed-avocado ooze leaked from his head, as he cried.

"Oh! How hard is your heart, Little Monkey?"

He swam away, and you hoped that was the last of him, but you saw him further out, swimming round and round in the belly of the pitch-black lake.

You wondered if you should tell Baba—he wouldn't notice if you didn't, for what do men know? He didn't know about Mama, how it was you who said to test the creaky branch, just then it broke. Oh, nasty!

Your baba came back from the forest with a clutch of golden baby bananas, but the sweet goodness of the yellowest bananas was lost in the throb of your stump. You didn't tell Baba about the croc and the god-loved heart. But something in his eye, the way Baba

    looked first at the croc

      with a misshapen head

        swimming round, round

          at the bottom of your tall, tall

tree, and then at you—
He didn't say nothing, but something still and black s t i r r e d in your core,
and
    s
       t
         a
           y
             e
               d.

The Zanzibar Trail

(*with Clare E Rhoden*)

1.

MY MIGRAINES come and go in color, sound and silhouette. I've had them since I was a bub. They drew my mother batty, the way I howled, clutching my head, the hues, bangs and shapes morphing. I was six when I first saw blood and brain matter. Before then it was turds—brown and speckled with the brightest blues, reds, purples. But blood, brain or turd, they all sighed and moaned, squealed and screeched—very frightening to witness as a child.

When unicellular organisms shape-shifted in shadow, extending, retracting, stretching pseudopods into luminous puddles, patches reached towards me as they grew, wailing all the time.

The growth in sound, tint and shape of my migraines seems commensurate with maturity. Because now I see anacondas, griffins, ogres and banshees. They pant and howl, ruff and shiver towards me. Sometimes I see flames, brightest in a fluorescent orange, licking in haste to gobble me. In agony or trepidation, I lie on the ground, on a bed, on whatever…shut my eyes and clasp my head until the torment fades itself out. This is how my darling Dalton finds me, wrapped on the kitchen floor in a Halloween that's my life, as a pecan pie chars.

"My dear Evelyn!" He coughs at the smoke. Whips out the pie and bangs open a window. He scoops me in his arms, rests me on a lounger and brings me a shot of Kentucky's finest. The bourbon's notes of vanilla, maple and marzipan smooth away the jack hammer on my skull.

"Sorry to be such a nuisance," I say.

"Rubbish!" my husband says.

160

"They're getting worse, you know. Since the pestly war when I nursed all those dying men at that military hospital in El Paso. Oh, Dalton, the headaches are so terribly eviler."

He takes my hand, and today there's sadness on that boyish face that never misses a beat to live life to its max.

"Indeed, I know, my dear Evelyn, and I think I've figured out what to do."

He tells me his plan, and it almost brings about another migraine.

2.

The next morning, I step into my brand new Ford Thunderbird, the newest 1967 model that Dalton swapped for my tiny two-door, four-seater. This hot rod is positively much sleeker. Larger than its 1964 predecessor, it purrs like a Lincoln, unless you want it to grunt.

I visit my sister Sue Ellen in her bungalow near Warfield where she lives with her husband Hunter, who's away in the oil fields. She's as astounded as I am by my husband's suggestion, yet is more amenable to it than I am.

"Why, Evelyn, that's the biggest escapade you'll have since the first and only adventure you've ever had."

"Which was?"

"Moving from Odessa to Parks Lagado!"

"Everyone treats me like the invalid I'm not." I give my loudest protestation yet.

"You *are* an invalid. Lucky that your Dalton has far more success in oil mining than my poor Hunter. That man of yours has a solid head about him."

"That solid head about him is mine. Gallivanting to the middle of nowhere in Africa is not Dalton's brightest idea right now, seeing how well he's doing drilling oil."

"Oh, don't be a bore. Drive by the thrift shop round the corner when you pull yourself together. They have the best tents. I can lend you my hard case to travel with—it's hearty as a house. You'll be able to pack just about anything in it!"

Another migraine grabs me just then—this one in the form of a multi-colored slug that's a monstrosity, and it's pushing itself onward, flowing around me in ripples of slime and howl. It has a monstrous jaw of flexible microscopic teeth that Dalton, if he were here, would have told me are called radula—he's good with trivia this way—25,000 of them, each scraping and rasping at me, cutting me up into tiny pieces of slime delish.

A Place Between Waking and Forgetting

3.

Back home, I show Dalton my purchase of the waterproof tent from a dollar shop, and he laughs at me to the edge of tears.

"But look," I insist. "It has sealed seams, no permeation."

"Rubbish, my dearest Evelyn." He looks serious for a moment, and I suppose he's about to say something sensible this once. "You must remember to pack the black coffee cup—black has always calmed you."

"Oh?"

"What's more important is this—will the tent have a writing desk for me? I don't think so. Tomorrow we'll buy something more fitting for our voyage."

"I'd rather you didn't doubt me this much, Dalton. A thrift shop doesn't mean that what it sells is unspecial. Do you know that this tent can pop up on its own?"

"And what good is that, my darling?"

"For starters, I can put it up on my own when a lion gobbles you in Africa."

At this he roars heartily, and proceeds to tell me the many ways a grown lion can kill me, none of which involves gobbling.

"First, there's the rank smell of rotten meat and blood, decaying flesh in its teeth. Not to mention the heavy musk of its fur and popcorn smell of its urine. That's enough to knock you insensible."

"Is that so?"

"Yes, my dearest Evelyn. And if that doesn't kill you, then the beast's weight will. Think of four-hundred-and-twenty pounds charging at you at fifty miles per hour, then a massive blow loaded with muscle swiping at you—still at those speedy miles per hour—and knocking you flat, before claws drag you down to a waiting jaw."

"Must you be so gross?"

He laughs harder. "If the claws don't cleft you in two, it's the teeth that will break your neck as the lion clamps its jaws around your neck and bites your throat."

"Oh, Dalton!"

"Now my dearest, if you don't die at once from the bite, then you'll surely die from blood loss, as the lion slowly picks at your favorite body parts to eat: your lungs, your heart and your liver."

"Dalton!"

4.

"We'll take a flight from Dallas Love Field to New York." Dalton points at the map, not because I'm a visual person who loves maps, but because he is.

He outlines a voyage that includes a Pan Am plane on multi-legs across America to Cartagena in South America, where we'll board a seaplane to West Africa, along the Gulf of Guinea. "It's the world's very first flying boat," he says.

"Ten stops, Dalton? That's not what I'd call flying. I wish you'd let me do the booking. I'm sure there's a more convenient transatlantic route than one that heaves us all over America, Europe, West Africa to East Africa, and entails bundling in tiny aircrafts, uneasy seaplanes. I'm beginning to suspect there are belligerent mules somewhere along the way in this plan of yours. Isn't there a British Overseas Airways Corporation that's running passenger flights? It was on the news the other day."

"You've done your research, my dearest Evelyn. But I don't want you having migraines over this matter," he says in that patronizing way of his that sometimes slips through, especially when he's doing his best to hide it. "Zanzibar, our destination, is now in unification with the mainland, Tanganyika, fresh off colonial independence. See? I know what I know, and I do have some trivia for you."

"Oh, do tell."

"The new country, this *unification*, is newly named Tanzania."

"Oh?"

"And the president, Julius Kambarage Nyerere, has recently announced an Arusha Declaration."

"An A-roo what now?" I blink at him.

"The Tanzanian government has solemnly declared a commitment to socialism and self-reliance. It's a sort of African socialism called Ujamaa. So don't pack up too many things on this trip, who knows they might get confiscated and declared property of the government in a communal spirit of togetherness, my dearest Evelyn."

"We're not affiliating with communists!" I say sternly, as I neatly pack stilettos, geometric shifts, miniskirts and boxy jackets with large buttons in loud colors, full skirted gowns with trim waists and low necklines into the hard case Sue Ellen lent me.

Dalton looks at my travel wardrobe, starts to say something that I'm sure will be patronizing, but I give him the look that silences.

"Not the turtlenecks," he says firmly, when I start to pack his clothes. He refuses the knit sweaters too, says they're just as useless as champagne flutes in a jungle.

He accepts the polo shirts, bell bottoms and stirrups.

5.

It's night.

We gulp Kentucky whisky and suddenly Dalton's eyes darken. He takes me like a demon, and it feels like an emergency. I let him do with my body as he pleases, and what I feel is inversion. It's as if I'm on a steep slope doing tight somersaults face down. It's both danger and glee.

I take my turn to indulge my curiosity about his strong hard body and we're on top of Mt Kilimanjaro. A rush of icy cold wind whips my hair. My blood is pumping hot through screaming veins whose pain and pleasure is fear, exhilaration and bliss. We're unified in a collective unconsciousness, and all I can hear is African music that sounds like the lute, harp and shekere—a dried gourd with beads—that Dalton made me listen to over and over. I see lightning, thunder racing at me in a new migraine that accompanies a roller-coaster orgasm.

We clutch each other, panting and as one, our bodies strong and free.

6.

Flying isn't fun when I'm wobbling in a tiny craft trespassing its way towards a blazing sun. I see myself plummeting over and over, shattering over and over, cremating over and over, the skeleton of each death a splitting atom in my attention.

In each moment, an explosion rips the plane, but the dying is different. A pressure monster flashes my neck clean off my chest. A throng of seats dislodges itself and crashes onto my thorax. A wing shard spears into my esophagus, pins me as I bleed. Startled bubbles straight from La Côte des Blancs—fermented yeast and liqueur de tirage—discharge a bottle in a wretched overhead locker and it thrums my head into mash. Flames gobble me alive. A bang incinerates my body. I plunge from great height, and die over and over in the wind, before the ground takes me at terminal velocity...

Life's about falling, flashes of memories. But these are the things I remember. What death feels like, stretched to the sun.

7.

On the seaplane, Dalton guides me to the lowest level shaft that sinks by lift.

"When sunlight spears the depths, you'll see a wonderland," he explains.

Indeed, beautiful white rays slip through the black, and I see a monstrous oarfish, long and bony without scales. It lingers at the window, ogling back at me as if it's a friend.

"That fish is as long as seven men," I gasp. "That's a lot of food!"

"Oarfish are gelatinous," says Dalton. "Not quite edible."

"They're flat as a road!"

164

"They're scaleless. See the crests, how they are embellished with crimson specks. When you startle oarfish, you'll feel electric shocks," he says.

He points at jellyfish and sea jellies, yellow, aqua and pink umbrellas, each the length of a ruler. I amaze at their long, translucent tentacles as they float past.

Nearer to the West African Coast, Dalton points in the distance at a coral jungle, multi-hued. Peach, red coral, orange, cyan, olive green, brown, tan, pale yellow, black, and purple—the color of my migraine.

8.

We take an East African Airways charter plane straight to Nairobi in Kenya, then we board an East African Railway that chugs and huffs to Mombasa along the Indian Ocean. Mombasa is an Islamic town full of stone houses and women wearing long black robes and covering their faces. It's a rubbish round trip that has no compass, and I'm even more cross when we board a monorail. Doors seal and the metallic snake shakes us to our fate. I think back to the maneaters of Tsavo in the late nineteenth century, the big cats that hunted railway workers and ate them alive. And from what Dalton's told me about the eating habits of lions…

I ask him again about the false firefly beetles, the brown spotted locusts and the giant millipede he's already told me plenty about, and I share with him my deepest fears about Africa.

"Baboon spiders," I say.

"Rubbish," he says. "Their toxin only burns for eighteen hours and it won't kill you."

"Whip-scorpions," I say.

"They are most ugly and have a nasty nip," he says. "But you'd smell their vinegar long before one attacked you."

"Driver ants."

"Contrary to belief," he says, "they don't eat people alive. *Safari ants*—that's what they're called—have a strong sense of smell and the Plumeria perfume you've poured on yourself, my dearest Evelyn, is enough of a deterrent. If it's any consolation, they prefer mice and baby sparrows. Do you know the Maasai use their pincers as stitches?"

"Oh, Dalton. I'd rather stay unknowing."

He looks at me.

"What you have the most to fear," he says, "are mosquitos. Malaria and elephantiasis are an unfortunate way to go. You die slowly and painfully, your fever-ridden body hotting up as your hallucinations worsen—"

The new migraine takes me in spins and whirls through which I crawl. They morph into the skeleton of a monstrous elephant carrying a decapitated calf, fully formed, still alive and bleeding inside its mother's bones.

9.

I clutch my head, close my eyes and think of the Rift Valley and the Ngorongoro Crater that Dalton showed me on a map. The thorn trees of the Savanna grasslands right here, he says in my head, his voice a sweet calm drone somewhere beyond hell.

Feel the curves of longing, he's now saying. Find the cosmos. He slips into my clutch fossils and fragments of bones and shells he's unbowelled from the earth.

We're in a dhow, and it's just like the National Geographic photographs with its mast and lateen sails. It has a sharp bow, ornately curved, and is a Dhoni—so Dalton tells me, though it's slim like a Persian Sambuk, he adds.

The Omani Arabs are wearing turbans. They're amenable enough but I wonder why they cradle muskets and spears as we sail. It's a leisurely dhow, but riding the ocean's belly isn't. I wonder about the water creatures below that Dalton is telling me about: the bioluminescent squid…

Just then a giant-toothed armored fish that resembles a colossal toad jaws the rear of our dhow, and it wobbles and leaks. One of the Omani Arabs points his musket and blows off one of the monster's eyes. He reloads, blows off the second eye, as one of his fellow Arabs spears the thundering toad through its throat. I grab Dalton as the men come at us on a fly, but they only urge us to move so they can fix the leaks with rubber and a spark.

Then they serve refreshments: sugared sweets soaked in cloves and honey, and dried lime tea (it's called Basra tea, Dalton tells me). For the strangest reason, I think of an Omani Park, a theme park with radiant creatures popping up to startle you along a boat cruise—

A migraine strikes and I'm sick all the way on the water's humps as we sail with the monsoon.

10.

A porter in Zanzibar grabs the hardcase, hauls it onto his shoulder and long-legs away with it as I yell cobalt murder. I try to give chase but the heel of my stiletto sinks into the white sand that deceives the eyes, and is not as soft and malleable as it looks.

My darling Dalton—who's accustomed to unbowelling minerals and fossils from the earth—unsheathes me and stiletto from the sand. With chuckles, he heaves me onto his shoulder like the porter who ran away with our luggage did.

"Creepy ol' Tippu Tip would bear you thus into his grimy lair," he says in a scratchy voice that's meant but fails to scare.

"Teepoo who now?"

"He was the wealthiest slave trader, so lusty for wealth, he shackled his own children in clove plantations, slaved them for profit."

"I don't know why you're laughing, because it's not remotely funny!" I writhe hard for him to let go, and we collapse in an ungainly heap over each other on the whitest sand. Only then do I laugh, though I'm devastated that we've lost everything we brought along, lost it ourselves before Ujamaa and African socialism could take it.

Dalton distracts me with birds. He points at a white-winged tern with a dark crown. The winger greets us with a burry call that closes on a nasal finish. "And that, dearest Evelyn," he points anew, "is a blue Pemba sunbird."

The bird is annoyed with my staring and makes a high-pitched jumble. *Tsik!*

Our guide finally appears. He's an even-natured fellow named Mwalimu. He's garbed in a cotton suit that he explains is called batik. Mwalimu is an intense man with whitened eyes, gold in the pupils

"Welkom," he says in an accent. "The universe-y be here. It be yours to explore."

He explains his name. "It mean teacher in Swahili."

He says not to worry about the luggage, and points at a monolithic stone building of several stories. "That," he says, "be telephony house."

"It's an exchange where you can cheaply make calls home," explains Dalton. "I suspect it's government-owned. Ujamaa, my dear."

Mwalimu takes us to his home in Stone Town, in a suburb called Mkunazini—which means the coconut shaver, he says.

Zanzibar is nothing like Parks Lagado or Odessa. Here is blinking sand and naked children scooting around, dogs, cockerels and donkeys plodding every which way along the road, and no-one is watching them. Women wear *chitenges*—that's what Mwalimu calls them: brightly colored wraps, unlike the black ones in Mombasa. These ones come along with waist sashes, puffed sleeves and head wraps. Women seem to adore them, despite the tropical heat.

A bearded scrub robin contemplates us from the lowest branch of a tall palm tree. It has a gaze as if it knows a secret we don't. We arrive at Mwalimu's stone house—cool, flat-roofed and wearing elaborate carvings on doors and windows made of black Iroko wood.

"It resist termite," he tells us.

Nonchalantly waiting for us on a sisal mat in the lounge is our luggage.

More children race fully naked towards Mwalimu. They gleefully call out, "Baba! Baba!" as they pedal at speed across the dirt.

"Batoto, calm-y down," says Mwalimu.

They stop short, not at his ask, but to gawk at us. Their chant changes.

"Mzungu! Mzungu!" and I can only imagine it means white devil.

We meet Mwalimu's wife Dada, who greets us like long-lost family. She cooks for us, without asking if we're hungry. It's a type of rice called pilau, full of cloves, nutmeg, cinnamon, cardamom, ginger and coriander, and comes stewed in chicken served with a side of coconut chutney. Dalton and I fall on it hungrily with bare hands, which is how we're meant to eat it. Mwalimu passes around a calabash of maize wine that makes me think ruefully of the Kentucky finest we left at home.

I squeal at an army of giant millipede marching towards me, some are round as baby kittens and long as a hanging rope.

11.

Dusk.

I ask Dada where we can pitch our tents. She laughs at me, perhaps misunderstanding my broken language. As I try to explain, I realize that my stilettos are missing, neatly swapped for a pair of closed sandals made of car or bicycle tires.

I try not to make a scene—our hosts have been so kind—but it annoys me that Dalton finds the whole situation amusing.

"It's a kindness," he guffaws, and I can only accept that there's order to his madness.

You only live once, he likes to say, and he repeated this to Sue Ellen when she dropped us at the airport in his car, having parked her own at our house because it was too old and too small to act as a shuttle. At the gate, waiting to board the plane, Dalton looked out the window, and then at me. "Your Sue Ellen," he said. "All this time…I don't know if she likes me."

Now I fall into a tropical forest in my new migraine, and outside its howl Mwalimu is saying, "Every tree be a realm of life."

I'm in the guts of a giant fir—the tallest tree at 100 yards high, needle leaved and coned. All around are lycophytes. Tall palm trees and cycads that are stout and woody, large crowned and evergreen, ferns all spored and branched, and they are all closing in on me. In the guts of colossal trunks I see dead people in stages of decomposition. Rank meat is falling off bones. My toes squish along a porridge of rot. I can't breathe…breathe…

I think of Sue Ellen back home in Odessa. The stupid suitcase she loaned me—an American Twister with red clips—which by now I realize is a terrible mistake, Rain falls in a torrent.

I long for roasted chocolate in steaming milk inside my dark, lucky mug that Dalton insisted I tugged along.

The tent pops up into an instant two-person cabin, waterproofed, seamed and roomy.

"I get a sense that our hosts are brooding. But I don't know why," I say to Dalton.

"We've declined their hospitality—guests sleep inside the main house," he explains.

"Oh."

I slide into my sleeping bag but don't go to sleep for a long time.

12.

We wake up to the low sweet coo of an African green pigeon. A tambourine dove answers back in a repetitive coo. Somewhere in the distance is the burry call of the tern with its nasal finish.

A pot-bellied urchin spills into our tent holding a hot serve of ginger tea (it's called tangawizi, says Dalton) in my black mug, and I know at once the Zanzibari have already necked in, fingered and toed our travel case with all its latches. The boy hands me the tea and touches my head with the utmost reverence. He says something that sounds like, "Shika-mooh."

"Baa-aa," says Dalton at once without batting an eyelid, then collapses in hilarity. In between breaths, he asks me, "Why are you a moo? Cows are Daisy, Maisy, Betsy. Never Evelyn."His mirth pools in a puddle at his feet, enough tears for a camel to drink.

"My darling," I say, with the patience of St Jacinta. "I am the linguist here. And judging by the hand gesture, Shika-mooh must be a greeting of paramount respect."

Dada greets us with more rice (for breakfast), the cinnamon and cloves in it a partner for a strange purple fruit. She gestures us out of the tent and into her airy stone house where the morning sun pierces my eyes.

A swarm of naked children has gathered to meet us. They loom like shades in a glitter of vision, pointing to wonders that fall in the rain, and this world feels like a hallucination. I marvel at swallowtail butterflies and cats with coats of jaguar. A long-tailed monkey grins on a nearby palm tree, snatches ants off a branch and crunches them.

Mwalimu places his long fingers on my arm. I see Dalton's frown as they all stare at me. In a distance, as if in a dream, Mwalimu is saying, "There be but a fragment-y here."

"There's more?" Dalton chuckles. He's in his element here. I think he chose this odyssey more for him than me. "You'll love this, won't you, my darling?"

Mwalimu lingers his hand a moment longer, not uncomfortable, but there's an odd weight. His eyes reflect the sunshine as he looks across to Dada. Something crosses between their gazes—I notice it, but my husband doesn't.

"For the true Zanzibar," Mwalimu tells us, "the trail you must-y see."

His words spark like a rainbow ribbon that wriggles across my vision. Dada gestures to my bare feet and hands me the ballet flats made of tire, as Dalton speaks with Mwalimu. They're gesturing, full of excitement, like boys, about the trail.

13.

We walk out into the sunshine, the ground wet beneath out feet. The tire-sandals clap echoes in the narrow alley. The floating hem of my orange skirt drags like the train on the monorail. I glance back and see leaves of virulent lime riding the paisley swirls. I see butterfly wings, petals. Somewhere along I stumble, and Mwalimu crooks my hand into his elbow. His arm is lead. Dalton strides ahead, energized and loud, his laugh the bark of a leopard.

How much time I can't say, by now my jacket's too hot. I pull at the oversized buttons and rip it open, but does it matter? Mwalimu helps me out of the clothing hell, drops it on the dusty trail among the coral rag scrub.

"Through here?" Dalton bends, zagging through a curtain of buttery vine, and an aqua sky opens before us. He whistles. "Isn't that something, darling?"

I shudder to a halt, open-mouthed. The whole of the archipelago lies shimmering, Zanzibar-scented, the ocean panting with life.

"This-y way."

I turn from Dalton and see a burst of green. An elephant is there, just there, its calf rocking from side to side in its mother's emptying pelvis. The air sways, and I see the emergence of a pinkly trunk. I sprint closer, the tire sandals slapping on mud. I reach down there, where the elephant and her calf stood but a moment ago. They're gone. Now there's only a cave yawning a vomit of small rocks onto the birth-sodden trail.

"No run, Missus."

I can't help it. I race, a new rhythm throwing me ahead. Spattering pebbles slide under my tires and I fall on my back, because, oh, the sky is reeling. A swallowtail dips from the clouds and lights on my hair. Blood trickles down my face.

"Be not move, Missus. No move."

Mwalimu comes close but not too close, holds a finger to his lips and then points. My eyes glide to follow his motion. A spew of rocks comes alive, coruscating colors billowing toward me. It's a mantle of flesh, painted slugs but quick, quick, like ants. I am rooted, unmoving perhaps in fear or memorization.

"Close eyes, Missus. Close mouth. Be not move."

Such a relief, not to see them surging, because the slugs are as beautiful as they are horrid to look at. I'm sure Dalton will later tell me what they are, this tide of worms, segmented khaki and coral and peach and mustard, and black markings for eyes.

I am a corpse, so still. Resigned. Let the grubs take me.

I hear Dalton's march towards me.

The giant slugs wriggle over me, soft and furry, a million tiny legs that tickle. Up my legs, along the foolish sunset skirt…

What are these? Land sea-worms? Army slugs? Troop worms?

"Tamu tamu," says Mwalimu.

How do I know without seeing that he's catching a wriggly one, biting it in two? The squeal is mine.

"Tamu tamu," he says again.

"It means delicious, dearest Evelyn."

But I am still making noises that may be distaste or loathing, above which I hear, "Evelyn! Look. Get up, quickly. Look, Cleopatra's Eyes! Oh, yum."

The sound of his bite is wet, my eyes still closed.

I feel the critters flowing from the posseting cavern down to the sand, pushing aside shards of pottery. Finally I bear to look. En masse they form an enormous blanket, surging and billowing like a coverlet of shapes. Not amorphous at all, more like a shawl of black, black eyes. I see what Dalton sees, what that old stager Livingstone saw when first he named these creatures. Moving in a mob, their colors merge and shift, the black coming together like a pair of Egyptian eyes, the corals and greens and blues like the face of a mummy's sarcophagus.

My precious Dalton lies flat with me, head between my feet, a prelude to pleasure, as the unstoppable tide of creatures takes us both.

Then we're right back at the front of Mwalimu's stone house, as if it were all a sensory escapade. All eyes are on Dalton and I—flat aground on the white Zanzibar sand that's hard as clay. Out here it's dark. A pale moon creeps hesitant light into our eyes.

What's this?

"Have we lost time?" I say to Dalton in a small voice.

He doesn't answer.

I look about. There are no hairy army slugs or troop worms wavering in and out of our clothes.

But I know what I saw, what I felt.

And the cream-yellow grub juice snailing down Dalton's chin is as real as moonlight.

He looks at me with the most tranquil eyes I've ever seen on that boyish face.

14.

I am pensive, alone in the tent, more worried than my Dalton over the delirium that lost us time. The tent's opening wobbles, and Dada steps in. She's holding Betelgeuse.

I blink. The dazzler twinkles the room, the stone sills starkly white in a liquid glare. I await the migraine's spring, but feel in its place a deep calm. An unruffled dune of golden sand. An emerald sky. The color of my thoughts is tranquil, as serene as the bejeweled bracelet, not Betelgeuse, that Dada is holding.

"Zawadi," she says, and I perceive that it means 'gift'. "For your journey."

The jewelry's hues are a riot.

I stretch out my hand, expecting a flash of rainbow-streaked, intergalactic agony. But the world composes itself to bliss.

"My word," is all Dalton says when I show him how the bracelet only glowers when I touch it.

"We go, my friends," says Mwalimu.

Dalton puts an arm across my shoulders, and we walk into the dusk. The path through Stone City narrows. Mwalimu steps ahead and I find myself, in utmost trust, calmly reaching for his shoulder. I walk behind him, look down at my too-white feet in the tire-flats and take the pace, steady, like breathing, so easy, so calm. Dalton's firm fingers grip my shoulder in turn, and we follow our guide in a chain through shadows past tree trunks among mangrove roots waving dead men's fingers.

A fallen baobab tree springs in front of us.

Dalton, in his playfulness, plucks a leaf off and disarms me by solemnly handing it to me. "Milady," he says.

"What are you doing?" I let go my grip on Mwalimu's solid shoulder to take the leaf.

"Welcome to the Realm of Realms," says my husband. "If you look closely, you will see that this ticket must ADMIT ONE. But there's a hitch—where's mine?"

172

"Oh, darling, must you jest now?" I peer into the darkness. "And where on earth is Mwalimu?"

15.

I blink, climb and fall down the fat baobab trunk to the other side.

Dalton cascades into me and we stare at the grotesque mirror before us. It's a grossness of dead hands stuck on a dastardly frame, lifeless hands from their bloodless color, yet distortedly moving and tossing at us a confetto of fluorescent creatures. Now the mirror is a fountain.

"Blue dragons—watch out!" yells Dalton.

He hauls me from the azure creatures. The wonders are endless. "Look, a nudibranch!"

He points at a giant worm near my foot, and it's glowing orange with hedgehog spikes of aqua. We amaze as turquoise eels slime for our flesh, angler land fish showing the way with a hangman's lantern.

I turn my face into Dalton's shoulder and his arms come around me. A wobble, and the path beneath us buckles into a picnic rug. Blue-green jelly fish fly up and over us as we stagger on the uneven ground.

"What—" My husband is bright-eyed.

I lift my head as the ground steadies, and see what's gotten Dalton wrapped in awe. To the side of the trail looms a massive door. It's studded and girded like the entrance to a medieval church. As we gawp, the door eases open to nothing but darkness beyond.

Behold.

The word reverberates through my skull, and I grab Dalton's sleeve. But we're entranced, and nothing can stop us walking toward that shadowy tunnel into the unknown. We step under the lintel, a glimmer pricking the pitchy distance. We jump at a creak from the door, then it thunders shut behind us. We're on hands and knees on the soft, trampled mud.

Darkness invades me. It's close and as suffocating as a wet burlap sack. Dalton draws me closer, so we're bunched like lemmings. On either side of us are a shuffle of steps that mark the passage of many feet. I clasp my hands together and the bracelet's brilliance resurrects at my touch.

My eyes adjust to the light's sharpness, and they fall upon a dreadful march. The clink-drag of chains and reels of exhaustion grind in a serried tide of barefooted slaves overawed in bondage. The head of the one closest to me is almost decapitated by the heft of chains. Blood drips down his body, leaving behind crimson footprints on the sand. The poor sod looks at us with the utmost bleakness, and I lurch forward in urgency to...do what? Feel him? Restrain his bleeding? Recompense his life?

But my fingers sieve through him and the rest of them as they ebb away, away toward the ruddiness of void. What I feel...is an elephant graveyard tucked in my gut...a disemboweled puppy crawling to my heart...a stillborn child hung by its own umbilical cord moaning for life out of my own throat.

"How can this—?" begins Dalton.

"How ghastly!" My own devastation, as the tunnel's mocking laugh booms in resonance.

Nothing is over, over, over.

16.

Wan light surges toward us. Unexpectedly, we find ourselves in a catacomb, the walls an ossuary of grinning skulls. My screech reverberates the cave, and we lurch back onto the trail, facing the warping mirror of deceased fingers.

"Dalton, what's happening to us?"

He frowns into the mirror's distortion.

"Perhaps I can help?" a new voice says.

We whirl to find a slender woman looking at us with curiosity. Her skin is the palest, the most translucent I've ever seen. Her luxuriance of bright red hair sweeps upwards in an elaborate style. She's dressed like someone out of a Dahlia boutique, the sweep of her silks way more unsuited to Zanzibar than my own garbs.

My stomach is unrecovered from its knots at the slave train, but Dalton appears himself again, or at least the version that commands the respect of the industrial and financial moguls.

"I fear, ma'am, we do need your help. We've lost our guide. Perhaps you'd be so good as to point us in the direction of Stone Town?"

She smiles, this woman out of time, and opens her hands in a questioning gesture. "The where is simple enough, but the when?" She tilts her head. "That's another question."

"If you wouldn't mind," I say, one woman to another. I'm fearful that I will spew on my feet any minute now. I hold out my hand in a gesture of imploring, and her eyes light on the bracelet around my wrist. It's instinct more than anything that puts my hand over the jewelry to hide it, and it shimmers at my touch.

"Oh," the woman says, pointing at the bracelet. She smiles, all at once friendly. "That is an answer I know, or near enough. Follow me. This way."

She turns, swishing the lilac silk of her bustle behind her. She casts a look over one shoulder at us, and totters ahead.

"Look at the night sky," gasps Dalton. Indeed, there's more sparkle than blackness. "Carina, if I'm not mistaken," he identifies the star. "And look, Sagittarius!"

Suddenly it's easier to keep up. The trail is smooth, the floor gently sloping like the ramp to an airplane door. On either side, scenes open like windows to other worlds, new and old epochs. That there is a village of thatch with smoke curling from chimneys. Here is a rolling plain of giant ruminants. Now a liquid coalescence of huge amoeba. Oh, a gallery of rock art.

"Petroglyphs, my dear," says Dalton, pointing, his voice thrumming with exhilaration. "Only look how fresh they are."

Something about the precision of the images makes my heart bound, silhouettes taking form in the leap of deer and finned creatures.

Our guide steps aside and there's Stone Town, its narrow alleys hiding from the heartless sun. The sun?

Night is gone.

17.

The star bracelet flashes, and I blink.

"I thank you," Dalton begins, turning to the woman, but she's nowhere to be seen. A clutch of gangling teens surrounds us, black faces spilling with laughter. One boy whistles through his teeth, another cries, "Baba! Baba! Mzungu they come!"

Then Mwalimu is before us—well, I think it's Mwalimu. His curls are twirled with silver. He's wearing a polo shirt and one of Dalton's bell bottoms with stirrups.

"Now you know," he says solemnly. "The Zanzibar Trail be a wonder and a dread. Batoto!" he turns to the teenaged children. "Batoto! Tell your mama our guests are starved."

Dada is already tumbling with ease and full of joy towards us and, also, in the spirit of Ujamaa, wearing my lipstick, a knee-high geometric shift and the lost stilettos.

Dalton's brows are raised in surprise, not at her, but at our escapade. He claps Mwalimu on the shoulder, and says, "Quite the trail, huh?"

Mwalimu grins, tilts his head. "It change you."

It dawns on me. "I haven't had a single migraine, darling," I say in wonderment, and open my hands to the benevolent sky. "I feel reborn."

Mwalimu nods, taking credit. Then he turns to lead us back into the core of Stone Town. "Come, my friends," he says. "There be one who would meet you. She name, Sue Ellen. She wait seven years for you. She seem, hmm, annoy. Still annoy long time."

18.

We're in a dhow, all three of us, with a fresh batch of Omani Arabs. Not the ones that killed a giant toad three ways: twice shot and once speared. I am frightened yet excited at the notion of lost time—what happened back there?

"Omani Park," I muse lightly to my sister, who seems to have recovered from her wrath now that we're headed back to Texas, even though she hasn't looked at Dalton once, let alone directly spoken to him.

"Omni what?" she says.

"The place where weird things happen," I say.

I think back to the letter Dalton wrote me from Montana in August, the one about a most marvelous wonderland he and I would build. Suddenly, the words form, and I grip my husband's hand so tight that it reddens.

"My dearest Evelyn—"

"OmniPark!" I gasp. "Let's call our park—the fun but eerie one you wrote me about—oh, Dalton! When we get home, darling, let's build it and call it—"

"OmniPark," he says in a most somber voice as I've ever heard from him.

Acknowledgement

'A Fiddle of Whisper Music' was first published in *From the Wasteland*, PS Publishing, October 2022

'Human Beans' was first published in *Life Beyond Us*, European Astrobiology Institute, September 2022

'Naked Earth' was first published in *Phase Change: Imagining Energy Futures*, Twelfth Planet Press, March 2022

'She Loves How He Glows' was first published in *Spyfunk!*, MVmedia, June 2022

'Sleuthing for a Cause' was first published in *Clamour and Mischief*, Clan Destine Press, December 2022

'The Devil Don't Come With Horns' was first published in *Other Terrors: An Inclusive Anthology*, Mariner, July 2022

'The Set' was first published in *Multiverses: An Anthology of Alternate Realities*, Titan Books, March 2023

'The Water's Memory' was first published in *Hadithi & The State of Black Speculative Fiction*, Luna Press Publishing, October 2020

'The Water Runner' (earlier abridged version) was first published in *Danged Black Thing*, Transit Lounge Publishing, November 2021

About the Author

Eugen Bacon is an African Australian author of several novels and collections. She's a British Fantasy Award winner, a Foreword Indies Award winner, a twice World Fantasy Award finalist, and a finalist in other awards. Eugen was announced in the honor list of the Otherwise Fellowships for 'doing exciting work in gender and speculative fiction'. *Danged Black Thing* made the Otherwise Award Honor List as a 'sharp collection of Afro-Surrealist work', and was a 2024 Philip K Dick Award nominee. Eugen's creative work has appeared worldwide, including in *Apex Magazine*, *Award Winning Australian Writing*, *Fantasy*, *Fantasy & Science Fiction*, and *Year's Best African Speculative Fiction*. Visit her at eugenbacon.com.

9 781947 879782